Mist

A Four Regions Story

Andrea Fink

To anyone who has ever wanted to write a book,
Do it. And learn something while you're at it.

Chapter 1

The howl of the spring wind tore through the valley. It was louder when she sat in the treetops. She would be able to hear every whistle and bellow closer to the Dark Region, as there would be little vegetation to block or absorb the sound, but there would also be less cover to keep herself concealed. The closer you get to the darkness, the more harsh the land. Instead, she settled with climbing the highest trees she could find and listening from the clouds. The air was crisper here, there was no sulfuric overtone. The fresh grass and new pine needles cut through the smell of the melting snow. The cold wind pushed the thick, dark waves from her neck and sent chills to her core.

A voice called from the surface. "Fern!"

Fern. What a dumb name. There were no ferns in the Mountains. It painted her as an outsider. Names in the Mountains were given based on the natural surroundings or circumstances of your birth. Flaming red hair? Your parents named you Red in whatever their language was. Born during a torrential downpour with thunder rattling in the distance? Storm.

Fern was born in the Null, or perhaps near the Null. Her parents never quite clarified. They were not very forthcoming with information about anything in their past. They were refugees—two part-humans who had escaped the Dark Region and found a home in the Mountains with a makeshift clan.

Her name had time to echo off a nearby foothill before she decided to look down. Her sharp green eyes could not see the being who summoned her through the thick branches, but she knew who it was. He had been her companion since she was just months old—another part-human in the clan. He was also the only person with a worse name than Fern. Her curiosity was focused on how he found her.

"What do you want, Kraai?" Fern shouted directly at him. She had been able to pinpoint his location from the snap of a branch. His name came from an old human trading language, Neder, which was kept alive in the Mountains by the dwarves. Since he did not look dwarvish, being average human height with soft facial features, those who heard it assumed it to be "Cry," which was a terribly unfortunate name for a child and even worse for the young man he was becoming. He did not look particularly demonic, either. The only thing that looked unhuman about him was his black hair, which rather than reflecting light, absorbed it. She would describe it as being dark as obsidian, but this black was darker. In reality, he was part-human and part-amalgamation like Fern. With no clan that would fully accept them, their families created their own.

"Come down," Kraai's voice responded.

Fern did not want to. She wanted to listen to the song of the Region of the Mountains. But Kraai's voice held concern, perhaps something he was not willing to yell freely. With a sigh, Fern slid from her branch, taking one last glimpse of the light filtered through high clouds. Her feet found another branch, which she jumped down from the moment she saw another acceptable foothold. When the supports started to be fewer and farther between, her callused hands grabbed at branches, letting her body dangle before dropping to the next waypoint. Within a minute, she was on the ground, looking her friend in the eyes. "What?" She crossed her arms. This was her first day out alone in nearly two weeks. He would have to have a good reason for calling her away.

"Your father is concerned. He saw beings in the area. He wanted me to bring you home." Kraai winced as he spoke, as well he should, being the bearer of bad news.

Fern, too, appeared mostly human. Soft features, no markings, tan skin that darkened when the sun was strong and paled as winter snows came in. A male appearing human was curious, but a female was suspicious. At least, that was how her parents presented it. "Is it not enough that you are with me?"

"They are not local clans." His chestnut eyes flashed. "They appear to be from the Dark Region."

Fern turned to take in her surroundings. Local clans were at least familiar with their families. The prevailing sentiment in the Mountains was to stay out of each other's business. Even if they knew about their human lineage, no other clan would dare reveal them, lest their own secrets be brought to light. Not only would beings from the Dark Region not honor this unspoken agreement of the Mountains, but bringing a part-human prize back with them would earn them certain honors. The vampires who lived there took particular enjoyment from human blood.

"I do not hear anyone, do you?" Kraai asked. It was a useless question, as Kraai's hearing was superior to Fern's. He also had a particular skill of telling exactly where the sound was coming from, while Fern was often thrown off by echoes.

"No," Fern said as her eyes continued to scan for any signs of intruders in the area—footprints, disturbed vegetation, anything off. She had been trained in sensing danger. It was imperative for her own survival. "I don't see anything strange, either." She turned to Kraai. "I don't want to go back yet. I haven't done any training." She scrunched her face. "Tell them you couldn't find me?"

Kraai's eyebrows raised as his lip smirked to one side. "They would not believe me."

It was true. Kraai could find her anywhere, anytime, and her parents knew it. "Come with me to visit the river, then we will go back. I must reconnect." Fern turned to move before she got an answer.

"Go into an open clearing—are you mad?" Kraai followed, hurrying his feet to catch up.

"Just for a moment, then we can leave." She took a ribbon and pulled her brown hair into a knot behind her head. The curls hadn't been brushed in days. Father said she looked wild, but said nothing when Fern retorted, 'Perhaps, but who is going to see me?' Besides, she *was* wild. She was never allowed to meet anyone or go anywhere. All she knew of civilized society was from books she read, stories she'd heard, and encounters with Kraai's extended family when they came to visit.

She pushed through the undergrowth in the direction of the river. She always knew exactly where it was—it called to her. She had been connecting with this water since she was a little girl. Mother had first taught her how to share her emotions with the water in this river. It was an old friend. But if she did not visit often, the water would quickly forget her. Such was the personality of rivers, the water did not stay long in one place, and neither did connections.

It was not long before Fern was kneeling on the riverbank. She dipped her fingertips into the water, letting them break the surface tension, swaying them back and forth in the rapid, shallow current. The coolness spread from her fingers to her hand, then up her arm to her heart. The water connected her to the glacial ice packed on top of this mountain. She closed her eyes and smiled, listening to the trickle as the water pushed past and over the small rocks in the shallow riverbed.

It still remembered her, at least a little bit. She reached to the bottom and tapped her finger. A wave sprang up from the spot, rushing downriver. Two more taps created two more crests, slightly larger. Then a snap from the other side of the river. She turned around to find Kraai staring into the trees on the far bank, eyes wide. Wordlessly, Fern thanked the water and backed away, careful to place her feet just so in order to not disturb the pebbles along the riverside.

When they were into the cover of the trees, they began to sprint. Never run home. Stay together unless they are on your tail, then split up so only one is caught. Never look behind, only listen—keep your eyes before you. If you have a good lead, throw them off your trail. They had both been taught these rules at a young age. They had only ever needed them a handful of times. When they came to a place where the undergrowth gave way to stone, they leapt from barren spot to barren spot, leaving no footprints or disturbed growth. A few hundred yards into this, they began their climb—first the sheer cliff of the mountain, then the trees they found where the ground leveled out. They had likely lost anyone in pursuit long ago, but they needed to wait to know for certain.

When they made it high enough to be completely enclosed by the branches, they stopped to listen. No noises save for the calls of birds and the distant rush of the river as it fell down the steep mountainside. They sat face-to-face in a cedar tree, their legs straddling the branch.

"Did they see us?" Fern finally whispered.

"Perhaps. I cannot be sure. I hardly saw them through the ground cover before we ran." Kraai's eyes were busy searching below them, darting from one spot to another, but he could see no more than Fern could—nothing but the branches and needles of the tree.

Fern broke into a wide grin and placed her wrist in her mouth to stop herself from laughing. The lingering adrenaline was making her delirious; her heart was racing, her blood pumping, her lungs recovering. The cool air chilled the sweat on her forehead. She threw herself forward and rested her head on Kraai's shoulder.

Kraai's chest gave three short shudders as he chuckled. He whispered, "I am glad you find this amusing."

Fern whispered back, still pressed into him, "We haven't had to run like that in ages." She stopped to continue catching her breath. "I'm just glad to know I am still faster than you."

Kraai placed his hand on her shoulder and pushed her off of him. When he met her eyes he smiled and said, "I had to let you go first. My mother would have my head if they took you and I came home unharmed. Also, I seem to remember *I* was the one helping *you* climb."

She shrugged. "I had been climbing all morning. My arms were tired. I can both outrun *and* outclimb you and you know it." Fern glared, daring him to challenge her.

Kraai reciprocated the expression. "Perhaps you should have been at the river instead of climbing first thing this morning—as you told your father you would be—then we would not be in this mess."

Fern's glare harshened, but her lips betrayed a smile. They stayed in the tree for an hour more, slowly getting louder in their conversation as they realized there was no immediate threat. They walked home as the sun was beginning to set, but the shadows were no danger for the two, whose demon blood allowed them to see well in the dark. It was actually in the dark that Fern preferred to be exploring, but it was also the time vampires could be out, ready to pick up on their uniquely human scent.

The woods grew thick in the area around their homes— three wooden cabins in a clearing. The air was warmer as they broke through the cloaked barrier that protected their location. Father's worried eyes and scowl greeted them.

He pointed at Kraai. "I told you to bring her home immediately." He turned his finger toward Fern. "And you were to be home before the sun went behind the mountain."

Kraai's mother, Iris, stepped out from their cabin. She was able to sense her son's presence, and no doubt could feel what was unsaid. She placed her hand on Father's forearm, lowering his hand, and whispered in his ear.

Concern overtook his face as he signaled them closer. "Get inside. Now."

Chapter 2

The main room of Kraai's family cabin finally calmed. There had been shouts and yelling, blame being placed on both of the young explorers, and whispered plans between the adults. Were they seen? The question they could not answer was the most important. They would have to assume they had been and act accordingly.

"How are the stores of cloaking potion?" asked Kraai's great-grandfather. The elf was the oldest in the clan, yet looked to be one of the youngest. His overall stature radiated elegance, but his mop of messy red hair clashed with the aesthetic.

Father shrugged. "I would need to look, but I doubt it's enough to last the three of us one week."

Fern found her opportunity. "I can get some at the dwarvish market tomorrow." Fern had never been to the market, but she knew many dwarven clans set up shop by the dirt road that formed the border with the Null on the third day of each week. The elves did their trade on the fifth day. Those days were safer to venture closer to their respective beings' lands, as so many were away.

All eyes turned to Fern as if they had forgotten she was in the room. The silent staring was on the verge of becoming uncomfortable when Mother spoke. "Absolutely not. You are not going anywhere."

Iris cocked her head, looking to Fern's mother. "Consider it, though. They will be looking in the mountains for the girl they saw. They will not be looking in the market."

"No," Fern's mother snapped through gritted teeth. "She is too young."

"She has seventeen years," Father's voice cut in. "I know someone who was working at the docks with just sixteen years, and the market is far less dangerous."

"No!" Fern's mother looked frantically between her husband and her friend. "She does not yet have twenty years! She is not leaving! I will not lose her. We can hide here. It is safe." Her voice was filled with panic.

Fern's lip curled as she forced her chair out and stormed from the cabin. She made sure the door slammed loudly behind her. As her feet crunched on the gravel between their homes, she heard the door open again and footsteps rushing after her. Quick steps with a sporadic hop—Kraai. Fern kept her eyes forward, beelining for her own home. Three more years. How could she stand to wait three more years to interact with the outside world? Why would someone with twenty years be more equipped than someone with seventeen? She stomped inside, clearing the mud from her boots, leaving the door open so Kraai could slip in.

"What is the reason for her fixation on twenty years?" Fern grabbed at the mess of hair on her head, having half a mind to pull it out.

Kraai closed the door softly behind him. "She is from the Dark Region. Twenty years is universally adulthood there."

Fern stared at Kraai, open-mouthed and finger pointed. Finally she scolded, "First of all, you do not take Mother's side on this." She lifted another finger. "Second, I would have been named twice over by now if I lived in the Dark Region, and it would be a better name than *Fern.*"

Kraai smirked. "And what name would that be? *Run* or *Hide*?"

Anger bubbled up inside as, in one motion, Fern grabbed a cup off the table and threw it at Kraai. He shifted to the side, allowing it to shatter on the closed door behind him. Fern huffed, hunched over and scowling, upset she missed him *again*. How were his reflexes always so sharp?

"You've been to the market before," Fern complained as she slumped into a large leather chair. "You've met with dwarves and elves in other clans. You are allowed to exist. Why do I not get the same?" Her eyes harshened. "And do *not* say anything snide."

Kraai held up both his hands in surrender, then turned them outwards to shrug. "Perhaps you look too much like your parents. They clearly ran from someone or something—they are in hiding, too. I suppose my face is not so recognizable, not on a wanted sign."

Fern gave a short chuckle. "A wanted sign. Really? You think my parents have it in them to do something that would put them on a wanted sign?"

Kraai summoned fire in his hand and threw it into the fireplace, sending the waiting logs into a blaze. He went to sit in the leather chair opposite Fern, his eyes too sympathetic for the joke he just made. "There is human blood throughout the Four Regions. Nobody else is being hunted like our parents are. There is more that they are not telling us."

Fern laughed again, this time from nervousness. Her parents, the bookish homebodies who are afraid of strangers. The paranoid woman and the man who picks up the pieces when she falls apart in fits of screams. The two she had found crying together on multiple occasions. What could they have done to warrant being in hiding for nearly two decades? Fern opened her mouth to refute the idea when the door opened.

Father stood tall and strong against the darkness from the doorway, the torchlight in their home casting a warm glow on his light face. Was there a secret hiding behind it? He slid something from his sleeve, ignoring the two younger occupants, and walked to a cupboard. He slid the key into the lock, turning twice to the left before opening it, revealing an assortment of glass containers, clear and colored, tall and short, all sorts of shapes and levels of fullness. "It appears we are short on cloaking potion, after all." His voice was flat, as if speaking to himself, yet he was loud enough to be heard across the room. "I suppose someone will have to go to the market to purchase some." He closed the cabinet, resting the key inside the lock without turning it, then removing it to slide it back into his sleeve.

Fern turned to Kraai to see if he had noticed the missing step. From the curious look on Kraai's face, it seemed he had.

Father stepped over to the living space, his eyes settling on the fire. "Your mother has had another of her fits. This one will have exhausted her thoroughly. Please make sure you are quiet tomorrow morning so she can sleep it off." He finally looked at his daughter. "You should sleep out here tonight."

Fern could only stare in response. She had been sleeping in the main space for years now, not wanting to share the one bedroom with her parents. After Father left to retrieve Mother, Fern turned back to Kraai. "Am I reading too much into this, or is he telling me to go tomorrow?"

Kraai's eyes lit up. "I believe the door is unlocked, you must simply choose whether or not to go through." He leaned forward, bringing his face closer to her ear. "I will be waiting outside the door just before sunrise. Do not forget the cloaking potion."

As Fern settled in by the fire for the night, her mind raced with ideas of what the market could be like. What would they sell? How does one barter? Would it be loud and chaotic? Or orderly and civilized? Would the cloaking potion be enough to conceal her? Or would she need to disguise herself further? The buzz in her mind lingered, not allowing her to sleep until well into the night.

She was startled awake by a tapping on the window. Morning light was beginning to shine in. She fumbled into her clothing as quietly as she could, hobbling to the potions cabinet while still trying to secure her hair. She climbed on the counter so she could read the labels in the dim light. A crystal bottle etched with a pattern of bumps seemed to be the one she was looking for. She lowered herself to the ground and brought it next to the window to confirm. She opened it, taking a long sip as the smell and taste of it hit her all at once. Pulling the bottle away from her lips, she spilled a small streak on the floor as she attempted to mute her gagging. It was the worst thing she had ever tasted. However, this was the price of a day of freedom, so she went back for one more sip before sliding it into her bag.

When she emerged from the cabin, Kraai, who had been staring off into the woods, did a double-take. "I see you have taken the cloaking potion. I could have mistaken you for some fine young woman."

Fern elbowed him, slightly harder than she intended. "I *am* a fine young woman, potion or not." She had no idea, though. All of Kraai's family her age were boys—she had never even *met* another young woman. How would she know where she stood compared to others?

Kraai took his own sip of the potion and Fern's recognition of him began to change. Almost as if her understanding of his face began to fade from her own mind. He still had all the same features, and when noticed one at a time they were identifiable as being his, but when put together, it did not make up Kraai's face. After a long and intense look, they left the clearing together, but not before Fern stopped to look back. Would Mother have another fit when she realized Fern was missing? Of course she would. She had half a mind to return home, but was overwhelmed with a need for novelty and pushed on behind the young man who did not look quite like Kraai, but most certainly was Kraai based on the banter that poured from his mouth.

Between competitions of *who can jump down the higher cliff* and *who can sprint fastest through thick trees*, it did not take long for the two to come to the foothills. The large field of grass that blanketed the ground near the border was too expansive for Fern to comprehend. It stretched out as far as she could see in both directions, running alongside a dirt road that did the same. She had seen it from afar, from perches atop the taller trees, but it did not seem so open or intimidating up there. She clutched at Kraai's arm, jolting him back toward the last of the dense ground cover.

"We will be seen," Fern said in a shaky whisper. Her eyes scanned across the field, looking to the carts and stalls along the road in the distance.

Kraai sighed, shaking his head. "If you do not want to appear suspicious, then do not act suspicious." He shook free from her grasp and rubbed his hand down her arm, interlacing his fingers in hers when he got there. They hadn't held hands in years, not since they were children. At some point it felt strange to her, so she stopped. But now it felt nice, comforting, safe. She tightened her fingers, squeezing his hand. Fern looked up at the face that resembled Kraai's; the combination of features was quite handsome.

They walked out into the clearing, Fern fighting her internal warning of leaving herself exposed. Normal beings did not have these warnings. They could go to the market, meet others, converse, all without looking over their shoulder. Today she was a normal being. Still, she used her free hand to raise the hood of her cloak, shading her face.

The first wave was the noise that could be heard from afar: hundreds of voices all speaking at the same time, carts creaking as they crept along the endless dirt road, feet shuffling, goods loading and unloading. The overlap was overwhelming—Fern could not distinguish one sound from another.

The next wave was the sights that overwhelmed as they climbed onto the road: the wide dirt path was lined with stall after stall, table after table, all filled with goods. Piles of metals, vials filled with liquids, textiles, books, jewelry, crafts, prepared food, and fresh fish. Those were just the stalls in the immediate vicinity. Down the road, the stalls appeared smaller and smaller, going all the way to the horizon where they disappeared somewhere before the sliver of visible fog that indicated the border of the Dark Region. It was easy to see the booths that belonged to those from the Light Region and the Dark Region—if it was not manned by a dwarf, the colors and fabrics that decorated the stall would tell the tale. The Dark Region forbade cotton, favoring wools and occasionally silks in dark colors. The Light Region used bright colors, embroidered with images that represented their products, and would be the ones selling goods that need light for production. And passing from booth to booth, either in a leisurely step or purposeful stride, were hundreds, possibly thousands of bodies—mostly dwarves, but also an assortment of demons, elves, and other beings shopping at the market.

The final wave was the smell that enveloped them as they began to pass between the stalls: freshly baked breads, salt water still clinging to dead fish, assortments of fragrant flowers, all accenting the base smell of too many bodies in one space—a stale smell like that of the entire clan shut into one cabin on a cold winter night, but multiplied.

Fern's attention bounced between one stall and the next, admiring the goods she did not have the coin to afford. She worried she might look suspicious with her cloak pulled over her head, but she was not the only one in hiding. Graceful figures glided down the road, hoods up, parasols in hand, hiding from the sun. Would they be able to smell her? Fern's free hand reached up for her neck, as if it would stop her scent from reaching them. Her other hand was still securely in Kraai's. She looked down and admired the way their hands fit together. Would onlookers make assumptions based on this physical display? Fern released her fingers, Kraai doing the same. Fern looked up to give him a smile, apologetic, perhaps? His lips twitched a half-smile in return before his attention was brought back to the stalls.

They continued to walk side-by-side past dozens of stalls. Kraai knew what he was looking for—the red-eyed elven clan from the Dark Region. They would be farther down the road, toward the darkness, where more stalls from that region had been set up. He stopped to buy some bread from one dwarven stall and some berries from a Light Region elf. They cut between two stalls and slid down the embankment into the Null, sitting among the field of ferns to break their fast. Fern was thankful, as she had been too excited, and too rushed, to eat anything that morning.

"Is it everything for which you had hoped?" Kraai asked as he ripped off a piece of the large loaf.

"It certainly is busy," Fern replied, looking back up at the road. She popped one of the red berries into her mouth. Sweet, but slightly tart. Not a wild Mountain berry at all—cultivated, selected for its unique flavor and soft texture. "I am spending most of my attention just trying to keep my bearings. It is overwhelming."

"You are making it quite evident it is your first time here." Kraai fiddled with one of the ferns, scraping spores off the bottom of a blade and rubbing them between his fingers. "Perhaps try to make it appear as if you do not have hunters after you. Relax. Let your guard down."

Fern threw a berry at his head. He caught it in his mouth. She snarled, "You let yours down first."

Kraai rolled his eyes. "At least do not look so interested in *everything* you see. These are normal market wares, not priceless artifacts. Conceal your curiosity."

Fern scowled, pursing her lips. "Fine." She stood, holding her hand out to help her friend up. Kraai held back a laugh as he eyed her arm. Her sleeve was powdered with spores. "Oh, come on." She swatted at her sleeve, sending the dust out into the air. "I don't harass you every time a crow caws." She reached down to pull him up, then surveyed the field around them. The sea of ferns reached as far as she could see toward the Dark, the Light, and the Seas. It rose and fell with the breeze—a green ocean. This was the first time she had seen the Null up close, where she had been born as her parents escaped the Dark Region. Perhaps *Fern* wasn't the worst name.

Kraai tried to assist Fern in getting back up the embankment to the road, but Fern shook him off, insisting on scrambling up on her own. Why hadn't she left him behind for this trip? Father did not mention needing a companion. She was better at running when she was alone. She could hold her own in battle. Probably. She hadn't ever truly *fought* anyone. Perhaps she did need Kraai to help sense when she would need to run or fight. He was better at reading the situation, listening for danger, and knowing when something was off. He was the alarm, she was the defense. He was the cry, she was the cover.

The sugar in her blood helped Fern relax. Not everything was a threat. Not everything had to be investigated. She glanced instead of perusing, helping them make better time to the stalls at the other end of the market. They had been here for some time. How long would the cloaking potions last?

Finally, Kraai stopped at a stall manned by a tall, slender female elf with dark hair. Before her were dozens of glass vials and bottles. Behind her were shelves stacked with more. The bottles were all clear, some simple, and others with elaborate etched designs. The liquids showing through were an assortment of colors, all with varying levels of opacity. The elf's red eyes held Kraai's gaze. "Cloaking potion?" she asked. Her voice was smooth, but the accent startled Fern. She had never heard someone speak like her before.

"Yes, I—" Kraai started, his brow furrowing.

"Yours looks as if it will wear off soon. Let me see what we have." The woman ducked under the table.

Fern stared at the glass vials. Color glinted in the corner of her vision. Off to the side, a table filled with gems and trinkets had been hit by the sun in a way that made the colors dance. They called to her—greens, reds, golds. She approached slowly, taking in all that was there and deciding which to investigate further. She glanced up at the woman manning the wares. Her hair was black, but greying under the hood of her red cloak. Her small eyes returned the glance, and the wrinkles around them only shrank them further. Still, something in them flashed. Fern looked down immediately and fiddled with items on the table. Had it been a look of recognition? Realization? The old woman looked human, as well—no distinctive demonic markings or vampiric grey hue, at least. Might it have been solidarity?

The woman's voice struggled to whisper, giving an almost croak instead, "Listen, but do not look up. Nod as if I am explaining the wares to you." The wrinkled hands lifted a pair of earrings—gold metal wrapped around red gems that dangled off of each other.

After a short freeze of panic, Fern decided to play along for now, but kept her ears alert to the sounds around her in case the woman intended to distract her. She nodded, letting her finger venture close to the gems, but not touching them.

The woman continued, rubbing her finger over the gems, twisting them in the light to reveal their shine. "I have been receiving letters for you, in case I ever crossed paths with your mother. I never thought I would be able to deliver one to you personally."

Fern dropped her hand to another trinket and lifted it instead, uncomfortable with the red glow that had been so alluring before. Now she caressed a dark green gem set in a necklace. Perhaps she should have been wearing gloves. She could leave now, but intrigue held her in place. "You know my mother?"

"Yes, but not as well as I knew your father." A smile flavored the old woman's sad voice. "Before he died, that is."

Fern set down the green gem. "Before he died?"

The old woman took in a sharp breath, laying both of her hands on the table. Fern fought the urge to look up at her, instead focusing on a dagger before her. The commotion of the market around them filled the silence until the woman spoke again. "So he does live. There had been hope but no proof." The woman straightened herself, pulling back her shoulders and lifting her head before reaching under the blanket that covered the table. The increased volume of her voice startled Fern. "So just the earrings?" Her hand reappeared with folded paper in her grasp. She placed the red and gold earrings inside the paper, wrapping them tightly and tying it with twine before handing the package to Fern. "Twenty-seven," she demanded, holding out an empty hand, as well.

Fern finally looked up into the woman's face. Something about it was familiar. "I don't..." she started as she fumbled her hand in her bag for whatever coin she could muster. She knew there would not be twenty-seven in there.

The woman gave a thin smile, red paint on her lips accentuating the expression. She winked and looked down at her empty hand.

Fern reached out to place the one coin she found in the woman's palm. From the woman's gold-trimmed sleeve fell more coins, giving the illusion Fern had placed them there.

The woman made eye contact once more, whispering, "Your cloaking potion has worn off. It warms my heart to see you alive and well, but you must go—quickly." The weathered face suddenly shifted to horror as pointed down the road, yelling, "Thief!" A clamor rose around them and all eyes went in the direction she pointed—the opposite direction of where Fern needed to go.

Fern wanted to stay, to ask questions about the family history she had never been told, yet her defensive instincts kicked in. She tucked the parcel into her bag, made sure her hood was secure over her face, then pushed her way slowly through the oncoming crowd with her face down. A hand grabbed her arm from behind and pulled her back without turning her around.

A voice whispered in her ear, "It is just me. Keep going." Kraai sounded worried. He never sounded worried. He let go, but stayed close on her heels.

They made their way out of the thick of the crowd and jumped off the embankment into the Region of the Mountains. Fern wanted to run through the field into the trees, but held her feet back in order to appear more relaxed, less suspicious. Her breath stuttered, preventing the deep breaths she was attempting. At least they could see if someone was coming from a distance, yet none were headed in their direction.

The day was not warm, but sweat beaded in her hairline by the time they reached cover. Fern tried to stop in order to regulate her breath, but Kraai stormed on. Fern followed, constantly looking over her shoulder. The cliffs, streams, and thick undergrowth did not seem to exist as Kraai hurried through them. They were nearly halfway to their clearing before he finally stopped. He held up his hand for quiet and listened. He scanned the forest around them. Fern heard nothing but the birds in the trees and a far trickle of a stream. Finally, Kraai's chest expanded as he took in a great breath.

"Someone smelled you," he panted. He pressed himself against a tree and slid down, sitting on the exposed roots.

"*Smelled* me? How do you know?" She envisioned a vampire creeping behind her as the shopkeeper kept her distracted, his nose brushing her cloak hood. Between these thoughts and the cool mountain air on her sweat, a chill took her.

"I just know." Kraai rubbed his face with his hands, burying it for some time before finally looking up at Fern.

"How close were they to me? Were they sniffing in my direction? Headed toward me?" Fern demanded. This was not a time for him to be vague.

"I just know," Kraai repeated, stone-faced, jaw set.

"No." Fern snapped. She stomped closer to Kraai, pointing. "You will tell me how close I was to being taken. I need to know if this risk was worth it. I need to know if I am going to be followed, if they can track me home."

"I cannot explain how I knew. I could just," he paused, gesticulating toward his head, "sense it. I was standing by a vampire and I could smell you in a way I had never before. I knew it was your smell, but you were not near me at the time. When the vampire turned in your direction, I just knew he was the one who picked out your scent."

"So you could smell me through him? Like some weird empathetic sense reading?" Fern withdrew her hand, stepping back.

"I suppose so, yes." Kraai's face held worry.

"And what, exactly, do I smell like?" Fern asked with a chuckle, trying to lighten the mood.

"Home," Kraai responded quickly, absently. He shook his head and laughed off his initial answer. "Like the cabins, the clearing. You smell like where we live." His words fumbled out of his mouth. He slowed his pace when he changed the subject. "But to him you were nearly irresistible. He wanted you without ever seeing you. Something about you was very important to him."

"But you were right next to him, why did he not pick you out?"

Kraai shook his head. "I have no idea."

Fern's hands fell to her sides, one resting on her bag. *The bag.* She rummaged through it while making her way back to Kraai, kneeling beside him. She pulled out the folded paper and held it between their faces.

"You bought something?" He asked, looking past the parcel and into Fern's eyes. "Do you even have coin?" His eyes widened. "You *stole* something? You were the thief?"

Fern tossed it in the air, then swiped it as it fell in front of her. "It was a gift." She shrugged. "I think." She caressed the hastily-tied bow with her thumb. It felt important. Something inside burned to come out, but was it the red jewels that radiated like fire in the light? Or the beautifully-scrawled words she had glimpsed on the paper as the woman was wrapping?

"Are you not going to show me what it is?" Kraai asked, breaking a long silence that Fern hadn't yet noticed.

It was a paper parcel with earrings inside. Why did it feel as if opening it would be turning a corner into something new? Why did it feel that, once opened, it could never be put back? Friction vibrated her fingertips as the twine rubbed against itself, breaking free of the bow. Her hands shook as she pulled off the ties and unfolded the paper. The earrings fell to the ground, bouncing in the moss below. Kraai's eyes fixed on them, but Fern could only see the paper.

Your father may be gone, but I am still very much alive. I had hoped to be able to return to you, but I must find a way that allows me to come back whole. I have found safety beyond the Golden Veil, yet I am trapped. You can find safety here, too. I know you are out there. I hope one day these letters will find you. I love you. —Em

Kraai's eyes, shocked by the earrings he was now holding, met Fern's confused ones. She needed answers. She leaned back onto her feet and sprang forward, setting off into a sprint, barely escaping Kraai's grasp as he reached for the edge of her cloak. She couldn't run faster even if she was being chased. Who had written the letter? Her feet slid over wet patches of ground, but her forward momentum kept her going. How did they know where her family was? Droplets fell into her hair, her cloak hood useless as it dragged the wind behind her. Why did the woman look so familiar? A low rumble shook the air. Was this letter truly for her? Sparks leapt on her skin as the sky churned.

Mother and Father were in the main room of their cabin, huddled by each other at the dining table. By the time Fern reached them, the sky had opened and she was drenched. Her mind had shifted from curiosity to anger. If they had told her more of the truth, there would not be so many questions.

Mother stood with fire in her eyes, shrugging off Father's arms from around her shoulders. "You had me worried sick! Now you come back in such a state and—" Her voice quavered through the strength she tried to project. Her eyes shot open with realization. "Where is Kraai?"

Fern responded by slamming the paper on the table. Water from her cloak dripped onto the floor, yet the paper was bone dry. The only magic she had used on the way back was to protect the letter. "What is this?" she demanded.

"Where is Kraai?" Mother repeated, her voice clearing of hysteria.

The door closed behind Fern. Kraai's wet footsteps squelched inside.

"What is this?" Fern asked again, emphasizing each word.

Father eyed the paper, then looked at Fern. "Where did you get this?"

Fern turned to Kraai, who was now directly behind her. She pried open his hand, retrieving one of the earrings. She threw it on the table so it slid, stopping as it hit the letter.

Father sat straighter, his eyes set on the new objects on the table. Mother turned toward them, as well, but did not seem to recognize what Father had. His hand shook as he reached first for the earring—the large ruby with smaller gems dripping from it, all traced in fine gold that held it together. A small smile of recognition formed on his lips. Next, he reached for the letter, opening it slowly.

Fern stared at Father as he read. She watched as his lips tucked away and his eyes squinted in pain. She stared as he handed it to Mother, and she read. Her eyes held confusion until Father reached into his pocket and dropped a piece of silver metal on the table—the bar he would rub with his thumb when he was nervous. It rang as it bounced off the wooden surface. Mother looked at the bar, then the letter, then in shock at Father. Father collapsed, falling to the ground, pressing his face against the floor. His body began to heave as he let out cries. In a change of roles, Mother wrapped herself around him, holding him tightly as he released whatever emotion had overwhelmed him.

The door flew open. The storm outside raged as Kraai's mother and great-grandparents entered with fear in their eyes. They stared at the heap on the floor that was Fern's parents.

His great-grandfather, who looked to be in pain, spoke first, "What is it?"

Mother looked up and slid the paper on the table closer to them. Kraai's tiny great-grandmother reached for the letter while giving a wide berth to the two who had already read it, barely grabbing it with her fingertips. As she skimmed over the words, her hand went over her mouth, but her eyes smiled. Her husband did not even read the letter, but wrapped his wife in an embrace. Their significant height difference was always most evident when they hugged like this. Iris took the paper from her grandmother's hand. Upon reading, her eyes widened, yet she had no one with whom to share the emotion.

Fern wanted in on the secret. "Who is it from?" Her question was loud, forceful. It broke the spell under which the letter had put them.

Iris' eyes found Fern. "The queen."

Chapter 3

They were seated in the living space, the elders on one side, facing the two young beings. A fire roared against the cold that pressed against the windows from outside; the rain had not ceased, now throwing itself against the glass window panes. Father had collected himself, now presenting a stoic attitude, a touch colder than his normal demeanor. "What do you know of the Dark Region?"

Fern looked to Kraai for a companion in her disbelief of her father's audacity. When she found him straight-faced and solemn, she turned back toward Father. "I am the one who gets to ask questions at the moment. Who was the old woman?"

"My grandmother. Next question." His face did not move.

"Who sent the letter?" Fern demanded.

"The queen. Next question."

"The Mountains have no royalty, only a council. Try again." Father had taught Fern how to play chess when she was young. She buckled to the exchange, knowing she would have to approach this strategically.

"The Dark Region does."

"So it is from Belle?"

Mother's fist slammed on the arm of her chair. "That monster is *not* the queen."

The sudden noise broke Fern's concentration. She racked her mind for a moment, trying to get back on track. "Then there is no queen, unless the princess has been named."

"The regent will never allow that. Not until she has nearly twenty years and is placed into her public trial."

Dead end. It was time to try a new approach. "The one who wrote the letter—who is she *to you*?"

Father took a deep breath before answering. "My mother."

"The old woman's daughter?"

"No. Daughter of Champion."

The name rang a bell. Fern closed her eyes to concentrate. Where had she heard that before? Was it a book? A story? Something overheard in conversation when she had eavesdropped? Em. Em. M? Her eyes shot wide as her mouth hung open. "Mask?" The dead queen's name echoed in the still cabin.

"Yes."

"No." Fern's eyes searched all the faces before her. Her lip curled in disgust as she realized the lies she was being fed. If Mask was his mother, then he would be king. But if Mask was alive, she would still be queen. And what would all of this mean for Fern? Who were these beings to her? "Mask's only child was killed by a siren, a seductress who posed as his wife."

Mother nudged Father. "I told you not to let her read those books."

Father chuckled. "I suppose it is time for the truth. Let us begin with names. I was born Son of Will. I was named Strike. For a short time, I was king in the Dark Region. I was stabbed through the chest with a wooden stake by a horrible siren." He looked over at his wife, smiling as he unbuttoned his shirt. "But not the one the books say." He pulled his shirt over his shoulder, revealing a large, circular scar near his heart. The raised pink flesh cast shadows on his skin as the firelight danced on it.

Lies. More lies. "If you were the son of Mask, a wooden stake to the heart would have killed you instantly. You are not a vampire. I have seen you in the sunlight. I have seen you consume sun-grown foods." Fern was leaning off the front of her chair now, on the verge of escalation.

"Vampires do not age after becoming a vampire. In order to grow, my mother made me human."

Kraai's voice chimed in. "The werewolf decisions?" His eyes were wide, taking in all this new information.

Father nodded.

"You don't believe him, do you?" Fern stood, snapping at Kraai. "Yes, it is an entertaining story, but you know it is not true. None of this is true. My father is not a king." She gestured to the plain cabin room around her, spinning. "Obviously." She raised the hood of her cloak as she left the cabin, her heavy footsteps the only sound left in the room. With cold rain stinging her face, she leaned against her home. She slid to the ground, letting water saturate her clothes once more. All she wanted was the truth—was that too much to ask?

The door squeaked beside her as a figure emerged.

"Leave me alone." Fern buried her face in her arms, propped up on her knees.

A hand fell on her back as a body slid to the ground beside her. "Your father speaks the truth." It was Kraai's great-grandmother.

Fern looked over to her. The old demoness was a full head shorter than Fern. "How would you know what the truth is? They probably lied to you, too."

The purple eyes beside Fern lit up with memories. "I used to work in the palace. It is where I met Lathron. He was called Son of Scribe in those days, but was named Empath for his trial, and I was Daughter of Brawn. We worked for Champion. When Emily—Mask—first arrived, we became her confidants." The demoness stood. "If you wish to hear more, you will have to come inside. Unlike some, I do not relish the rain." She moved toward her own cabin, not Fern's where everyone else was still congregated. The bait had been placed before her, now she had to decide if she would take it. The click of the cabin door was her cue. She sprang to her feet, splashing through the growing puddles.

The dining table, distinctive with its large mended crack down the middle, already held a pot of tea. Sneak sat alone, staring at the door, waiting in silence. The light from the fireplace bounced off her purple hue, casting a long shadow for such a small being.

Fern sat down across from her, scooting one of the cups closer. The tea would not be ready yet, but she didn't know what else to do with her hands. She was about to ask the demoness to continue, but Sneak beat her to it.

"I would like you to listen to all I have to say before you have another of your outbursts. I appreciate your fire, but you would do well to sit with information before you erupt." She stared down Fern, waiting for something. When a rebuttal did not come, she began, "I could write a book with tales of the first week or so Mask was in this world. It was determined to be her trial—she pretended to be someone else, wearing a sort of mask. I was named shortly after she was. I suppose I was sort of a supporting figure in her trial. Lathron and I lived in the palace until I conceived my second child, then we moved to the Mountains where nobody cares how many offspring you have." She gave an unamused look for an aside. "Nobody cares about anything you do out here." Her face straightened with a smile. "Yet we stayed good friends. She would come visit often—she and Will, he was her husband. Originally engaged to her sister, but that is a story for another time." She placed her hand on Fern's. "What you need to know is that Mask and Will had a child. A son. Vampires had never conceived before, so this was unexplored territory. He was a vampire from birth. He did not grow once he left the womb, so Mask made the decision to use a few drops of a potion that was used to turn werewolves human. It stripped the child of any demonic abilities from his father's side and any vampiric abilities from his mother. For all they knew, he was completely human. That is until—" She paused and looked at the tea. "Oh, I am terribly sorry. The tea was ready before we even went to your cabin. Would you like some?"

Fern snapped from her rapt attention and nodded, scooting over the cup. Fire licked the outside of the pot as Sneak poured, and the liquid steamed as it escaped the spout.

Sneak poured her own cup, set down the pot, and continued. "Until he found he had retained one power. It was the same power that Mask had retained when she became a vampire. The same power *her* father was known to have—a family trait spread through generations. The power of conjuring lightning."

Thunder clapped outside, shaking the pans above the fireplace into song.

Sneak looked out the window with a grin. "Well, that was fortuitous." She turned back toward Fern. "Conjuring lightning is not as common as manipulation of water or conjuring fire. In fact, it is an incredibly rare talent. They were able to convince the region that he was both demonic and vampiric, through his retained power and his artificially greyed appearance. Of course, if they found out the truth, there would be many opposed to him being in the palace, but vampires were hopeful when they thought one of their own was on the throne and another was an heir. They were against Mask for killing another vampire—even if he did deserve it—but believed she would either come around to their way of seeing the world or would be killed and they could try again with the son."

Fern steadied herself to make sure her voice would not be abrupt or loud. "What does this have to do with the letter?"

"The letter is from Mask to her son's child. When Belle stabbed Strike with a wooden stake, he was standing in front of a window portal. Belle thought he did what vampires do and disintegrated to dust as he fell from the second story. He actually fell here,"—she spread her fingers on the dining table, right down the crack—"and we were able to heal his wounds before he succumbed to them."

Fern's eyes shifted momentarily to the table, then focused back on Sneak. "Belle didn't kill the king. His wife did—the one who had seduced him."

"When the villain writes the history, she can blame whomever she would like. The wife, Wave, ran with her twin daughters and friends. Not all of them made it away from the palace."

Fern sat, staring at the rain streaking down the window. She took long sips as she processed the story. Without looking back to Sneak, she asked, "If my father is Strike, then the wife must have died in order for him to remarry."

"Wave might have been part siren, but she was also proficient in water magic as a water demoness." Sneak gave a sympathetic smile. "Your father never remarried. His wife was able to escape with one of her daughters and one companion who knew where to find safety in the Mountains."

Sneak had always been kind. She was one who would always speak her mind, even if the honesty was jarring. Fern knew Father and Mother could lie, even Kraai could be capable of deceit, but not Sneak. But what did this mean? Her father is a king in hiding—that story had been confirmed. Her mother, though. A siren? That would mean… "I am a siren?"

"On your mother's side, yes. Not enough to allow you immortality, but enough that you might want to avoid salt water unless you have always wanted a tail. And water demon, of course, as you knew. We assume your father contributed human blood, but also that demonic spark."

Fern nodded, taking another long sip from her cup. It was empty, but she took no notice, dealing with a new reality. More questions raced through her mind, but she did not want to ask just yet—she already had too much to sift through. All she could muster was to say, "Thank you," and leave. The sky was as still as Fern was numb. Trapped moonlight gave the stagnant clouds a silver glow from below. Slow steps brought Fern to her cabin where her parents and Lathron were speaking in low tones. As she opened the door, the calm voice of Lathron broke through.

"I believe it is best we all retire for the night." His voice was quiet. "She is not yet ready to speak."

A small piece of Fern wanted to snap, to spit venom about him reading her emotion when she did not want to be read, but that part of her was drowning under the weight of the new revelations. All she could do was drag her body to her corner by the fire and lie down.

When the sounds of their hushed words and footsteps departed, Fern was alone with her thoughts. She watched the yellow flame dance, hypnotizing herself to avoid the horrors whispering in her mind. Of all the words in this new history, the one that pierced through was *siren*. The scum of the Four Regions. It was not uncommon to hear someone called *a siren's toy* when they are weak-willed or *shady as a siren's cove* when they are up to no good. They lived lower than the lowlanders. They were literally and figuratively beneath Mountainfolk. Yet Fern was one now; rather, she had always been one. Her heart pounded in her head as her dirty blood pulsed through her veins. The rhythm lulled her to sleep, finally overpowering her disgust.

Chapter 4

Each fork laid against a plate, each cup being placed back on the table, each scrape of a chair on the wooden floor cut into the still morning silence. None of the three spoke. A buzz tingled in the air—an electric energy that Fern knew her father could feel as well. She glared at him every few bites. Her eyes never made it to her mother. The woman was a stranger now. They both were, but at least hunting those who walk on land was not in his blood.

Anger bubbled. Screams tried to push their way out of her throat, but she held them down. Her face grew hot. It had been twenty minutes without so much as a word.

The seal broke. "You're a king!" Fern shouted. It wasn't a question or a demand. The tone was more accusatory.

"The king is dead," her father, Strike, said without looking up from his plate. "I had to give that up to keep our secret. The king was a vampire who was stabbed with a wooden stake. He no longer exists."

Fern turned her glare to her mother. "You're a queen." This was all she could handle for now. The other part of her lineage would remain taboo.

Her mother, Wave, actually looked up. Her eyes were striking as they glared back. "Princess consort. The advisors would not allow a foreigner to be called *queen*."

The barrier broken, Fern tried to keep her emotions out of her next question. "When were you going to tell me?"

Strike finally turned his attention away from his plate, as well. "After the danger had passed."

"What danger? They do not know I am human."

Wave cut in, firm. "Belle wants you dead. She told me I had to kill one of you when you were infants to keep the lineage tidy—that is why we ran. She has your sister, and once she is named, you will no longer be considered a threat."

The entire night, Fern had neglected to give even a passing thought to the person on the other side of this. Another patchwork being whose blood held a secret. Would she be as repulsed by their human blood as Fern was by their siren blood? Did she know she had a sister? "And what if I am named first?"

"Then you become queen and we will all be subject to Belle's vengeance," Wave said. "Again."

"But I would be queen. I could just"—Fern flicked her hand in the air—"do away with her."

It was Strike's turn. "You don't just 'do away' with Belle. She has haunted this family for seventy years." He stood from the table, taking plates of half-eaten and pushed-around food that nobody had actually touched in some time. "Besides, you will not be queen because you are not going to the Dark Region. Your grandmother has offered protection in the Light Region and we are going to accept."

Fern's eyes bolted open, pleading for a contradiction from her mother. Finding nothing, she begged her father, "The Light Region? Father, no! I will not go! I wish to stay here in the Mountains! Besides, the letter never said she was in the Light Region! Do not send me there!"

"She is beyond the Golden Veil," Strike said. "That tells us all we need to know about her location."

"And that veil is in the Light Region?" She paused, reflecting. Of course it was. Those pretentious sunbrains had an obsession with gold. "Why does she not simply leave? What is keeping her there?"

"The Light Region has more secrets than even the Mountains and they keep their secrets at all costs. They do their trade and commerce closer to the border, so most who visit from other regions have no need to go near the veil. Many citizens of the Light Region live their entire lives outside of the veil. It is said that anyone who leaves the veil will not remember what they saw inside of it, except Light Region royalty and others trusted with the secrets. Some leave remembering nothing at all."

"Is that what is keeping Mask? The threat of forgetting?"

"I have no idea. She can tell us nothing outright in letters—they are all checked when they leave the veil."

"And what of their palace? Is it beyond the veil or before it?"

"There are two palaces—one outside the veil and one within. Their royalty takes up residence in both. If they must meet with foreign diplomats, discussion occurs in the silver palace, yet they disappear to the golden palace frequently."

Fern's interest was piqued. They had no books about the Light Region like they did about the Dark. All she knew was from overheard conversations with Sneak and Lathron's son, the one who did business there on occasion. He was always very brief with his accounts. It had seemed like the Dark Region but with more sunlight—royalty, trade, the wealthy feeling superior to working classes.

Strike and Wave, these familiar strangers, told her all they knew about this place she was to live. It was clear that Wave had never been before, but Strike had visited on diplomatic trips. Of course he had—he was a prince visiting the mirrored royalty. What hoops he must have jumped through to continue the charade of vampirism in a region where the sun shone sixteen hours each day.

By the end of their lecture, Fern's apprehension churned with the newfound excitement. It would be an adventure—a way out of hiding. She could go about as she pleased beyond the veil, she assumed. She would meet other beings. She could learn magic from skilled individuals. She would have more books than the infrequent gifts of Kraai's cousins. Fern's imagination ran away with the prospects, but there was no guarantee of what was even there. The only promise was safety according to the grandmother she had never met. What that safety consisted of was still unknown.

Fern's mind was racing with the new round of information when Kraai came in, letting in the midday light that warmed the clearing. Both of her parents gave a weak smile, then rose to leave at the same time. They must have seen the confusion on Fern's face.

"You two have much to discuss," her mother commented. "It is best if we leave."

As they walked out the door past Kraai, his lips smiled, but his eyes did not. He moved slowly toward the table. Fern's chest tightened as a worry darkened her mind. Why was his face so stern? His slow steps came to a halt before her as he bent in a dramatic bow. "Your Highness," he managed to say before a laugh burst from his lips.

His lowered head was just close enough for Fern to reach out and smack him. "You dolt! You had me worried that you had some terrible secret, too."

"Well, I do." He sat in Strike's seat, pushing a teacup out of the way. "Nothing so life-changing as finding out you are an heir to one of the Four Regions, but I do have some secrets in my blood."

"What, are you a siren, too?" Fern asked, rolling her eyes. She watched Kraai's face lose its humor, and hers dropped to match it.

He looked away.

"It is hard enough for me to accept all of this. The least you can do is laugh when I try to jest about it." Fern sat in silence as long as she could before her nerves got the best of her and she stood.

Kraai did not look at her, but spoke before she managed to step away. "I am not human."

Fern lowered herself back into her chair. "You have no human blood at all? Then what are you?"

"Demon," he revealed.

"Demon? On both sides?" Fern knew his mother was mostly demon, with traces of dwarvish and elvish blood, but the father had been a mystery.

"My father was a worker at the palace—a crow demon. A shapeshifter." His eyes finally met Fern's.

Fern's brow raised. "Then your father is alive?" The story had been that his father, a part-human, was dead. She was intrigued by the new narrative.

"My mother believes so." Kraai raised his hand for an aside. "Needle, by the way. She was called Needle in the Dark Region." He lowered it and continued, "She was pregnant when they escaped the palace. She could not tell him where she had gone without risking Belle finding out. She did not know if he was under her power."

"Did he know she was pregnant?"

Kraai's voice became vacant. "He did."

There was no word in Fern's vocabulary to encapsulate everything she was feeling at once. Actually, there was one. It was an old human word her father would whisper under his breath. She had never heard another being use it. Perhaps it was more modern than the Four Regions, brought here by

Mask and learned through example. It didn't matter, though. Fern was forbidden from using it. Apparently it was incredibly vulgar. She let the word escape under her breath.

"Agreed." Kraai's eyes focused across the room. Besides a sigh every now and again, the room was completely still for a few minutes before he spoke again. "So you are going to the Light Region?"

"I believe I am, if only to hear this ridiculous story from another source. It still does not feel real."

"Which part?" Kraai huffed a short laugh under his breath.

"Honestly, I am more at peace with being a hunted princess than I am with being—" Her voice fell away as her eyes found her lap. They did not rise again to meet her companion's.

"I need to ask you something." Hesitance coated his words. "But you must promise not to think about it too much."

Fern nodded without changing her focus. She felt the urge to bathe in scalding water just thinking about it.

"Have you ever used your song on me?" The question held no contempt, yet no true curiosity. It almost sounded worried.

"Absolutely not. I do not even have my songtone." Fern had happened upon a book about sirens in Sneak's cabin when she was a little girl. For weeks she hid it under her pillow and would read it late at night to scare herself, never realizing the information she learned would be this relevant. "I would have to undergo a transformation before it is given to me by the male—" Fern halted and looked into Kraai's face. The angle of his brow confirmed her suspicion. "Why would you think—?"

Kraai held out his hand to stop her. "I asked you not to think about it."

Fern knew she could not adhere to that promise, but would not bring it up with him again.

"I am going with you." He cut through her train of thought.

"No. She said I would be safe. Not two people. Not even my parents were mentioned."

"But nobody is after me. I am completely insignificant. Insignificant beings venture into the Light Region all of the time, into the veil even. I would be just another traveler." He tried to hide his excitement about the adventure, but there was no fooling his closest friend.

"Then why don't you stay here? Our families are in more danger than we realized."

"We need to be sure it is not a trap."

Fern gave a light chuckle. "I do not believe my grandmother would be an accomplice to murder or kidnapping."

Kraai's face was set in stone. "That is exactly what your other grandmother has planned. Why put it past this one?"

"Because this one is not a siren," Fern snapped. She did not mean to yell.

His eyebrows raised only slightly. "But she is a vampire."

He was right. Fern had never met a vampire, but while the hatred for sirens had been implied, the fear of vampires was explicitly taught. They were the enemy. They drank human blood for sport. Blood like Fern's. She could feel her heartbeat quicken in her chest. Her eyes shot around her field of vision as she searched for answers in the familiar space. How would she walk directly into the grasp of a vampire? How could she trust anyone outside of her clan? She felt warmth on the back of her hand.

Kraai's hand was on hers, his face trying to mask his worry with a supportive smile. "I will see you safely there. If we encounter any trouble, we will run together, as we always have."

Fern attempted her own smile. "As we always have."

Chapter 5

A heartbreaking goodbye stuck in Fern's mind as they made their way down the foothills. She had expected her mother to break down, to cry and scream in one of her typical fits, but instead she had been vacant. Any emotion had left her completely. Her father gave her the final embrace. She felt a warm drop on the top of her head as he kissed her hair. She had to fight to keep her own tears in.

Iris fussed over Kraai, rummaging through his bag, making sure he had all of the things he needed for the journey. Their goodbye was not as hard. He would be back soon enough. Fern had no idea when she would return to the Mountains. *If she would return to the Mountains.*

They padded down the grassy slope, keeping their eyes peeled for the cart Iris said would be coming for them. An old friend, a trusted acquaintance, who was well known for providing safe transportation for smuggled goods and valuable cargo, would be in the driver's seat. Fern watched Kraai as his eyes scanned the border. She could not see his face, but she could see each of his features—the features she knew so well from years of companionship yet never took the time to appreciate. His hair, black and downy. It made perfect sense now that she knew his lineage. His eyes, warm and alert, always searching, watching. His lips, full and permanently half-smiling. He did not look himself, but the smirk was unmistakable.

"It is rude to stare." He shot a glance sideways, the smirk still resting on his lips. "Are you going to help me look or not?"

"My apologies." Fern's eyes found the road. "I am simply in awe of the cloaking potion. You hardly look yourself, but I know it's you."

"And how can you tell it is me?" he asked. "What gives me away?"

Fern nearly said her last observation out loud, but stopped herself, instead saying, "I know you too well to see your features and not be able to put them together. It just takes more time with the potion; recognizing you is not instinctive."

"It bewilders me, as well." Kraai kept his eyes ahead, skipping over rough spots in their path without losing his focus. "I can study your face and see the familiar pieces, but I cannot put them together to see you. I can see the mess of hair pulled up on your head, the sharpness of your eyes, the angle of your jaw, the shape of your lips—" He stopped in his tracks, squinting his eyes and looking down the road. "I think he is coming. There is a cart kicking up dust. I believe an animal is pulling it."

Fern could not see anything but the dust but kept pace when Kraai quickened his steps so they would get to the road the same time the cart would cross their path. As they drew nearer, Fern could make out the long, white beard she had been told to look for. They came to the road just before the cart approached and Kraai waved his arms above his head. Fern nearly reached out a hand to stop him, instinctively wanting to prevent him from giving away their position. Instead, she grasped the strap of her bag tightly.

"Excuse me!" Kraai hollered over the sound of the approaching wheels. The cart must have been ancient—slow and rickety. It would be a wonder if it could carry three beings in addition to whatever cargo it held.

The driver stood to get a better look, his horse trudging on slowly. "How far do you need to go?" He pulled the reins and he came to a stop. He was about as old and tired as his horse, his voice creaking almost as much as the metal cart. His back was hunched, but even if he stood upright, he would not even be as tall as his vehicle.

"How do you know we need a ride?" Fern asked, staring up at him.

The dwarf looked down the road behind him, then in front, then back to them. "Two kids from the Mountains want to see the world. Hard to make it far on foot. Hitch a ride on a passing cart. Happens quite frequently."

Kraai quickly reached into his bag and pulled out the note his mother had written. He held it up to the driver.

The driver took it, opening it up and squinting hard as his eyes skimmed the page. When he reached the last words, his eyes widened and he stood straighter. With surprising clarity to his voice, he said, "Ah, get in, you kids. Anything for old friends." He gestured his thumb to the space behind him.

Kraai immediately made his way up, hopping over the side and landing in the back of the cart. He looked to Fern, who hadn't moved.

"What will we owe you?" Her eyes narrowed with concentration, trying to read his face. Mother required she ask this before getting on, though she couldn't articulate why.

The dwarf squatted so his eyes were more level with Fern's. His movement was very graceful for how old he appeared. "I owe your families much more than a ride into another region, but that is of my own appreciation, nothing formal. When the siren paid back her debt to us, my associate and I were free from our last owed task. Her power destroyed those assassins and, with them, destroyed my past life."

Fern looked to Kraai, who nodded. But it couldn't be true. Her mother did not have assassin-destroying power. And if she did, she did not have the mental faculties to use them. She pulled herself onto the driver's bench, then held out her hand, "Fern."

The dwarf smiled, his hand grasping hers. "Journey."

Fern gestured her head behind them. "That's Kraai. Tell me more about my mother."

Journey whipped the reins, a sparkle in his eye. "I thought you might be her daughter. Had an awful sense of déjà vu when I saw you. Strange I would bring her from the Seas to the Dark Region, the two of you from the Dark to the Mountains, and now you from the Mountains to the Light. Just one more leg to bring the whole thing full circle." He chuckled to himself. "You see, the main road through the regions is an oval, so it"—He shook the train of thought from his head—"is not important." He shifted in his seat, his face considering something before he began. "I was the one who brought her to the mist, then to Capital. Little did I know the darkness she would bring to the region with her. Sweet, if not a bit inexperienced. She was bright, I'll give her that, but she knew so little about the world outside of the water."

Journey told the tale of a young woman completely foreign to Fern. He had been assigned to keep tabs on her whenever he was in Capital, making sure she would be easily accessible when they needed her to make good on her owed task. He spoke of the way she became comfortable with workers on the docks, how she would steal away during the day to party in the sunlight, how she fell in love with a mysterious stranger. Just snippets of the life she had lived. This woman could not be her mother. There was no way any of those vignettes could be from the life of the woman she knew.

"But when I saw her—blood-soaked hands, clutching a child to her chest, hellbent on walking out of the Dark Region—I knew something had broken inside of her." Journey took a breath and let it out in a shudder. Fern thought he would continue, but he did not, just bit his lips together, worry on his brow.

Broken. What an apt way to describe her mother. And her father, constantly trying to keep the pieces in one place, ridden with guilt. The chain of events, all of the events that broke her mother, must have been his fault. At least, that must be how he perceived it. Why else would he stay with a shell of a woman, happy for the moments when she would seem normal? There was so much love in those moments, though. Perhaps that alone was worth it.

The wall of trees approached, the front line of an army guarding the unknown lands. The apprehension must have been clearly written on their faces as they scanned the massive evergreens. Journey cut in, "You are right to be worried, but not just yet. Beyond the trees are just farms—as far as you can see, they grow food in orderly rows. We will not get to the grandeur of it all until we reach the cities. The magic in the Light Region permeates everything—it floats in the air, mixes with the water, grows in the plants. There is no danger to it, there is only danger in the beings who control it. They do as they wish, when they wish. While it may seem like light and happiness, there is darkness within every being. There is a reason the fae folk were not trusted in the human world."

"Fae like the elves?" Fern asked.

"And then some. The elves in the mountains keep to themselves, but the fairies and elves and"—he waved his hand—"everything else in there make sport of trickery and illusion. Outsiders are fair game, hardly protected by the laws that create some semblance of order here. Learn the rules quickly and you will be left alone."

"And what are the rules?" Kraai asked, sneaking his shoulders between them on the bench from behind.

Journey smiled wide. "You must ask the fae about the fae rules or you must learn them the hard way."

Fern looked the dwarf up and down. "You will not tell us?"

Journey stared right at her, his face tilted forward, brow raised.

Kraai piped in. "You *cannot* tell us?"

Journey's lips snuck into a tight-lipped smile before he returned to his task of driving the cart.

Just as they crossed between the two trees that stood on either side of the road, Fern looked to Kraai, who mirrored her concern. What were they getting themselves into?

The blinding sunlight caused them all to shield their eyes, Kraai even going so far as to collapse into the shade of the driver's bench. The clouds that had covered the sky on the border of the Mountains and the Null were gone. In their place was the clearest blue accented by the radiant sun, which gave a strong warmth Fern had never felt from sunlight before. In fact, the tingle on her exposed skin was growing uncomfortable, too warm. Then, suddenly, it shifted to a pain like a hot blade peeling thin layers of skin off her face and wrists. She frantically pulled her sleeves down and looked to her lap, letting her loose bits of hair fall to create protection.

Journey took a long breath, capped with a sigh of sympathy.

"Will it wear off?" Fern asked, still staring at her hands.

Journey gave a cough for her attention.

When Fern looked up, the dwarf was nodding his head. He pointed forward, his sleeves rolled up exposing his forearms, soaking in the sunlight but no worse for wear. Fern looked forward, too, letting the peeling sensation take over her face once more. She fought the instinct that told her to flee from the pain. She reached up to touch the skin of her cheeks—it was still perfectly intact. As she realized this, the sensation faded. She turned around, about to tell Kraai that he needed to adjust to the pain of the sunlight, but when her lips formed the first word, she choked on her own voice. She tried again, but the words came out as a cascade of vomit that she turned to spew over the side of the cart, though it disappeared before it hit the ground. The taste of bile in her mouth lingered, however. She turned, wide-eyed, to Journey.

He nodded, the smile under his facial hair somewhere between amusement and commiseration. "Welcome to the Light Region."

Fern jumped into the back of the cart, finding the cowering Kraai. Without a word, she grabbed his hand, pushing back his sleeve as she pulled him to his feet in one motion. She dragged him forward as he dug in his heels, but a bump in the road caused them to lose their footing, slamming them both onto the driver's seat. Fern held Kraai's arm there, sprawled onto the bench, in direct sunlight.

Kraai screamed, "What are you doing?" He tried to pull his hand out, tugging at his sleeve.

Fern held firm, placing her body weight onto his hand with one of hers and fighting to keep his sleeve up using the other. She saw his skin peeling, like a tree being stripped of its bark. She pretended to not hear his shouts of pain, gritting her teeth and holding him still.

He continued to struggle, to scream, pleading for her to stop. His eyes reminded her of a trapped animal facing its death.

Tears welled in Fern's eyes—why was it hurting him so much more than it had hurt her?

Finally his free hand found his arm, feeling it, and the tension he had built subsided. The peeled skin disappeared, leaving only his tan hue. He stopped fighting. He looked to Fern, his face streaked with tears, staring, reading something on her face, before he wrapped her in his arms. He mumbled into her hair, "This is not going to be easy, is it?"

Fern returned the embrace, shaking her head into his shoulder, rubbing the salt water from her eyes. Another jolt underneath their feet separated them.

They continued on, but nobody spoke about what had happened. They couldn't. Out of the corner of her eye, Fern caught Kraai rubbing his arm absentmindedly, then looked down to find herself doing the same. It *had* happened.

They stopped by a small stream so the horse could drink and Journey could have a meal. They sat with a view of long rows of bushes, but no beings in sight. Kraai shared some of the food his mother packed for them—dried meat and some foraged bilberries that were a bit worse for wear after the adventure thus far. Fern scraped the mashed berries from the paper they had been wrapped in and, when she had finished, licked the juices off her fingers. The acidic bite made her wish for those sweet red berries from the day at the market. She saw a grin cross Kraai's face. "What?" Fern asked.

"Nothing." His smile grew as he went to take another bite of the meat. "It is nothing."

Journey cut in. "So you two are headed into the veil?"

"We are." Fern turned, smiling to indicate her appreciation, but preparing herself to guard her speech. "We think someone is in there who can help us with something. Do you know anything about what is in there?"

"It is said that anyone who goes in will not remember what they have seen." Journey said these words almost as if it were a joke, not a warning.

"But the royalty surely remember, otherwise they could not rule their entire kingdom," Fern pointed out.

"They are privy to the secrets of the veil. Many of those close to The Monarch will know these secrets." He stared at

Fern for an uncomfortably long time, then brought his voice low. "Even some commoners have learned these secrets."

Fern froze. Her mind raced with implications—to have the ability to remember what was beyond the veil could allow her passage in and out. She could determine if it is truly safe. She could return to her parents when it was safe, not having lost the part of her life lived in there. "Can one of those commoners share the secret?"

Journey's face betrayed annoyance before settling into a smile and saying, "That is for another time. For now, you look a bit parched. Here, have something to drink." He searched behind him, shaking jugs of water before finding the one he was searching for.

Fern *was* quite thirsty. She reached for the jug. The heft of it was from the ceramic container—it only had a small amount of liquid inside. As she tilted it toward her, it jerked from her grasp, falling to the ground. Before her face now was Journey's outstretched hand and serious expression. He stared at her as the jug rolled away, toward the field of bushes. "You should refill it from the stream. You are a water demon, yes? Be sure the water is clean." Journey slowed his words, enunciating in his raspy whisper, "You never know what might be in the water."

Fern wasted no time leaving the uncomfortable exchange, carefully stepping down into the field to retrieve the jug. She met the horse by the stream—if it was good enough for the animal, it *should* be fine for their consumption. She could see straight to the rocks at the bottom, not even dirt or sediment riding the current. Still, she reached into the stream, letting her fingertips get a better read of the water. It was not the bite of glacial cold, but rather a refreshing coolness that greeted her. Despite being an unfamiliar stream, the water responded to her touch, connecting to her. She moved to dunk the jug into the water, but turned back to the cart. The dwarf's eyes remained on her, his head shaking so slightly Fern could hardly see it.

She set the jug on the bank, lying it on its side. She conjured the feeling of purity, of cleanliness within her. It was a routine she had carried out many times retrieving water for her family, but not an easy task when she felt so dirtied by her own blood. She asked the water to move and it leapt from the stream by her hand funnelling itself into the container. After moving the jug upright, she bent over the water, taking a handful to her lips. It tasted clean enough.

After she fumbled to hoist the jug from the ground, Kraai scurried to her side, awkwardly lifting the jug and carrying it for her. Neither of them had strength as a particular skill. Neither of them had ever considered needing to be stronger than an enemy—just faster and smarter. When they returned to the cart, Fern closed her eyes, feeling her body for any strangeness from the water, and said, "The water was fine. I don't see why you insisted I purify it."

"*This* water is fine enough," Journey agreed, hopping down from his seat. His tone implied he was going to continue, yet he only made his way to retrieve his horse.

Kraai's eyes met Fern's. She was glad to see she wasn't the only one confused.

The group continued on, Fern and Kraai finding comfort in the back of the cart while Journey drove. Kraai offered to take the reins, but the dwarf shook his head, saying, "This old girl listens to nobody but me anymore. Besides, we're dropping off some cargo soon enough. We can all rest in that town if dealings go well."

"And if they do not go well?" Kraai asked.

"Then I will be too disquieted to rest, and we will have to drive through the short night and much of the long morning."

On the unending road, they could admire the beauty of the farmlands—stalks of green that bent and swayed in the wind, purple bushes that drew the attention of the eyes with their precise rows and calmed the senses with their aroma, animals fat from the expansive fields of grasses in which they grazed. When they grew bored of the scenery, Fern and Kraai would play games they learned as children—counting games, acuity tests, guessing what the other was thinking. They had cycled through all of the old standbys and seen enough fields to last a lifetime before they stopped once more to stretch their legs and for Journey to make one final check of his goods. The cart came to rest by a field, but Fern's face lit when she saw what grew. Kraai followed her eyes and, upon seeing what she had noticed, went down toward the red berries that they had enjoyed at the market.

Fern already knew these would be her favorite part of this region—a place that could produce such light and sweetness in one bite could not be so bad. She watched Kraai reach for the closest bush, as her ears picked up on two distinct noises— from before her, a snap like that of a rope drawn tight, and from behind, Journey yelling, "No!" before vomiting. Vines had reached from the base of the bush, coiling themselves around Kraai's wrist. The muscles in his arm went taut, his feet trying to plant themselves to resist the pull.

Within a heartbeat, Fern reached for the knife in her bag, running to where Kraai continued to struggle, being drawn toward the ground that was pulling the vine back. By the time she got to him, she had to slide the blade in the sliver of space between the soil and where his arm now stood. As she pulled him back and away, she worried that the blood on his arm was her doing, but the remnant of the plant left on his wrist was covered in thorns. When she had finally guided him back to the cart, his clenched hand was purple, the vine still holding strong to his forearm.

Journey, recovered from his incapacitation, scowled at the young man. "We need to leave. Burn that off and treat your wounds on the road. I do not want to be here when they come looking for a buried thief." He hoisted himself to the driver's seat and whipped the reins in one swift motion.

Fern held Kraai's arm, pulling at the binding, the thorns cutting into the soft flesh of her fingertips. His fist still clenched, she could hear him breathing through the pain. She could feel his heart racing as she braced herself against him. She remembered what the dwarf said. "Kraai, burn it off."

His free arm was banging against the side of the cart. The veins in his neck bulged.

"Kraai!" Fern shouted into his face. "Burn it off. Now."

His wild eyes finally found her. His hand slapped onto the vine and a burst of flame erupted between his fingers. Fern fell back to avoid the heat. Ash fell from his arm, leaving only pocks that oozed with thick blood. His head toppled backward, resting forcefully on the side of the cart. He brought his arm to Fern, his fingers blooming open to reveal a mangled berry coating his palm.

"You dolt," Fern scoffed. "After what that plant did to you, I'm not touching that." She wiped the pulp off his hand with a scrap of cloth torn from one of the threadbare blankets that covered the cargo. Fern ignored the glint of metal that shone underneath as she tore another piece to clean the wound with some of the clean spring water. She would do what she could to stop the bleeding and pain with magic, but the wounds were too deep to heal completely. "Don't get us into any more trouble."

"Me?" He feigned offense. "Trouble?"

Her hand rubbed over his arm, the warmth of his skin blending with the warmth from her concerned touch. "I seem to recall shouts of discipline from your cabin much more frequently than from mine." She tugged just-too-hard in dressing his wrist, which was still speckled with shallow holes, causing him to flinch in pain. "But I'm serious. I have to live here now. If there's a chance I get to live my life in public, I don't want my reputation ruined before I even get to the veil."

His eyes rose from his hand, a protectiveness emanating from them. "Not a toe out of line. I promise."

Chapter 6

Journey's dealings took them to a city called Carthage. By the time they finally reached it, the cart cast long shadows on the road behind them. Kraai was asleep, likely from all of the excitement, but Fern sat attentively on the driver's bench, cloak pulled over her head, thrilled to see a city for the first time. It sat where a river from the Mountains joined with a river from the mountainous area of the Light Region. Looking at the "mountains" Journey gestured toward, Fern would hardly classify them as even foothills. Not a flake of snow, even in the springtime.

The city was bustling with life—boats making their way to and from the city as they passed over on bridges, fresh torchlight casting shadows into doorways where people came and went. The marketplace had been a temporary thing, but this city was where people *lived*. It would be this way tomorrow and the day after. People greeted each other, waving and smiling. The familiarity of the exchanges made Fern sink into her cloak.

The buyer was waiting for them when they arrived, a dark blue cloak covering her golden dress. Grumbled words between Journey and the elvish woman took only moments, and the cargo was shifted into another cart quickly with the help of her two burly assistants. Kraai, awoken by the shifting of the cart beneath him, jumped in to help.

When Journey returned, he whispered over the side of the cart, "It is best if we leave the city. You may be recognized here."

Fern nodded, disappointed but understanding. She was a half-day's journey from safety. Why ruin it now? She kept herself mostly in the back of the cart, peeking out to take it all in. The homes were pressed against each other, layers stacked on top of each other. Lights in the windows gave glimpses into the lives of the residents—most were dark, but some kept the glow of a single candle, refusing to rest even though the sun did. It would have been hard to sleep in this city; the noise was enough to put Fern on edge. Kraai slept beside her, completely unaffected by the clattering, shouting, and overall chaos around them.

As they left the light of the city, Fern could see more and more stars. It was a completely different arrangement than the ones in the Mountains. Would they change gradually like they would back home? Or was it a drastically new starscape each night? The rhythm of the cart and overall boredom eventually lulled Fern to sleep.

A pain in her back woke her in the middle of the night. She was used to sleeping on the floor, but the metal lost heat quickly in the night, adding to her discomfort. The cart was stopped somewhere quiet. Kraai was still fast asleep, but Journey was nowhere to be seen. Fern peeked over the edge. They were by another field, the horse gone. For a moment, Fern was gripped with panic. Had their guide abandoned them? She scanned the area, looking for some sign—perhaps they found a stream or grassy field and were sleeping nearby so the horse could rest and regain its energy. There were no signs of them, but there were stars. Not stars—they were too low in the sky. A dozen or so balls of light, moving just over the top of the plants in the field.

Fern snuck over Kraai and out of the back of the cart. She pulled her cloak tight over her body, still trying to recover the warmth she'd lost in her sleep. Something about the lights called to her, drawing her forward. With her first step toward the field, a hand grabbed at hers. She nearly screamed, but when she turned, she saw the dwarf with his finger held to his lips.

"Do not let them know we are awake," he whispered, hardly loud enough to be heard. "I got their permission to rest alongside their field, but they will vanish if they know we are watching."

Fern sat on the ground, resting her back on one of the cart's wheels, tucking her knees to her chest under her cloak. "What are they?"

"Fairies." Journey leaned against the wheel, as well, just barely taller standing than Fern was sitting. "They do not reveal themselves when other beings are watching."

"I thought the Four Regions were made so all beings could come out of hiding."

Journey looked down at her. "You know as well as I that many in the Mountains are still wary of others." He turned his attention back to the lights before them. "The fairies have always been secretive, their particular magic still a mystery. It is powerful, though. If you ever find yourself wondering 'how' in the Light Region, you can assume the answer is that the fairies are behind it."

Fern thought about the vine trap, the words that can't be spoken, the burning flesh. Powerful magic, yes, but terrifying. She followed one bobbing light with her eyes. It was too far away to make out a form, but it seemed to dance among the greenery. The cool breeze rattled the leaves, but the sound was so foreign. It was not all-encompassing like in the Mountains, but capricious and playful, passing on the wind. The smell was fresh, though, clearing the last of the sleepy fog in Fern's mind. She could probably stay up, keep Journey company if he decided to continue moving forward, toward the veil.

The dwarf was in a trance, though. His hand mindlessly stroked his moustache and the top of his beard. His attention was focused on the fairies. Their light reflected in his eyes. Fern watched them, too, drifting nearer and farther, across the field and back.

Before Fern knew it, an elbow was jabbed into her side. She started awake and the lights were gone, replaced by the warm glow of the sky taking on the light of a rising sun.

"Looks like they noticed us. Good thing they were not *too* upset." Journey pushed himself to stand, brushing dirt off his side. "Sometimes when they put the sleep on you, they bless you with terrible nightmares."

Fern stood, too, using the cart behind her to lift herself up. She wanted to peek over the side to see that Kraai was still safe, but when she turned, her attention was held by the horizon. Golden light burned her eyes, but she could not look away. It was as if the sun was being shone through a wall of amber after reflecting off solid gold.

"Ah, it is beautiful, is it not?" Journey led his horse back to the cart. "The best sunrise in all the Four Regions is the sunrise through the Golden Veil." He hoisted himself onto the driver's bench. "Best sunset is in the Seas, but only if you can catch the green flash." He took a sip from a jug, then held it out for Fern.

After climbing into the hold and stepping over Kraai, she made her way to get a sip. The air was dry, and she had apparently been sleeping with her mouth open. As she brought it to her lips, it was again forced from her hand. It fell into the cart, spilling water all over, soaking the blanket Kraai had used to cover himself.

He was awake instantly, throwing the wet cloth off of him. "What is—?" He looked to Fern, to the jug, and then to Journey. "I just—" He harumphed, kicking the blanket to the corner where the water was still spilling out. He rubbed his eyes. "You could not think of a kinder way to wake me?"

"You—" Fern started. "I—" She looked to Journey, then gave up on talking to Kraai.

"Do you trust me?" Journey asked, looking Fern dead in the eye.

Fern held his gaze but narrowed her eyes. "Not particularly."

His face beamed, a smile able to be made out somewhere beneath his facial hair. "Even if you did…" His eyes fell to the jug, which was now out of water to spill.

Fern followed his eyes, bending to pick up the sopping blanket and wring it out over the side of the cart. She righted the jug, summoning out the little bit that remained and cleaning it before drinking. Once the discomfort of her dry mouth was eased, she actually felt quite refreshed. That was some of the best sleep she had gotten in ages.

They drove through another city, Gordium. This one was even larger than the last. It took hours to make it from one side to the other. Kraai was in awe, sitting on the driver's bench watching everything pass by. Fern, however, decided to keep to the back here, bundling herself in the half-dry blanket in an attempt to hide herself while still being able to take in the surroundings.

The most impressive building was the palace. While the accents and decor on most homes were bright colored paints and gold, the palace shone silver. The facade was a grey granite that had impurities that sparkled in the light. The long metal roof provided a smooth but warped reflection of the nearly-cloudless blue sky above. There were more windows than Fern could count. While this was impressive on other buildings,

Fern knew that just the royalty called this entire structure their residence.

Royalty like Fern. She could live in a place like this. If she had ventured the other direction, toward the darkness instead of the light, she could have fought to claim the throne. She could have too many windows to count. She could have thick walls to protect her from threats, plus an extra wall to keep beings away from the actual walls. She could have so much decoration just on the outside of her home that people will stare at it in awe as they drive by in the back of a cart.

She could, but she wouldn't. She was on her way to safety. She was on her way to put her mother's fears at ease, to save her father from constantly having to suffer her fits. Would this be enough to fix her, though? Or might the unknown make everything worse?

"Sort of gaudy, is it not?" Kraai's voice startled her. She hadn't noticed that he climbed down and was now sitting next to her, resting his head next to hers on the side.

Fern pulled away. "Yes, it is." She turned around, slumping down into the blanket. "It hurts to look at it too long."

Kraai put his arm around her and squeezed her shoulder. "They will be alright."

Fern turned into his chest, tucking the blanket to her nose to hide her expression. "I know." But she didn't, and neither did Kraai.

Chapter 7

The horse slowed its pace as they drew near. Journey had to fumble with the reins to keep her going in the right direction—toward the glittering curtain. Finally, the animal planted its hooves, snorting her disapproval.

"I suppose it is on foot for you two from here," Journey called over his shoulder to his passengers in the back.

"Are you not coming with us?" Kraai asked.

Journey's entire body tensed before he shook his head. "But before you go, would you like something to eat? A drink of water?"

Fern gave him a sidelong look. "Yes to some food, but we will do without the drink."

Journey took some of the food he had procured in town and handed it off to Fern—a significant amount of food. Finally, he took one berry from the small basket that sat next to him, pouring water from his small cup onto it, then threw it to the ground. "Not that one." His eyes met Fern's and once his stare burned into her, he broke and looked up to the veil behind her.

She nodded. "Thank you. For everything."

"Anything for your families." Journey smiled as he finally allowed his restless horse to turn around. As he left them, he shouted over the creak of the cart, "A pleasure to meet you both."

The duo turned around. The veil stood before them, tall and looming. They could not see inside, but rather a hazy, golden reflection of their own figures waving in the light breeze.

"Will we remember this moment when we come back out?" Fern asked, knowing her partner did not have the answer.

The warmth of Kraai's hand reaching out and holding hers did nothing for her nerves. Would this be his last memory of her? Her hand tensed, and his squeezed back.

"So we just...go?" She stared straight ahead, inches from the wall. Its metallic smell wafted toward her and away as it bent and moved through the air before them. Even if she wanted to look away, she would not be able to.

Kraai also kept his eyes on the veil. "I suppose so."

"We just have to step forward." Each word came out slower than the last.

There was no response for some time. It felt right to rest in that moment, watching swirls of sunlight catch and dance. Not a bad last memory to have with someone.

"As we always have?" Kraai asked, a devious smile on his lips, as he cocked his face toward Fern.

Fern dared him back with her eyes. "As we always have."

It was only two steps from one side of the veil to the other, but in that moment, time seemed to stretch. Sound ceased completely as her head passed through the substance. Any worry Fern held instantly melted—not just her nerves about forgetting everything, or the fear of the unknown that lay ahead, but *everything* that had been weighing on her did not seem to matter anymore. Not her dirty blood, not her parents' lies, not the soreness in her rear from sitting in that old cart for so long. Her shoulders sunk. Her jaw loosened. The crease in her brow melted away. If this feeling were a spell, she would cast it every day. The one breath she was drawing in this time felt clean, and when she let it out she could see glimmers of light swirl with the breath that came out in a hazy, grey cloud.

When they reached the other side, hands still joined, the pleasant feeling lingered. Fern floated with her next steps. Kraai stepped lightly beside her, his eyes wide.

A loneliness crept into a corner of Fern's mind. It was not a sad loneliness, more like noticing that a friend was missing. She looked at her hand that still held Kraai's—he was still here, present. She admired her other hand, watching her fingers trail through the air. *The air.* Why was it so dry? She sensed no water around her. Her fingers searched, flexing and grabbing in front of her eyes, as her mind wandered to an incident in the Mountains when she mixed an emotional spark with dry vegetation. She would need to keep control of her emotions here. Yet, she had no control. She was in a fog of bliss. An alarm went through her mind, telling her that she needed to take command of herself, but the noise got lost—how could this be bad?

The road continued on before them, rolling grass hills on each side, but before they made it very far, two orbs of white light floated toward them. Unconcerned, Fern watched the lights dance around each other, coming to a stop just feet before them. In a blinding flash, two tall females appeared in their place. Were these fairies? Their skin was like porcelain, one white as the crest of a wave, the other the shade of earth after a fresh rain. Both had straight black hair. Their eyes glowed with the same light that had approached them.

With smiles on their faces, they held out cups. "Welcome, newcomers," the darker one said with a voice of honey. "You must be exhausted from your travels. Please, have something to drink."

Her thirst became instantly apparent. Her throat was as rough as bark. Swallowing her saliva felt as if she had pine needles lodged in the back of her mouth. Her hands lifted from her sides, finally letting go of Kraai.

A snap in Fern's mind cut through the fog. The eerie dryness of the air. A slap of the drinks from her hands. A stare from the dwarf. Fern could see now the force with which these two were smiling, the lack of expression in their eyes. Her instincts had been shut off by the veil, but now they were screaming at her. Her hands stopped moving forward, and instead she reached to the side to press down on Kraai's outstretched arm. "We are quite alright. We had our fill of drink before we came through."

Kraai's head snapped to look at Fern. She could see the clouds lifting from his own eyes, his brow coming back down in its normal resting place. "Yes." His voice found clarity as he spoke. "We are not in need of refreshment at this time. Thank you."

The two beings before them continued smiling. This time the lighter one spoke, holding the cup demandingly toward Fern, the light in her eyes burning brighter. "We must insist. It is considered an insult to refuse a drink in this place. You do not wish to slight us, do you?"

Fern glanced at the cup in the hands of the fairy who stood before her—it looked like plain water in a glass. How could she tell, though, unless she felt it?

Fern once again took Kraai's hand, gesturing to him as she said, "We come from the Mountains. Our clan drinks only from the streams. Perhaps you can lead us to one where we can drink as is our custom, and you will be providing us refreshments, as is yours." She cocked her head to the side, pulling as much worry into her eyes as she could muster, trying to disguise it as sympathy.

The glowing eyes blinked once, twice, then turned to their companion. They stood, frozen. Not a muscle twitched, their forced smiles still sculpted on their faces. The only movement was a light pull of their hair from the gentle wind. It reminded Fern of a fish she had seen frozen in water—a moment forever suspended, as if the creature would move again once the ice thawed. Fern grew restless watching the nothingness unfolding before them. Do they move? Interrupt? Run? When Fern shifted her foot, the crunch of grinding rock into the road seemed to break whatever spell they were under.

The fairy before Kraai turned, continuing as if no time had passed, "Yes, we will bring you to the stream. Please, follow us." The skirts of their long, golden dresses grazed the dirt of the road, hiding whether their feet were truly on the ground. They moved in a way that convinced Fern they were actually hovering above it.

Fern looked to Kraai, hoping to ascertain if she should be concerned. By the expression on his face, it was evident he was searching for clarity, as well. His fingers squeezing her hand spurred her forward, and they followed their silent guides off the road and into the lush green of the grassy fields to their left. Fern could sense the stream as they approached. She could feel the churning of the water as it tumbled over itself, fighting to follow the command of gravity. Yet that was not the only command it followed. There was another force at work she could not grasp. The babble of the water when it entered earshot gave no more indications. Fern had studied streams and rivers; she had befriended the ever-changing currents near her home. Even the rivers in the Light Region outside the veil had stories to tell, yet this one held its secrets. She did not trust this water, yet she had promised to drink from it.

It was over a hill that they finally saw the stream—narrow and quick, clear and crisp. Fern smiled at her guides who, upon reaching the bank, stared wide-eyed at the newcomers. She knelt on the mud at the edge of the stream, the coolness soaking into her breeches. She leaned forward over the water, planting her left hand upstream, letting the loose tendrils of her hair fall into the current. She closed her eyes, communing. *What are your secrets?* No answer. *I must know your secrets. I wish to trust you. I wish to show you that you may trust me.* Again, the water did not answer, but not because it did not want to disclose the truth, but because it did not know its own secret. The water held no information whatsoever. Yet it did hold something else. Fern dug her fingers into the top layer of the riverbed, pushing her attention past the water, trying to discover what else was hiding in this stream. Her eyes shot open. Magic. The water itself was enchanted. Fern turned her hand to the side, opening her fingers, letting only pure water through. Her chest trembled with the effort. She reached in with her right hand, feeling the water free of magic. It shook, quivering against her skin—a warning of nearby danger. The magic made them forget. *The magic in the water made them forget.* She thanked the water, reached in and drank a handful of the water free of enchantment.

Kraai watched her closely, waiting for guidance. Fern moved her body out of the way, leaving her left hand to filter the magic out, gesturing to the space where she drank. As he bent down, Fern got a clear view of their guides, their eyes calm, their smiles gone. A breath escaped them both at the same time as he drank.

"We thank you for the refreshment," Fern said as she rose, pulling Kraai up with her to ensure he would not go for another sip. She wiped the remaining water on her mud-stained pants. "Now we must find a relative we believe is living here."

"We would be glad to show you where to go," said one of the fairies.

The other continued, "If you would tell us whom you seek." Their smiles were now pleasant, the glow of their eyes less intense, dimmed further by the rise of their cheeks.

"A vampire," Fern began, but she stopped upon realizing how ridiculous it sounded to search for a vampire in the Light Region.

The light in the dark-skinned fairy's eyes went out, leaving beautiful brown irises staring. "She has been waiting for a visitor for so long."

The other fairy turned, asking, "How do you know they seek *that* vampire?"

"Do you not feel her spark?" The brown eyes did not leave Fern.

Fern's heart leapt and a tingle found its way up her spine. Mask was truly here, and Fern was going to meet her.

"We shall send you to Antillia, the city in which she resides. Her home is by the sea, but if there are clouds in the sky she is often out. She carries a black parasol." The brown eyes smiled as her hand rose, about to snap. "Deep breath. Do not exhale until your feet are on terra firma."

Then the fairies were gone. The world around them melted, the light never fading, but the color shifting. The blue of the clear sky sunk below the horizon while the direct light of the sun refracted into a white blanket above. Distant bird calls crescendoed into a collection of noises that could not be identified. The stone street rose to meet their feet and, upon contact, all of the sights and sounds found clarity. Fern let out a shaking breath, then filled her lungs with the new environment, taking in the salt air that slapped her face in a sudden gust. She staggered back, collapsing into Kraai.

"Best not fall in." He hoisted her up and gestured to the sudden drop behind them. "Not sure how your body will hold up in the sea."

Fern found her footing, then leaned to get a better look off the wall without moving the rest of her body. Waves crashed against the wall, sending a spray into the air. Fern recoiled, stepping back and away. She was not sure how much salt water it would take for her to develop scales and a hunger for flesh. In only three steps, she bumped into someone. Her first reaction to the sudden presence at her back was to swing her arm around in an attack, but halfway through her turn she realized she was the one in the wrong—*she* was the one who backed into *them*. Her swinging hand found its way behind her head, grabbing at the back of her neck as she said, "I'm terribly sorry, I—" Her mouth gaped.

Under the shade of a black parasol, the woman's complexion matched the pale grey of the sky above. She wore a luscious red dress, trimmed with black lace, and matching lace gloves to complete the ensemble. "I'll let it slide because you're new here." Her smile revealed sharp teeth that made Fern's heart shudder. "Just don't run into the wrong fairy or you might not even get the chance to apologize." The woman continued walking, her steps long and graceful so her large skirt bobbed with each step.

It was her. The blonde hair. The scar on her neck. Her grandmother, so young and beautiful, yet so dangerous simply in what she was. Every instinct forced her to stay silent, to not draw attention to herself, to not remind a vampire of her existence.

"Wait!" Kraai's voice called from over Fern's shoulder.

The vampire turned, the bottom of her dress turning in an echo of her motion. She stared at Kraai, about to say something, then squinting to further assess him.

He nodded at Fern, who nodded back before fumbling to open the bag at her hip. She dug her fingers inside—she should have given this a special pouch, some protective encasing that would be easier to find. Instead, she grazed the bottom of the canvas, scraping against tiny particles of rock and soil from her travels thus far, until her fingers touched upon a cool gem. She pulled it out pinched between the back of her index finger and the pad of her middle. She let the earring fall into her free hand, noting the glow was absent in this light. With a deep breath, she held it out toward the vampire, who still stood yards away.

The elegant woman walked closer, angling the parasol forward to block where the sun hid behind the clouds. Her gloved hand reached out slowly, too slowly in Fern's mind.

Fern began to shake, her breath stuttering as the predator crept closer.

"You needn't worry, child. I have lived among humans for years now and have yet to bite a—" Her voice faded as her fingers touched the earring. Her eyes widened and she took in a deep breath through her nose. Recognition melted her brow. "But you are not just any human, are you?" Something sincere flashed in her expression. "I believe we both have questions that need answering. Come with me." She turned, taking the earring with her, caressing it with both hands as she rested the shaft of the parasol on her shoulder.

Fern looked at Kraai. He showed no fear, yet something in his countenance indicated he did not want to follow the woman—a sadness lingering on his face. When he caught her looking at him, his face turned to a smile and he nodded her forward, hopping close behind.

Chapter 8

The woman's house stood but thirty feet from the sea wall, across a wide stone road that Fern struggled to cross due to a constant stream of carts and carriages. The people on the street dressed in strange fashions—men with trousers that reached nearly to the ground and hats that rose toward the sky, which they touched when acknowledging Fern's presence. The women were in wide gowns with layers of cloth that could never be functional in the Mountains. Looking down at her own attire, Fern realized how much of the road had caked onto her shirt and breeches. She looked a right mess, and Kraai was not much better.

They passed through an iron gate in the wall that met the road. The residence itself was simple enough, a stone structure that reached two stories toward the sky, but the decoration made it grand. Stone statues and intricate masonry graced the facade. A shorter, yet not quite dwarvish, man stood guard in the doorway.

The vampire collapsed her parasol and handed it off in one smooth motion on her way in. "These two are with me. Privacy and refreshment would be lovely."

The man nodded, giving only an emotionless glance to the two guests before following the lady of the house inside to go about his work.

Fern expected heavy stone and darkness to surround the lodging of a vampire. Yet this place seemed *pleasant*. She would have no fear entering it if she did not know it housed a blood drinker.

Kraai placed his hand on the small of her back, whispering in her ear, "I am right here. I do not believe she poses a threat to us."

Fern grumbled back in equally hushed tones, "Says the one without human blood." His hand pushed forward, gently enough that she could resist if she wanted to, but strong enough to assure her that he was still there.

Inside, the house was decorated with more color than Fern had seen in her entire life. A mural covered an entire wall, depicting strange machines beyond Fern's understanding. The other walls held tapestries, paintings, and large velvet curtains, closed and letting in no light whatsoever. All of the light came from torches on the walls. Some of the torch light shone on the red dress, highlighting its silken texture. The woman wearing it smiled, gesturing to a door off the main room. "Please."

With each step toward the waiting woman, the room grew colder. She was ice incarnate. Fern reached behind her, waving her hand until it found Kraai's. When had she become such a child? Still, she held tight, not wanting to lose him for a second in the beast's lair. They brushed past their host, turning to go into a large room filled with books—piled on tables, lined on the walls, even strewn about, open on the floor. The click of the door latch threw another warning through Fern's core.

"Might I get you something to drink?" the host asked, pointing back toward the door.

"No," Fern said rather forcefully. "Thank you."

"Good girl." A sharp tooth peeked out of her smile. "You read, yes?" The vampire rested her gloved hand on an open book.

"I am not one for reading," Fern replied. "Not to the extent my mother and father are, at least."

A sharp intake of breath and the greyed face contorted, biting her lips together. It was terribly unflattering, given Fern's understanding that the creatures were inherently beautiful. She almost scoffed at the reaction but was distracted by Kraai's hand leaving hers.

Kraai caught the collapsing woman in a kneeling embrace. Holding her firmly, he said in her ear, "He was similarly affected when he heard you were alive."

A vampire in tears. Fern wanted to roll her eyes at the ridiculousness of it, but the image before her reminded her of her parents the day she went to the market. It was so...*human*. Every vampire was once something else. Had she held on to who she was before? Could she? An urge to pull Kraai off of her faded as she recognized that the woman needed him more than she did, so Fern perused the books that looked to be in various states of use: *The Lord of the Rings, Portal Magic vol. V, U.S. History 2000-2050, Advanced Potion Antidotes*. She went back to the history book, looking closer at images on the open page. There were buildings that stretched into the sky like mountains, but not a painting—it looked so *real*. How was it possible?

"That is where I am from."

Fern jumped at the voice that came from over her shoulder. She hurried three steps away before she even took a breath. She now realized how cold her back had become. How long had the vampire been standing behind her?

Kraai stood between them. "I believe introductions are in order." He faced their host, bowing lightly. "My name is Kraai. I am a great grandchild of Lathron and Sneak."

"Needle's child?" The woman reached for Kraai's face, pushing his hair out of the way. "She made it out of the palace alive?"

"She did," Kraai confirmed, letting her examine him.

"So she must have been the one to guide Wave to safety." With the word *Wave*, her focus shifted. "Which would make you my granddaughter, I suppose." Her hand led her in Fern's direction.

Fern backed away, but responded as politely as she could muster, "I suppose. My name is Fern. And you are Em? Mask?"

"I was Mask in the Dark Region, but here I go by my human name." Her eyes glowed with warmth. "Emily."

Fern had had enough of this wolf in sheep's clothing. "But you're not human."

"Put that together yourself, did you?" Emily shut one of the books with a slap that rumbled through the wooden table upon which it sat. "A vampire would not have been foolish enough to become trapped here. The small human piece of me did. I would be ashamed to use the name Mask while a prisoner in another region."

"Why *did* you come here?" Kraai asked.

Emily gestured to leather armchairs with a wooden table in between. "Sit." She bent to the fireplace, removed her gloves, and snapped. A spark jumped from her fingertips to ignite the wood. After hovering her hands over the newborn flame, she replaced the gloves and found her way to one of the leather chairs opposite. "You both know I had a sister. A twin." Though she directed her speech to Kraai, she paused to look at Fern at the word *twin*. "She was in the human world, made fully human in order to save her life, but not allowed to return here."

Ever the good student, Kraai nodded along. "Using the potion from the werewolf decisions, the one later used on Strike."

"Exactly. I had struggled to accept what I had done, stealing her away from her world without choice. Will helped me through it, but a part of me always wanted to see her, to talk to her, to be sure she was alright. We were under careful watch, though. Nobody was going to the human world through the Dark Region." Her eyebrows raised dramatically. "Not after all of my family's shenanigans."

"We know the history," Fern interrupted, though keeping how recently she learned the history to herself. "Why did you leave your family in danger to come here?"

Stone faced, Emily looked Fern dead in the eyes. "My sister was here. Within the veil."

Did she have to offend Fern by telling her lies? "There are no humans in the Four Regions." Fern looked to the curtain where a sliver of daylight let itself in, trying to see what was outside.

"According to everyone outside the Golden Veil, you would be right. Here, we know differently. That is one of the secrets guarded so strictly." She drank from a metal chalice that seemed to have appeared from thin air. "Some humans come here as a reward for their service to the Four Regions. After dedicating their lives to helping track down and send back magical beings that were in the human world, they get to live out the rest of their days here." She put her cup down and gestured to the room around her. "Well, not *here* here, but within the veil. My sister was part of that group. It turns out my mother's friend initially wanted to recruit my mother due to her knowledge of the Four Regions, but my mother had me to take care of and could not go bounding off after vampires, then became ill before I was an adult. My sister, however, was a perfect candidate—raised in the Four Regions, familiar with the beings that lived here, and not susceptible to a vampire's charm. When she became too old to continue and had trained her replacement's replacement, she was allowed to come here. I came to find her. I needed to seek forgiveness. Humans have such short lives; I did not have time to figure out how to get around the memory issue. It was only after entering and...you know..."—she raised the cup back to her lips, staring down into it with intent—"that I found out I would not get to leave with my memory. I've spent all the time since trying to find out how to leave while remembering my time with my sister."

"You didn't even know her." Fern continued to look away, continuing to keep tabs on the vampire from the corner of her eye. There *had to* be more than memories of her sister keeping her here.

"Exactly. But I wanted to. I grew up without siblings, without a father, knowing something was missing from my life. I got to spend years with my father before he passed, but never knew the person with whom I shared a womb."

"Is she here now?" Kraai asked, checking around the room as if she was hiding just out of sight.

"No, she died two years ago. Complications from an old battle injury. I've dedicated my time to trying to find my way out ever since."

"They couldn't heal her with potions?" Fern recalled the potion that had healed her father's heart the day he died. "I thought humans were easy to heal."

"They are sent here to live out their days, not to extend them. They are given every comfort and pleasure the region provides, but saving their lives through magical means is a punishable offense. It's happened only once. Both the healer and the healed were put to death."

Fern couldn't keep the sarcasm from her voice. "But she is *really* dead, right? Like, my father was dead, and you were dead, but we saw how that worked out."

"Fern!" Kraai's voice cut through her sardonic wall.

A pang of guilt pulsed through her, until she looked at Emily and saw what she was. Her face hardened once more.

Emily's lip curled toward Fern before she turned to Kraai. "It's quite alright. Vampires don't have feelings, do they? As long as we are going off stereotypes, you better watch yourself around the *siren*." The last word lingered on her lips, filled with venom.

Fern sat to the edge of her seat. "That's not fair, I don't even have my songtone!"

"And I have never tasted human blood besides my sister's—animal only." She paused as the words sunk into Fern's mind. "She is dead, burned, and buried. Now it is my turn to ask questions. Between your mother's size the last time I saw her and the rumors of task traders having people hunt down a mimic of the princess, my assumption has been that you are a twin, as well?"

Fern leaned back into the chair, tucking her feet up. Being on-edge was exhausting so she forced herself to relax as much as she could. If she was going to be feasted upon, it would have probably happened by now. "I am. My mother escaped with me and Kraai's pregnant mother."

"And Sway? Stalworth?" Emily leaned forward, her turn to be on edge.

Fern looked to the ceiling for answers, trying to recall the story she had been told just days before, yet that seemed like an eternity ago. "I don't remember names, but one of their friends killed the other while under Belle's influence."

Emily's hand found her lips and her eyes again fought to keep composure. "Such a bright girl," her voice cracked. "He is probably gone, too. I can't imagine he would have been able to stand the pain of knowing he killed the woman he loved." Her haunted eyes went wildly around the room. "I should have been there. If I had known that Belle would give up her—"

She cut short and shot her eyes to Fern. "How did she manage to gain access to the palace?"

Fern cast her eyes to the floor. It felt like a secret she should keep, based on the look on her father's face when he told her, but the pleading in Emily's eyes was enough to break her. "My father invited her in. Welcomed her in an effort to make amends."

Shame crossed Emily's face. "He always was too trusting. Always looking for the good in others." Her lips turned to a snarl. "But some beings have no good within them, and Belle is one of them."

"He is not so trusting now." Fern's body tensed, feeling shut in by even the thought of her restrictions and rules at home.

Kraai's brow furrowed. "All of those restrictions placed on you are not your father's. Do you not notice that he always defers to your mother and what she wants?"

Fern considered this, recalling the times her father had demanded discretion, privacy, even paranoia—they were times her mother had said something or had one of her fits of panic. He always conferred with her before setting down a ruling. *He* was the one who all but told her to go to the market. She had a sudden wish to go see her father, to know him in this new light after thinking he had been her jailor this entire time, but the realization that she would not see him sent a knife into her chest. As she hunched in her seat, she felt Kraai's hand on her forearm. Warm. Comforting. *There*, for now. Fern snapped back to the conversation. "How long may we stay?"

"Fern, you can stay as long as you would like. I feel as if things will be safer for you in a few years, or at least once your sister is named. Although, Belle is quite fond of revenge, so you might want to stay until she has completely forgotten about you." Emily took another sip from her chalice. "Or until she dies. Only another, what? Sixty years? If nobody takes her out before then." Her focus shifted to Kraai. "But you, are you staying? You are not being targeted too, are you?"

"I came to be sure Fern was safe." His grip on her arm tightened for a moment. "I will stay until she feels she is."

"I will have James make up some rooms…" Emily turned to give a surreptitious glance. "*A* room?" She waited for a response from the confused guests, but received none. "Two rooms it is. Far from my room, if that will help you rest easier."

Had her own grandmother just suggested she share a room with Kraai? It was hard to think of this woman, so youthful in appearance and attitude, as her grandmother, but she *was* nearing her nineties. She was even better preserved than Kraai's great grandfather.

Emily had business to attend to, but allowed the two to remain in the study until the rooms were ready. The moment Fern and Kraai were finally alone, she held his arms, forcing him to look at her face-on.

Fern opened her lips to speak, but felt the bile build in the back of her throat. Forcing the sensation and words down, she instead said, "If there was ever a time for you to read my mind, this is it. I figured it out."

Kraai gave a sympathetic smile. "It does not happen on command, and even when it does happen, that is not how it works. It is about emotions."

"And scents?"

Kraai nodded his head off to the side. "And scents that one time." He brought his focus back. "But I will follow your lead here. Are you suggesting that we might leave here with our memories?"

Fern checked with her stomach as her response formed in her mind, would this trigger the reaction? Upon a lack of queasiness she said, "As of now, I believe so."

As Kraai went through some of the books, Fern found a piece of parchment and quill. She attempted to write *"Do not drink anything here,"* but her hand cramped as she began the first stroke, causing a spasm that ended up knocking over the inkwell. After blotting the ruined parchment with the sleeve of her shirt, she tucked herself back into a chair, massaging her hand until it became usable once again.

James entered, bowing lightly to Fern, who looked at Kraai confused.

"Princess. Remember?" Kraai's broad smile indicated he took great joy in Fern's discomfort.

Fern smacked him on the arm with the back of her hand, then moved to follow the man up the stairs and down the hall. He indicated two doors next to each other, then left. No introduction, no explanation, nothing. Fern chose the door on the left and entered, shutting it behind her immediately for some privacy at last. The creak and close of another door indicated Kraai had done the same.

Fern lay on the bed, brushing her hands into the fur blanket on top. She pinched the hairs between her fingertips, rolling them together and straightening them back out. It was the only thing she could think to do, feeling trapped in this room. She nodded off for some time, awakening to the sound of footsteps in the hallway that stopped outside her door.

She sat bolt upright, grabbing onto the bedpost as her head spun from the drop in blood pressure. Why hadn't they knocked? Why were they just waiting? Fern sat in silence, only hearing the clatter of carts from out the window that faced an alley.

Finally it came, three light knocks.

Fern brought herself to the door, opening it a crack while keeping her foot in its way so it could open no further. A familiar face greeted her.

"I do not know what to do with myself here," Kraai whispered through the small opening. "Do you think we would be allowed to leave and explore the city?"

Fern rushed to the bed to grab her bag, pulling it over her head and shoulder as she pushed her way past him and into the hallway. "I don't know, but I would rather just go now and ask later." She still had mud on her knees, ink on her sleeve, but she didn't care. They had been travelling to this place for days—a set route, led by others. She wanted to choose the direction she moved, even if she did not know where she was going. She needed out.

Chapter 9

Antillia was the most beautiful city Fern had ever seen—not a hard contest to win considering she'd only ever seen three. As they walked, a wall of buildings, stone and wood alike, stood to their right, while on their left was the sea. It was nowhere near as gaudy as the buildings of the other cities outside the veil, and the decoration was even more attractive because of this. Boats and ships dotted the water's surface, suspended where they were as smaller boats transferred people and goods to docks along the sea wall. Being near the Light Region's sea meant they were in one of the lightest places in the Four Regions. When the sun's lens dipped below the horizon, it would set into this water, and rise again from it the next day. Fern stretched her arm and held her fingers to the horizon, measuring—two hours to sunset, though, likely more due to their relative distance to this edge of the world.

The cobbled streets had no give—after an hour, walking on them began to wear on Fern's feet and knees. She longed for the squish of dirt, the bounce of downed branches and leaves. She waited for a kick of pine or spruce in the air, but instead she got the salt of the sea. It burned her nostrils. There was not a single tree along the entire seawall. Well, there were some pitiable ones allowed to grow in holes in the side of the road, but they seemed to be more like overgrown bushes than actual *trees*. Nothing like the powerful two-needled pines, or the spruce whose needles change color as you climb. No, these were ornamental—not even decorative in the way some elves kept trees that changed color when the temperature dropped and lost their leaves—but they were appealing enough to look at. The most common type had tiny pink flowers that covered every branch. As the sea breeze would come in, petals would fall and be swept away, riding the current of air up and over the row of buildings. Though lovely, they were not sturdy trees—they would not hold up in a true windstorm.

Kraai and Fern walked without conversation and without destination. Fern fought the temptation to turn down side streets and duck into alleys, she needed to see this road to the end. Did it turn away from the sea? Did it have a way out? Visually, she could not see the incline, but her calves let her know there was a change in elevation—nothing a girl from the Mountains couldn't handle, but significant as the road narrowed and the constructed sea wall gave way to sheer rock cliffs. The curve of it toward the sea revealed chalky white rock and an outlook that Fern decided would be the end of their journey for the day.

She turned to see Kraai just behind her and she smiled, lowering her head and bracing a foot. Kraai did the same but before he could fully ready himself, Fern was sprinting forward. The cobbled street had become a dirt path, the buildings turned to houses turned to empty fields. A small part of Fern wanted to be afraid of being out in the open, but she could see any predator approaching from this vantage point. Besides, what vampire would be out in the light of day, now that the evening sun had burned away the clouds?

The path kept along the ledge, a small strip of grass between them and the ever-growing drop. Fern pumped her arms, keeping to her toes as much as she could, but frequently slipping over the rocks in the path and needing to keep her footing so she wouldn't tumble into the sea. She felt Kraai behind her, and could hear his intensified breathing as they climbed. But Fern was faster. She ran at full speed as long as she could, which was just long enough, as she found the path ended at that point where the cliff jutted out above the water. She planted her feet, but her momentum carried her forward, her torso bending over the fifteen yard drop as her arms flailed to keep her balanced on the ledge. One foot began to slide on the very end of the path. Her heart froze. Images of scales and blood-soaked lips flashed into her mind as her arm was nearly pulled out of its socket by a tug from behind. She turned her body toward the counterforce, falling into Kraai as they both tumbled into the road and grass behind them.

Fern laid on top of Kraai, her side pressed into his front. She could not move as she processed what had almost just happened. Would there even be anybody to perform the ceremony here? Was she about to be trapped in the sea within the Golden Veil?

"Your elbow is in my gut." Kraai's voice broke her reflection.

Fern rolled off, her back falling onto the ground beside him. "Sorry about that." She looked into the sky, watching clouds blow in from over the sea. "Thanks, I suppose."

"You suppose?" He sat up, looking out over the water as he rested his arms on his knees. "You owe me. If I would have fallen in, I would be dead."

"It's not so bad. It is hardly thirty feet. The water would break your fall." Fern pressed her hands into her eyes.

He got to his feet and inched toward the cliff's edge, peering over the drop. "That is at *least* forty feet. And if I did survive the drop, I am not sure I would survive the lack of ability to swim." He let out a staccato guffaw. "I mean, you never learned to swim in deep water, either, but I bet the fins would help. Or perhaps your ability to manipulate water."

"What? You don't think you would suddenly sprout wings and fly over the water?" Fern finally sat up, continuing to ground herself in the solid land beneath her.

Kraai was now a bit further from the edge, but still looking out into the water. "If I could shapeshift, I would probably know it by now."

"What if it only happens when you're in danger?"

Kraai turned to face his friend. "And you do not believe I have been in danger before?"

Fern rolled her eyes. "Name one time—and I mean *real* danger."

His face was flat. "Dwarven lands, when we had thirteen years."

"Oh, that wasn't *that* bad." Fern forced an eye roll.

"The handaxe came within inches of my head!" He moved his hand over his right ear, barely grazing the ends of his hair.

"Then lodged in a tree, which means we clearly had enough cover."

They stared at each other, eyes slowly getting wider until their smiles joined in and both began to laugh. Perhaps it was the adrenaline of what had just happened, but Fern laughed so hard she found it difficult to breathe. It was made even worse when she saw Kraai doubled over. They sat for minutes, trying to compose themselves, then finally managed to take complete breaths while wiping their eyes.

"You did not manage to get your acorn, did you?" Kraai asked, finally able to stand.

"No, and we still don't know why that tree is always guarded. We're faster now than we were back then. When we get back, I think we should try again." Fern's face dropped. *When we get back. If* we get back. Kraai would, hopefully with his memories intact. But would Fern ever be able to leave? And if she did, would she keep her memories?

Kraai let out a long breath, shooting a look of sympathy at Fern before turning back to the water. He once again inched toward the edge, putting far too much trust in the ground beneath him.

"You are too young!" a voice called from below.

Fern scrambled to her feet to make her way to the edge.

The voice, a woman's, rang out again. "You have too much life left within you! Come back when you are older!"

Kraai cupped his mouth to shout back, "I do not plan to jump!" He lowered his hands for a bit, then raised them again. "But I appreciate your concern!"

Resting her hand on Kraai's shoulder for balance, Fern looked out and saw the source of the voice—a woman in the water. She had a full figure and voluminous brown hair, decorated with an orange flower Fern had never seen before. Her skin was only a few shades darker than Fern's, but the water gave it a warm glow in the last of the setting sunlight. The woman's amber eyes grew large as she noticed Fern alongside Kraai and she tucked back under the water, saffron scales trailing behind.

Fern stopped breathing as she stumbled backward. She tripped over her own foot and was, once again, on the ground, her scraped hand covering her gaping mouth.

Kraai ran to her, concern on his brow. He held out a hand to help her up, but when she did not take it, he sat beside her, putting an arm over her shoulder and pulling her into his chest.

Fern shook as she breathed out the words, "There are sirens in the Light Region." She turned her head to look Kraai in the eyes. "They will tell Belle that I am here."

"They are within the veil, so they may be bound by the same enchantment that plagues everyone else in here." He looked away as his voice trailed off. "Which is good, because I believe she recognized you."

"Kraai," Fern warned. "Do not jest about this."

He shrugged. "I felt a twinge of recognition before she disappeared. Not that she necessarily knew *who* you were, but that there was something in you that was familiar to her."

Five focused breaths later, Fern said, "Let's get back to the house."

Their descent was not as enthusiastic as their climb, but almost as quick as they wanted to be in a populated area sooner than later, and dark fell quickly now that the sun was below the water. They felt safer when they were passing in front of houses on the narrow cobbled road, torchlight flickering onto their path, but the city itself was still a ways off. As they reached the area with a proper seawall, Fern breathed a little easier. The roadway was fully illuminated by light from windows and metal poles with fire burning on top. They made their way to Emily's house, hearing a loud splash as James opened the gate for them.

Emily, seated in a chair along the side of the main room, reading a book by the fireplace, gave a warm smile as she stood to welcome them.

Before she could say anything, Fern cut in, "There are sirens here? Bloodthirsty, conniving, disgusting sirens?"

James went to whisper in Emily's ear. Fern hadn't realized just how short the man was until Emily had to bend down to listen.

Emily nodded, then turned her attention back to her guests. "It seems they noticed you, as well. They are waiting just outside. Apparently, there is concern that *you*"—she nodded to Kraai—"plan to kill yourself by sacrificing yourself to the sirens." She bobbed her head side to side. "A reasonable assumption to make if you went to the end of the road where one goes to jump to their death in a sacrifice to the sirens." She turned to Fern. "And they thought that *you* were going to accept the sacrifice they declined." She raised her eyebrows. "Am I correct in assuming that was not your plan?"

Fern and Kraai both let out together, "Yes."

"Good." Emily began to walk to the door, not bringing her parasol with her this time. "I will go clear up this misunderstanding." She left, leaving the door open.

The cool night air rushed in. This was not a sea smell—it was crisper air, mountain air, a land breeze. Fern basked in the feel of it in her lungs. Then, a thought. She snapped to Kraai. "They thought you were going to kill yourself by jumping to your death and being fed on by sirens? Why is that something they would assume?"

Kraai shrugged. "The path *did* end there."

He was right. Her mouth dropped at the thought. Of all the ways to die, that had to be the least appealing.

They both stared at the open door, waiting for Emily to return. Time moved at a pace that would rival a glacier. Finally, they heard the sound of shoes on stone—a light, steady rhythm.

Emily started as she found two sets of eyes staring upon her return. "Honestly, don't try to scare me like that. I'm not used to having other people in the house." Her voice was tinged with annoyance. "I have settled their concerns"—she looked directly at Fern—"but the sirens wish to meet with you tomorrow."

"With me?" Fern nearly screamed the words.

"Yes, they wish to speak with you about your siren ancestry. I told them you did not seem all too comfortable when I brought up the subject and that you did not yet have your songtone. They wish to discuss it with you."

Fern's skin began to tingle. "First of all, you had no right to tell them how you think I feel about being part-siren. Second, I do not wish to have *anything* to do with them. How do you know they aren't going to kill me? They would probably jump at the chance to make Belle happy."

A smile of smug satisfaction spread across Emily's lips. "Oh, dear, they hate Belle more than you do."

Part of Fern wanted to leave for her room and end the conversation, not to give validity to the foolish notion that she would even consider meeting with the sirens, but another part needed to defend her stance. "No. Sirens will do anything for power. My mother told me as much. If they think killing me or bringing me to Belle would bring them power, they would do it."

"There are two shoals." Emily broke apart each word, as if to drill it into Fern's frazzled mind. "One believed themselves superior and declared war on the other shoal, attempting to keep their kind pure"—she lifted and bent her first two fingers on that word—"whatever that means. Many were killed, slaughtered in their sleep, caught and left to die by fishermen under the sirens' spell. Some escaped and made their home here. They do not consume flesh without consent, they do not actively lure people to their deaths. I believe they can help you." She moved close to Fern, trying to hold her hand until Fern yanked it away. "Just talk to them."

"They can help me do what? Become more like them? I do not wish to *be* one of them."

Emily repeated, slowly this time, "Just talk to them."

Fern's attention was drawn to the scar on Emily's neck. If anyone knew about navigating the world as someone with less-than-ideal blood, it would probably be her. Fern let out a long groan. "I'll consider it."

"Fine." Emily held her hands up in surrender. "Think about it while you bathe—you are both a mess. I'll have nightclothes sent up for each of you, and something fresh to wear tomorrow."

Kraai bowed his head lightly. "Thank you." As he righted himself, he continued, "For everything. This is all very gracious of you. I know my mother would be glad to know we are in your care."

Fern grit her teeth. She knew it would be polite to thank her, but she couldn't bring herself to do it. Instead, she gave a half-hearted smile which turned out more like a snarl.

Emily didn't seem to notice. She gave a head nod back to them both before going to the study, the small train of her dress trailing behind her, sliding smoothly across the polished stone floor.

James appeared, gesturing for the two to follow him once more. They were led to a room in the same hallway as their bedchambers. James opened the door, indicated the tub in the middle with one outstretched arm, and then left. Did he ever speak aloud? Did he ever *emote?*

Fern looked inside—a simple tub, filled with water. "You want to go first?" she asked Kraai.

"You're the one with grass in your hair. You go first." Still, he walked inside the room to look inside the tub. "You think…?"

Fern walked over and stuck her fingers into the water. It was enchanted. She didn't have the energy to free more than a handful. "I'm not going under."

Kraai nodded and left Fern alone in the room. She undressed, throwing her clothes in a pile on the cold floor beside her before going into the water. It was lukewarm, warmer than she preferred. She was used to bathing in the stream, ice cold current flowing across her, connected to the glacier at the top of their mountain. Kraai would stand guard by the riverside, keeping lookout. Fern would usually wear a slip while bathing, in case someone came by and they had to run suddenly, but now she could be completely nude. She felt vulnerable, but she wanted the water to pick up on that, to know she was also uncomfortable and confused. Even so, she could not commune well with the water while it was trapped by the enchantment. She did not sit and relax as she might have in regular water—it was the shortest bath she had ever taken. Besides, she couldn't figure out how to wash her hair without contorting and possibly slipping under the water. She could try her water magic, but if it behaved erratically while over her head, she could end up in just as much trouble. The last thing she wanted was a mouthful of lost memories. She decided to ask Kraai for help. She found a towel on a shelf by the door and wrapped it around her torso. She nearly jumped out of it, as well as her skin, when she saw someone standing outside the bathroom door.

Kraai turned around, but his eyes drifted down to the exposed skin on Fern's shoulders. He shook his head and snapped back to her face. "I thought I would keep guard while you bathed—do as we always have." He reached out to her hair, still in mess atop her head, and pulled out a clot of grass, dropping it in front of her face. "Do you need help with this?"

Fern pursed her lips, letting out a sigh through her nose. She didn't know if he always knew when she needed something because of some innate empathic ability or because he knew her so well. "Yes, please."

Fern sat on her knees, facing away from the tub, arching her back so her hair fell over the side and the ends dipped into the water. Kraai kneeled beside her, using a pitcher he found by the towels to pour water over her hair. Every time he reached over to the other side of her head, Fern could smell Mountain air trapped in the fibers of his shirt, released by the warmth of his body. She suddenly understood what Kraai had meant when he said she smelled like home. When her hair was sufficiently clean, Fern took her pile of clothes in one arm and scurried down the hall to her room, leaving Kraai with his hands aflame under the tub, attempting to warm the water to his preferred scalding temperature.

When Fern opened the door, an ivory nightdress waited on the bed. The light from the fireplace danced on the shining fabric. She grazed it with her fingertips. The cloth felt to her hands how cream felt to the lips. She pulled it onto her body and relished every inch that touched against her skin. She could get used to this. The gown fell to her mid-calf, but there were no sleeves—just two straps that held it onto her shoulders. It would do for now. It wasn't like anyone would see her. She turned back to the door to see another dress hanging on a hook on the wall. Black, laced along a bateau neckline, with a skirt that was four times as wide as the bodice. *Oh, no.* Emily expected her to wear *this* tomorrow? Fern let out a laugh at the ridiculousness of the idea. No. She would wear her own clothes. She would wear her brown, her leather, her cream shirt with ink on the sleeve.

No, that won't do. There was something about this place that made her care about how she looked. Perhaps it was the fact there were others around to see her. She grabbed her pile of clothes and walked back to the bathroom. She knocked to see if Kraai had finished.

A clear "come in" came from the other side of the door.

Fern opened it, her eyes finding rising steam from a tub that still contained a naked Kraai. He was facing the other direction, but she could see water glisten on his arms, shoulders, and upper back. Her eyes lingered just a bit too long before she remembered herself and held up her hand to shield her view while turning to the wall. "I am so sorry, I thought you might be done so I could wash my clothes."

Kraai did not stir, his voice bouncing off the wall on the other side of the room. "You do not like what your grandmother picked out for you?"

"It was a dress. A black dress."

"Ah, two negatives. I'll get out so you can get those stains out. But first, some help with my hair?"

Fern didn't dare move closer, but she peeked in order to raise water from the tub to rinse his hair. She tested on a small volume first to be sure it would listen to her. The water was so easy to manipulate, she felt bad doing so. Without the enchantment, this water might fight her, might ignore her, but now it was completely at her disposal. She turned away once more as she heard Kraai leave the tub. He walked over to her, the slap of his wet feet on stone growing louder. When he reached next to her head in search of a towel, she turned to look directly at the wall. Fern's face grew warm.

"All yours."

Fern forced her head to look to the tub, only barely catching a glance of Kraai's exposed torso, as he had only covered his waist with the towel. Years of having only just enough food for their families had built his body in a way that he had clear definition to his lean core. The sheen of water only accentuated each muscle. She fought the urge to look again. Yet, she couldn't help feeling his eyes were on her, as well. Remembering what she was wearing, she shrunk into herself and gave a hasty, "Thank you. Goodnight."

Chapter 10

Fern arrived to break her fast in clothes that were *mostly* clean. There was no removing that stain from the sleeve. At least it was a grey blob instead of the black mess it had been the night before. She might have stained the porcelain of the tub, though.

Kraai was already downstairs, picking away at his plate of eggs and bacon. He always managed to eat more than Fern, but was so *slow*. He could have been eating for twenty minutes already and Fern would still finish her food before he did.

Also seated was her grandmother, no food before her, but drinking from a chalice while conversing with Kraai. She noted Fern's arrival, but did not make a formal acknowledgement of it. Kraai did not take his eyes off of Emily. They were discussing something about dancing from what Fern could gather.

She went to the table where the foods were laid out. It was not overflowing, but certainly more prepared food in one place than Fern had ever seen in her life. It could have easily fed both Fern and Kraai's families for one of the Mountain holidays. It was even the kind of food they would have on those special days—eggs had to be bought from the market and boar was a challenge to take down, so both were saved for special occasions. Perhaps Emily was making a big show for her guests' first morning there. Fern piled eggs high, grabbed some bacon, and topped it off with a yellow-red hemisphere she assumed was a type of fruit. She didn't *plan* to run away today, but she opted for a full breakfast just in case.

"So anyone who wanted to come could come?" Kraai asked, a dainty clump of yellow egg on the end of his fork.

"Technically, no." Emily waved her goblet to the side and shrugged. "But if somebody wanted in, we usually wouldn't turn them away. We made sure to have empaths around at all times to pick up on any funny business."

"Funny business? Such as?" Kraai asked between bites.

"The usual—assassination plots, kidnappings. Things I don't have to deal with as much here."

Kraai straightened, forcing down the bite. "You believe assassinations to be funny?"

Emily closed her eyes and shook her head.

Before she could speak, Fern cut in with a mouth half-full of food. "Funny business means something deceptive." She swallowed and loaded another forkful. "Father used to say it sometimes." She shoved the next bite into her mouth. She would not admit to herself that hunger had made her cranky the day before, but she did have a sudden improvement in mood as the food hit her stomach.

Emily finally acknowledged Fern, eyes wide. She said her words, searching for them as she went. "I know you have had a long journey, but I do wish to know how my son is doing. I'd like to know about your life growing up, too. I know we have time to discuss these things, but I have not had word from anyone except Will's mother since I came here, and she had no information for me."

Fern shoveled even more food into her mouth, giving herself time to consider her next words. As much as she wanted to blame Emily for everything that happened to her parents, she needed to be in her grandmother's good graces. Fern felt sick as she swallowed the food and her words. "Perhaps another time," is all she managed to say.

A half-smile crossed Emily's lips. "The sirens still wish to speak with you." She took another sip from her goblet. The white napkin she used to wipe her lips was tinged a dark red.

"And I wish to speak with them." Fern kept her face flat, though a tremor of fear shook through her. She had questions that needed answering. Kraai's gaze caught her attention. "Do you take issue with that?"

He shifted his last few bites around the plate before mumbling something unintelligible.

Fern slammed her fork down. She didn't intend for it to make such a loud noise as it hit the plate, but she used the effect to her advantage, yelling louder than initially planned. "If you have something to say, say it."

The rising and falling of his chest could be seen from across the table. "I am coming with you." His words were sure, but his eyes were not.

Fern wished she hadn't already used her fork for emphasis as she tried to put more passion into her voice. "Absolutely not. I will not have you go near them again."

A flash emanated from Emily's side of the table. Fern looked over to see sparks trickling down her fingers, the tips digging into the singed metal of the tabletop. "You will need to get over your prejudice if you are going to remain here"—she scooted out her chair, rising to leave—"and if you are ever going to be able to live with yourself."

Fern's own lightning swelled within her, her hair fleeing her skin from the charge. That was normally the cue that she should leave the situation to prevent an outburst, but she couldn't buckle to *her*. She stood, knocking her own chair back from the force. "Of all beings, you should share my feelings.

Your *life* was taken by a vampire, your family and your crown by a siren." She could feel a pulse in her hand as she gestured, so she tucked her hand beneath her other arm.

Emily squinted her eyes, a small smile forming on her lips. "Do it. Let it out. You're furious. Use your anger." She quickly scanned the room. "Kraai, you'll want to move away from the table."

Fern tossed her glance between a smirking grandmother and a scurrying friend. "I am not using that power. It signals my location."

Emily shot her own hand out beside her, a thin bolt of lightning shooting from her hand to the metal table, without breaking eye contact. "Well, now they know *I'm* here. Your turn."

Years of lectures about holding back her power came rushing into her head. Mother's cries, Father's stern words. Lightning was common in the Mountains, but if storms were frequently centered around them, it would clearly give them away. She had no control over it at times, especially when she was overwhelmed, but she did her best to contain it. "I can't."

Emily's face reset to its calm composure, seemingly forgetting the past minutes of heated dialogue. "The sirens would be thankful to know Kraai is safe. He will go with you, unless you wish for me to arrange a meeting where he is alone with them."

New fire raged in Fern. This woman was manipulative, conniving. What else should she expect from a vampire? She let out a scream of frustration as her hands shot to the table. While Emily had thrown a streak of lightning, Fern's hands released a proper bolt that appeared as thick as her arm. The table jumped when it struck, a deafening thud ringing out as gravity returned it to the floor. A weight in Fern's chest lifted and, after taking her first full breath in ages, she looked to Kraai. "We'll do it together?"

Kraai stared at the table in awe, then shifted to Fern. "As we always have." He looked to Emily, who was already ascending the stairs, maintaining his absolute admiration for the scene that unfolded before him.

From the upper landing, Emily called out, "They are waiting for you outside."

Fern's eyes shot to Kraai and she mouthed, "Now?"

Kraai nodded, rising from his seat without touching or even drawing near to the table, which still buzzed with energy. He walked to the door and held his hand out for Fern.

Fern looked from her hands to the table, and walked beside Kraai, refusing to touch him. What if there was more lingering within her? That power could kill.

They walked into the new morning air, the sickening smell of the salt water once again overpowering her. She took a moment to double over and retch before composing herself. She could not show fear, or even discomfort. She would have to be stone, unwavering, changed only by the most persistent waters and wind. Stone did not run or hide as Fern had been taught to do.

They crossed the road to find three heads atop shoulders bobbing in the water. Each set of wide eyes was brilliant in its own right—the rich brown that seemed to glow in the light, the sharp green which made Fern ache for home, and the radiant amber that burned like a setting sun. This was not what Fern imagined the sirens to look like—their colorful tails were supposed to be in sharp contrast to their washed-out skin, but two of these sirens were far from pale. Fern scanned the surface, looking for more hiding beneath, but could see little through the ripples caused by the breeze and the coming and going of boats.

The siren they had encountered before approached first, signaling for the other two to remain behind. The uneasiness in the siren's eyes confused Fern. Her appearance did, too. In the

Mountains, sirens were said to be physically weak and skeletal—children were told to eat well so they don't look like a siren. This creature was far from that. She was large and strong; if she were on land, she might even be able to hold her own against a dwarf.

Fern abandoned Kraai's side to walk to the seawall, but did not dare to get close enough to be hit by rogue spray. "How did you know who I am?"

"I have no idea *who* you are," the siren began, giving a look of suspicion that ventured lightly into disgust, "but you cannot hide *what* you are from another siren. No siren in the Light Region has ever had a black aura, so we could only assume you come from the Seas."

Fern stood straighter, raising her jaw as high as she could while still looking at the woman in the water. "I am of the Mountains." She fought the urge to list off the litany of slurs against the Seas she had learned growing up. "I have never touched salt water. And I do not know this *aura* of which you speak."

The orange siren's brow furrowed. "And so you would not, having never received your songtone." She turned to her companions, nodding. As they made their approach, the orange siren pushed back her long, brown hair and introduced herself. "I am called Lute." She gestured to the siren with sharp green eyes and wild red-orange curls. "This is Carnyx." And finally, the siren with even tighter dark curls that reminded Fern of her mother. "And this is Sistrum."

Fern's mind attempted to figure out the musical meaning behind these siren names, forgetting to reciprocate the introductions until Kraai stepped beside her. "I am called Kraai, and this is Fern."

Fern spun, pushing Kraai back, managing only to say, "Don't!"

Lute leaned to look around Fern to Kraai. "Hair like the plumage of a crow." She narrowed her eyes. "Or is there more to it than that?"

Kraai gave a cordial smile, running his fingers through his hair. "You are very perceptive."

Lute accepted this answer and turned her attention back to Fern. "I have never been to the Mountains, but I have heard the Null is known for its ferns."

"It is." This line of conversation sent a prickle up Fern's spine. Her gaze shifted to Kraai, hoping for any kind of read on these sirens, while her hands grasped at the loose fabric of her sleeves, desperate for something to do.

Kraai shrugged, gesturing his head back to the water, forcing her back into conversation.

Carnyx spoke in an accent reminiscent of one of the Mountain clans Fern had the misfortune of encountering. "Secrets remain secrets beyond the veil. No need to be so reticent."

Fern raised her brow at the fire-haired siren, green eyes meeting green eyes sidelong.

Carnyx looked away for a beat, a slight smile gracing her lips.

Fern knew the veil had nothing on the Mountains when it came to keeping secrets. "If that is the case, I would appreciate you being more forthcoming. How did you know I was a siren? What is this aura? And why is mine black?"

Lute returned to her speaking role. "Every siren gives off an aura. When you receive your songtone, you can see the aura of other sirens—it is a gift that helps us recognize our own kind when we leave the water. And the color is genetic; it is the same shade as your tail. Every siren begins with a black aura in their mother's womb, but it changes before they are born. We have only ever heard of one other that came into this world with a black aura." Her eyes glowed just a bit brighter with the last sentence.

Kraai's voice piped up beside Fern. "What does an aura look like?"

Carnyx flashed a smile at Kraai that made Fern queasy. "Have you ever seen the particles that come off a fire? She seems to burn from the inside, releasing a black ash and a dark glow."

Kraai looked Fern up and down, his jaw going slack.

"Don't pretend you see it." Fern rubbed her hands over her skin, hoping to brush off the invisible ash that surrounded her. "I cannot even see it."

Sistrum finally spoke, her voice deep and rich. "One cannot see their own aura, but we can allow you to see those of others. Would you be interested in receiving your songtone?"

Fern stepped back, knocking into Kraai in her haste. "No. I never wish to undergo such a transformation."

Sistrum laughed. "Is that shoal in the Seas still forcing young sirens to transform to earn their tone?" Her eyes looked down, her smile fading as she realized something. She shook the distraction from her head and looked back to Fern. "All you must do is hear the song of the males. No tail required."

Carnyx chimed in, "But if you *do* receive the tail, you can come see Atlantis. It is more beautiful than anything they have up here."

A splash rising up between Lute and Carnyx suggested a swift jab from the lead siren to the red-haired one. Lute smiled warmly. "A songtone can be granted to you if you wish. We would appreciate knowing to whom we give this power, so you would have to tell us more about yourself—what you would do with it." She eyed Kraai for a moment before reconnecting with Fern.

Fern shook her head with a laugh, pointing to Kraai. "First of all, no." She then directed her finger to the sirens in the water, anger swelling. "Second, I do not want to be like—" She was cut off by a shock on her arm.

Kraai's hand had grabbed at her sleeve, discharging the power that had built up within her. He shook his arm while letting out a breath through puffed cheeks and gritted teeth.

Fern turned, wanting to grab him, but reeling her hands back when she realized *she* did this to him. "Kraai! I...I didn't—"

He waved his hand and shook his head, letting out one more deep breath before saying, "Wanted to stop you before you got too charged. That was a pretty rough one, though." His eyes widened as he finally regained his composure. He turned to the sirens in the water. "She will consider it." He put all of his charm into his smile. "How can we reach you if we wish to speak with you again?"

Fern did not turn back toward the water; she was busy looking Kraai up and down to check for lasting damage. Kraai kept his eyes on the sirens.

Lute nodded. "Emily knows how to reach us." She then called out, loud enough that Fern could not ignore her, "Even if you do not wish to join us, it is your right to have a songtone should you wish to have one. It *is* a weapon. While some will use it to harm or manipulate others, it can also be used to defend yourself."

Fern did not respond, finally feeling well enough to touch Kraai, grabbing his arm to turn him away from the water.

He managed to give a brief, "Thank you for your time," before Fern finally managed to move him.

When they entered Emily's house, Fern exploded, "I will *not* consider it! Why would you say that?"

Kraai matched her intensity. "You heard her. It is a weapon. You need more than a basic handle of water, lightning you cannot control, and an ability to run. You are a princess with a price on your head!"

"And you want me to seduce men to keep myself safe? Is that it? Use a power that lures beings to their deaths at the hands of man-eating monsters? You realize that is what they are, right?"

"You do not have to eat anyone! You do not have to kill anyone! You do not have to *use* the songtone! Just have it so I know you are safe when I am not with you!"

The last words caused all the fire inside Fern to die. She wanted to ask when he was leaving, but the words caught in her gut. Instead, they stood in silence, Fern's eyes filled with hurt and Kraai's with pleading.

"I hope I am not interrupting something," Emily cut in from the top of the stairs.

Fern turned away, "No. We are done here." Letting her hair fall into her face, she rushed up the stairs, ducking out of reach when the vampire held out a hand. When she reached the upper floor, her strides resembled those she took when outrunning a predator. The door to her room was heavy for her quaking arm, but she managed to close it with force before she collapsed onto the bed in sobs.

The chaos of her own thoughts was a scary place. There was too much now. Before, Fern had a companion in this, but he would leave—it was still his plan to abandon her in this new place. Now she would have to handle adjusting to life in a new region on her own, no member of her clan to support her. There would be only strangers, monsters surrounding her while she counted down the days until she could leave. She looked to her wrist, watching the three veins in the light skin of her hand creep down and disappear into her arm. The blood in there was tainted with the blood of monsters. Her demonic lineage was a source of pride—she had a connection with water that was rare in the Mountains. She traced the lines, feeling the water pulsing within her, but paused when she realized something else. Salt. She threw her face back into the bed, clawing her fingers into the fur, feeling the skin of the animal under her nails. She breathed a deep sigh. It has always been there. Salt water, deep inside her. She hated how it called to her.

Chapter 11

The light knock woke Fern from her doze. She rubbed her eyes with the heels of her hands, and they came to focus right as her veins moved into view. The hidden power within her. A second series of knocks came from the door. She was not ready to face Kraai just yet. She could not let him know how much she needed him. Hardened independence was a virtue where they were from.

"Come in," she said anyway. There was no use outright ignoring him. He likely already knew how she was feeling.

As the door opened, an unexpected voice said, "Fern?" Her grandmother peeked her head in a small crack. "Kraai sent me to check on you."

It was in that instant Fern decided she would rather have it out with Kraai. "I'm fine."

Emily let herself in, closing the door softly behind her. She gave a pressed-lipped smile. "And we all know what 'fine' means." She sat down on the bed, leaving a good distance between them.

"I'm good." Fern pulled down her sleeve and dragged it across the dried tears on her face. "Great, even. Nothing to worry about."

"Good." Emily smiled. "Great. Then you are in a mental space where you're ready to talk about your powers."

The fake grin Fern had managed fell to a snarl. "I will *not* be receiving a songtone."

"That's your choice, but that is not what I came here to discuss."

Fern looked to her grandmother. "My control of water?"

"We will get there." Emily held up her hand, a charge arcing between her finger and thumb. "But first I want to know about your spark. Your father, despite being mostly human, could kill with a strike of lightning. I want to see how much of that lies in you."

Is that where her father got his name? Striking someone down? Was he a murderer, too? "I don't care what my father did. I do not want to kill anybody."

"You may not have a choice. Your father didn't. Someone was going to kill the three of us—me, my husband, and my son. When fire was not enough to stop him, the attacker managed to—" She paused for a steadying breath. "He killed Will, and your father…" Emily's eyes searched the room as she bit her lips together. After another breath, she continued, "It is a useful skill if you cannot run."

"But I *can* run. I can run farther and faster than anyone I've ever come across."

"When is the last time you outran a vampire?"

Fern lifted her chin, smug satisfaction dripping down her expression. "Last week, at the market."

"Without help?" Emily's eyes pierced through Fern's pride.

"I could have done it on my own."

"I will take that bet. Outrun me and I will drop the subject, leave you to run for the rest of your life if you so choose. If I catch you before sundown, you will train with me until I am satisfied that you can defend yourself if the need arises." She stood from the bed and began to walk to the door.

"Now?" Fern leaned forward, adrenaline coursing through her veins.

"Why not? I must go dress for the sun. It will give you a good head start. I'll see you sometime this evening." Emily winked as she closed the door behind her.

Fern was glued to the bed, half-poised to start, half in disbelief as to what she was about to do. She could outrun her grandmother easily, right? She stood warily, looking around the room for anything she could take to assist her. Nothing worth the extra weight slowing her down. She clutched her cloak and looked out the window—two floors straight down into an alley, but there was another residence on the other side. She moved back into the room, opting for a running leap. As she hung in the air, she reached for a windowsill on the building opposite. Her fingers barely grasped the ledge, but she managed to at least slow her descent, sliding the rest of the way to the ground and landing lightly enough to not make a sound above the overall din of the city.

Left would take her toward the cliffs. Fern had been that way before—no cover. Her best bet was to go right, and to go quickly, knowing her grandmother would anticipate that move. She tried to tread like a mountain cat, but the slap of her soles on cobbled streets gave her away. At the end of the alley, she was faced with another choice: straight into the next alley, right to the water, or left to the unknown. She made to go straight, then changed direction just before entering the alley—more people lingered on the main road. More commotion to envelop her, more smells to mask her. She slowed her sprint, hoping that she could blend in as a citizen, yet all eyes seemed glued to her. Their stares burned. Did they know this challenge? Did they know more than that? Fern threw up her hood, blocking out the stares of strangers, as her feet sped up once more.

After a few blocks, the city gave way to more countryside, but unlike the cliffs, this area had cultivated vegetation—rows of small trees, covered in tiny white flowers, terraced along rolling hillsides. She climbed to higher ground, the lush green glowing in the afternoon sunlight. The neat rows would provide some cover, and the branches encroaching on the empty spaces might deter the vampire pursuing her. She ducked down the fifth row and ran, the dirt under her feet muffling her pounding steps. The long, unending lines drawing together toward the horizon was unsettling. There was enough room under the branches to cross through the rows if necessary, but Fern had hit her stride, each tree rushing by her eyes increasing the intoxicating dizziness, the thrill of the chase.

Fern finally slowed to a stop, her lungs aching. She crouched, hands on her knees, her human heart pounding in her chest. There was nothing before her, only the line of trees curving around the bend of the hill. She turned to find the same behind her. Using the sleeve of her shirt, she wiped the beads of sweat from her brow. The air whipping across her face helped cool her before, but now she was standing still, baking in the sunlight and her muscles still giving off the heat of exertion. It had been at least an hour since Fern left the house—she had to be miles from the town by now. With her head start, there was little chance that Emily could track her, but even that small chance made Fern uneasy. The vampire knew the town, the landscape, the people. As Fern's body cooled, she looked back at the town, considering her next move, but her heart stopped dead when she found a hooded face only a foot from hers.

The face was familiar, but she had never been this close before, this attentive. The skin of one of the cheeks was not smooth, but rough and scarred. Fern wanted to reach and touch it, but remembered her goal. She made a futile attempt to flee, but a strong hand gripped her arm.

Emily squeezed, not painfully, but commandingly. "We train tomorrow." She let go and turned to leave.

"How did you find me?" Fern demanded.

Emily half-turned back to Fern and stated as a matter-of-fact, "You wouldn't go near the water or the cliffs, so I started in this direction. The air is still today and your scent lingered everywhere you went. I had been close these past ten minutes, but I thought I'd wait until you stopped so I wouldn't have to tackle you. Didn't want to injure my granddaughter the same week I met her." Emily ducked between trees, clutching the hood to ensure it stayed over her head.

Part of Fern hoped a branch would snag it and the sun would burn her grandmother, another part scolded her for the thought. She hated that the vampire had found her, especially since her grandmother had not even lost her breath. It had been so simple for her. If they had been in the Mountains, it would be different. Fern could climb, could throw her scent. But she wouldn't be running in the Mountains, not for a long time. She was running here, and perhaps a better grasp on her powers would be necessary.

It was over two hours before she returned to Emily's house. Despite the majority of the trek being downhill, she *had* run far, and her legs were jelly.

Kraai was waiting outside, sitting by the side of the road. He watched her approach with worry on his brow. "Did you run away? Your grandmother said she went off to search for you."

"Technically, yes," Fern said as she wrapped her arm around his shoulders for support. "But not in *that* way. I wouldn't leave you. Don't worry." She jabbed at him with her free hand. "You're not free of me yet." She paused, considering. "How long was my grandmother gone?"

"It was perhaps an hour between when she said she was going out to find you and when she came back to say she was successful. Possibly less."

An hour to track Fern and get out to those orchards and back, not including the ten minutes she had apparently been on Fern's tail. How fast *were* vampires? And why did Fern's parents give her the indication she would be able to outrun them?

Fern spent the rest of the day in her room. Between the frustration of losing and the dread of spending more time with her grandmother, she could not bring herself to be around anyone else. Thankfully, Kraai sensed something amiss and came to visit just as the sun was setting.

"You are upset," he stated. "You give off a different essence when you are upset. What is it?"

"I start training with my grandmother tomorrow," Fern grumbled. "She wants me to learn how to protect myself with lightning. Apparently I'm no match for vampires." She would leave out the part about *how* she knew that.

Kraai's brow raised. "You are a princess on the run from assassins. The best of them might be after you." He came to sit next to her on the bed. "Having a way to fight back would be useful."

"I have water magic. I can fight with that."

"Water magic is wonderful." Kraai paused, keying Fern in that the next word would discredit the compliment. "But you refuse to touch salt water—what if there is no fresh water nearby? Or if the water you find is not familiar to you?"

"There is water in the air. I can find a way to use that." Fern closed her eyes and felt the water vapor creep near her face. This water was free, unbound by gravity or the enchantment of the region, and impossible to manipulate.

"You have tried that before. It has never worked."

Fern opened her eyes, turning toward her companion. "There just has to be something I'm missing, some knowledge I don't yet possess."

"Just try working with the lightning." Kraai looked into her eyes and placed his open hand on her back, rubbing in large circles, the heat from his hand penetrating her vest. "You can use it if the water ever fails you." His hand stopped. "Which it will not, but just in case."

Fern smiled weakly as her face fell into her hands. Kraai continued his back rub as the tension released enough for her to feel ready for sleep. Just as she began to nod off, her head snapped up. "Have you had anything to drink today?"

"I have not. I will not drink anything without your leave while I am here."

Fern had been sipping water all day, filtering out the enchantment. She rushed to a pitcher of water on the bedside table and poured the water through her fingers and into a cup. The process was becoming much more efficient, taking less energy than the all-out drain of filtering an entire stream. She handed the cup to Kraai. "It should be good."

Kraai looked up at her. "*Should* be?"

"I can't guarantee because nobody can tell me exactly what I'm doing, but I've been drinking it, so we're in it together."

He lifted the cup, pausing at his lips. "I *am* fire demon. We do not require as much water as you do. I can go a few more days without drinking. Do you still want me to have this?"

Fern's confidence slipped, her hand shooting out to take the cup back. "On second thought, we can wait. I'll keep practicing and have it even better perfected by the time you're *actually* thirsty."

Kraai handed back the cup and stood, glancing at the door. "I should go. You have a big day tomorrow." He wrapped her in a hug. "I cannot wait to see you having two ways to best me in a fight. You can already douse my fire magic; I wonder how weak I will be against that spark when you learn how to control it."

Fern melted into him. She had hurt him with her electricity today, what felt like an eternity ago. She had hurt people before when she hadn't managed to contain her emotions. If she could control this power, perhaps it wouldn't discharge when she was touched. Perhaps she wouldn't be so afraid of it— afraid of herself. Their hug lingered until Fern realized their breath had synchronized, slow and deep. This was weird, right? She let go and pushed away, looking down at the floor. "Goodnight," she said in a hush.

"Goodnight." Kraai's voice was warm, but lost.

Even after he left, Fern could still feel his warmth on her skin, his scent lingering in the still night air.

Chapter 12

"Stop!" Fern yelled at her grandmother, who was berating her for the umpteenth time. She was still exhausted from the day before, and the day before that. The only thing she had successfully accomplished in the week of training was letting herself explode in rage and having an unpredictable attitude the rest of every day.

"Do you want to learn or not?" Emily responded from across the field, loud enough to be heard, but calm.

Fern *did* want to learn. She saw how powerful this magic could be. That is also what scared her—if she learned how to amplify it but not how to control it, she could be more dangerous than ever. "Can you just trust me to fuel my own emotions?"

The grassy valley was half-shrouded in shadow, the half from which Emily would shout her commands. "I will stop talking when you give me a fork striking there, there, and there." She pointed to the three tallest peaks. There were no structures or people in the vicinity, so all the strikes would be discharged to the ground or, in a few circumstances, to Emily. She was always able to funnel the power through her and into the ground, with no damage done, save the char on the grass.

Fern had been using the charge that was present in the sky, but it seemed to have all vanished. She would have to conjure it within herself. Lies about her identity, one grandmother determined to kill her, another breathing down her neck, her longing for the Mountains, Kraai's desire to go home without her, a sister she had never met—all of it built and churned within her, the thoughts grinding against each other and creating a buzz within her, the hairs on the back of her neck rising away from the charge. She burst, reaching her hand in front of her. Time slowed as she watched the bright light reach toward the peaks, and she guided a different finger in each of their directions, splitting the bolt. Fern would never grow tired of the sound, the crack that she felt radiate in that now-empty space in her core.

"Let's head back." Emily pulled down her sleeves and covered her head with her cloak's hood before leaving the protection of the shadow.

"But we are usually out here for hours." Fern looked at the shadow's end on the second hill. Typically they would stay until the shadows were nearly gone, but there was still plenty left.

"Are you complaining?" Emily asked with a teasing smile. "Besides, I have some homework for you." She passed by her granddaughter, starting the long walk back to the house.

"I don't wish to practice at home. It wouldn't be safe." Fern kept her feet planted.

Emily kept walking, never waiting for Fern's moods to subside to do what she was planning to do. "You won't have to do any magic. You'll see when we get there."

Fern's curiosity took over. She scurried to catch up to Emily. There was one advantage to these training sessions— Fern got to let all of her emotions out. She would leave feeling lighter, almost happier, despite her circumstances remaining fixed. Her mood would rise and fall throughout the rest of the day, subject to change with any stimulus, no longer bound by the restrictions she had forced on them, but the highs were higher and she could linger there for some time.

The two walked back in silence, slowly increasing in speed. This part was never discussed, but by the end Fern would be pushing herself to keep up with Emily, out of breath by the time they arrived home.

Kraai would always be waiting by the doors, hoping to hear what had happened during training that day. But they were early and he was startled when the two entered the study. "Is something wrong?"

"No, I just thought Fern could use some theory to go with her practice," Emily said as she removed her outdoor gloves and donned the pair she used exclusively for the library. She made her way to her desk, upon which thick books with large covers were stacked. She picked up the one on top. "You should start with this one." She handed it out to Fern.

Fern took it, the weight of it almost too heavy for her exhausted arm. It was titled, *Physics*, and the front cover was riddled with black drawings. The image beneath the scribbles was of a single drop of water. She grabbed with her other hand, too, just as it was about to fall. "You want me to learn medicine?"

"No." Emily glanced Fern up and down. "Though, as a human, first aid might be useful." She shook off the tangent. "Physics is the study of substances and energy. Open to page 237."

Fern let the book fall onto a table with a loud smack. She turned to the back cover, more drawings—mostly shapes and squiggles. The sheen of it was unlike any book she had ever read. "Where did this book come from?"

"We get some books from the human world from time to time. This is an old textbook—students would use them in classrooms and schools. Page 237, please."

Fern opened to the page, the texture of the pages surprising her. They almost seemed to squeak as she rubbed them between her fingers. She found the page, running a finger over the heading. "Static Electricity and Charge?"

Emily nodded. "To start. You will work your way up to the kind of power you're dealing with, but this explains how the charge works in nature—it might help you better understand how to use it."

Fern stared into the book, flipping through the pages: a picture of a man and a flying cloth on a string, ovals circling around a ball, plusses and minuses printed on objects, and several equations with numbers, words, and letters. A twinge of fear rang in her, prickling her skin. "I don't have to do mathematics, do I?" Her mind flashed to long nights of her father trying to teach her sums, the fire burning as he explained a concept for the thousandth time, and her mother either sitting silently with her thoughts or lightly crying—she never even attempted to teach Fern the subject.

"No, just understand it conceptually. Get a better idea of its nature and its rules."

Fern jumped in her skin when she heard Kraai's voice directly behind her. "Is there one of these for fire?"

Emily squinted, thinking. "Not quite, but you may appreciate the chapter on thermodynamics." She held up a finger. "Only when Fern is not working, though."

"How do you know about these things?" Kraai asked.

"My teachers in the human world said I had a knack for science." Emily took off her library gloves, setting them on the table, and picked up the ones she wore outdoors. "If I had the means, I would have gone on to further study, but life brought me here." She gestured to the room around her. As she left, she added, "Happy reading."

Mother had taught Fern to read, adamant that she go through nearly every book they could get their hands on. All but *Macbeth*, that is. For some reason she was never allowed to touch the two near-identical copies that sat by Mother's bedside. The rest, though, were mandatory reading. Fern was never that interested in sitting still and taking it in, and often skimmed most of the texts, finishing as quickly as she could so she could go outside. She knew *how* to read, though, and that is what her mother wanted.

This book, however, was an entirely new language. Fern discovered that the back of the book held definitions, but even some of those were beyond her comprehension. This was going to be worse than the texts written in old English.

Kraai continued to read his book in a large, comfortable reading chair. He was the reader. He would spend hours reading and re-reading any book he could get his hands on. Mother was quite fond of him because of this. She would say that books were their escape.

Fern longed for an escape. This region was stifling—the unending sunshine, the heat, the salt flavoring the air. She did have relative freedom, though. The market happened twice a week, and Fern got to attend both times, completely exposed. There were whispers and glances, but Fern could not be sure if they were looking at her or at her grandmother, the vampire out in the sunlight, the absent queen. Would they have any idea who Fern was by context?

Despite the gossip, the townsfolk were nice. Fern had to learn the art of engaging in unimportant conversation—talk about the weather and the upcoming change in seasons, superficial questions about how Fern was enjoying life inside the veil—these filled the time during transactions or while moving in close proximity to others down a crowded street. Vendors loved sharing Light Region specialties with Fern as a gift of welcome; her favorites were the wide variety of cultivated fruits. The markets here were lighter, happier than the one she had attended in the Mountains. But her heart would sink when she saw happy families navigating the stalls together.

Kraai said something, but Fern was too deep in thought to make it out.

The page before her was a blur. She looked up to find Kraai leaning over the desk. "What?" she asked, still half-lost in her own mind.

"I asked what 'electric field' was." He pointed to the title of the section she had been attempting to read before she got distracted.

"Oh, um…" Fern shook the sleep from her head, her eyes finally making out the shapes of the letters. "Something about tiny particles being charged." She looked up with pleading eyes. "I'm not retaining any of this. Can we take a break?"

"I just finished this"—Kraai held up his book—"so that sounds like a great idea."

Fern did not even close the book. She would have to re-read that passage for the hundredth time when she got back, unsure of what Emily had wanted her to get from it.

The afternoon sunlight baked Fern's skin as they walked along the embankment, but the sea breeze kept her cool enough. It was still late spring, but Fern was nervous about what would happen when the sun's intensity increased in the summer. The salt water churned as it hit the stone that held the land in place. As long as they stayed closer to the buildings, the spray wouldn't hit her. Perhaps a few droplets, but she had discovered that was not enough to change her, thankfully. It was a terrifying few minutes the day they discovered that, with Kraai having to convince Fern every ten seconds that she was not, in fact, sprouting scales.

"You like it, then?" Kraai asked as they were discussing the day's lesson.

"Not the reading."

"But the power, you like knowing how to use it?" Kraai grabbed her hand as they approached a large crowd of people.

Fern appreciated the touch—somewhere deep in her mind, she was still nervous about being around others, especially large groups, even if she knew she was fairly safe here. She squeezed his hand as they weaved between people, not daring to let go. As they left, she agreed, "I do like the power. It is something else I can control. I can channel this power from the sky, and if there is none, I can create some myself, unlike water which cannot be conjured."

"Have you given any more consideration to the offer of a songtone?" he asked, his face locked forward.

Honestly, Fern had not. She had forgotten that meeting as quickly as she could and thrown herself into training with her grandmother. She looked around at the beings they were passing. She could control water, control lightning, perhaps she could control half of them, as well. It was an enticing prospect, especially now that she was no longer in hiding. They would be forced to keep her secret should they ever leave the Golden Veil, but there was no saying what they might do within it. She could stop someone from attacking her, or even call others to come to her defense. But would it be like controlling Mountain water—they could refuse if they did not want to do something? Or would it be like the enchanted water—they would be unable to resist, confused, and scared? Fern slowed her pace and looked to Kraai. "I don't want—"

"I know." He pulled her aside into a narrow alley that held a steep flight of stairs. "I have an idea and I would like you to hear me out before responding." He sat, patting open space on the next step down for her to join him.

Fern sat on the stone stair, again impressed by the lack of dirt and dust on the ground here. "If I don't like where it is going and leave, does that count as a response?"

"Yes. Now listen. You can receive the tone and never use it. Your mother never used her songtone, as far as I can tell—it is a choice to use it, like you choose to manipulate water. What if you got your songtone and tested it out on someone willing, someone who can tell you what it is like to be on the receiving end? Then, you can decide for yourself if it is something you would want to use again." He raised his eyebrows, waiting for the response.

"And you would be this willing victim?" Fern asked, mostly averse to the idea, but also somewhat curious.

"I would. I mean, please refrain from consuming my flesh, but I would be willing to be under your command so we can both understand the power better."

Fern thought it ridiculous to even consider this, but she had once been so against using the lightning. What if she had been wrong about this power, too? She replayed what Kraai said in her mind and asked, "*Both* understand?"

Kraai gave a guilty half-smile. "I have some news. Do you want the exciting part first? Or the part for which you might scold me?"

Fern closed her eyes and let out a sigh. "All of it. Just go."

Kraai began slowly, "Well, you know how my father is a crow demon from the Dark Region?"

"Yes. No more questions, just tell me."

"Your grandmother put me in contact with some elves who might make me able to shift. If they can, I would like to know if I am still susceptible to a siren's song in my crow form, so I can know if it is safe to go and find my father."

The ground shifted beneath Fern. She leaned against the wall, hoping to stop spinning. The stone was cold against the back of her head. "The Dark Region? You are going *into* the Dark Region?"

"That is where he was last seen by my mother."

Fern peeled her head back up and made eye contact with her friend. "The region of vampires currently ruled by a siren?"

He shrugged. "It is also the region where my father might be. I never got to meet him, Fern. He has not left my thoughts since I heard he could be alive. I want to know my father, and I want him to know me. He did not get a choice to be part of my life. Besides, I do not need to fear vampires as much as I was raised to—I am not human, remember? And the siren part is where you come in. I need to know how to protect myself."

"Can't you just ask the sirens here to test it?" Fern asked, upset with him for wanting to leave her and with herself for being upset with him. Did she truly not want her friend to have this missing piece of his life?

Kraai looked to the glistening water before them—the sun was glinting off the beautiful hue of blue in the shallow marina. "I do not know if I trust them."

"You seemed to before," Fern reminded him. How could she forget his insistence?

"Enough to meet with them." He turned to lock eyes with Fern. "But not enough to give up control of myself."

Fern searched his pleading expression. "And you trust me that much?"

"I trust you with that and more." He grabbed both her hands, stroking the backs with his thumbs. "Will you do this for me?"

Kraai never asked for much. He was always there to support Fern. He was in the Light Region for her, the keystone of their relationship after a childhood of helping her hide. She wanted him to be safe wherever he went—and if that meant accepting part of her that she wished to keep hidden, then she would do that for him. She would do almost anything for him.

"Of course." She took back her hands. "If you get some new fancy power, I'll have to get one, too. It's only fair."

He cocked his head. "You will have the song *and* the lightning. Not exactly balanced."

"I had the lightning before," she noted as she rose, brushing off her pants out of habit despite there being no debris on them. "But if you want to count it, you might be leaving with siren immunity from your bird magic, so…" She shrugged. "Even enough." She reached her hand down to help him to his feet. "Let's go tell my grandmother to arrange a meeting."

Although the two of them did not directly say they were going to ask for a songtone, Emily's eyes lit up when Fern asked to meet with the sirens again. Perhaps she knew. Maybe she was the one who helped guide Kraai to his decision—the two of them had been talking a lot in private, including whatever conversation about his crow ancestry and the possibility to shift. A piece of her envied the relationship Kraai had with her own grandmother, but part of Fern wasn't sure she wanted that closeness with the vampire. The woman who, by leaving, left her family to ruin.

Once the sun set, Emily left the house wearing a long robe, her hair braided and pulled around her head in a crown. Fern did not want to follow, but was curious as to how she would contact the sirens, so she snuck upstairs and into one of the rooms on the left of the hallway where she would be able to see out a window that looked over the water. Her grandmother stopped at the edge of the embankment and threw off her robe, revealing an absolutely shocking amount of her greyed skin. She had a form-fitting piece of cloth that covered most of her torso, but her arms and legs were bare. Those walking by hardly seemed to notice Fern's nearly-naked grandmother leaving the robe in a pile on the road and casting herself into the water. The splash broke the reflection of the moon on the surface. Fern watched for some time before realizing the vampire would not surface for air, as she did not need to.

It was hours before Emily returned to tell Fern she would be meeting with the sirens at the edge of town at noon the next day.

Chapter 13

"I thought you would come around," Lute said, her arms thrown over a rock that laid where the cliffs began their climb. "I did not think it would be so soon, but I know you hear the call of the sea." The siren had arrived alone, but the water behind her could have been swarming with the entire shoal for all Fern knew.

Fern looked down at her wrist, rubbing her fingers over the heel of her hand where the salty blood peeked through the lighter skin. "I can't deny that it is a part of me." She blinked up, staring directly at the siren in the water. "But that isn't the reason I'm doing this."

"Enlighten me." Lute rested her head on her hands.

"I am doing it for protection. I am doing it to keep my friend safe as he navigates finding someone important in a palace full of sirens." Without breaking eye contact, she reached for Kraai's hand and found it waiting right beside her.

Lute's eyes widened and shifted to Kraai. "You plan to enter the Dark Region? You will need more than practice with a tetarto-siren to take on Belle."

Kraai looked side to side with a light chuckle. "Nobody said anything about taking on the regent of a region. I only wish to meet someone."

A glance at their combined hands and Lute hushed her voice. "If you go anywhere near the princess, you will fall victim to Belle's wrath. Not to mention the princess herself has her song."

Did Lute assume Kraai was going to go see Fern's sister? "We don't care about—" Fern stopped herself. This was not the important point. "You know who I am?"

"After our last meeting, the other sirens and I pooled our knowledge. We know Mask—Emily—and her story. We know of her murdered son. We know much of Belle and how far she would go to gain power. It is because of this we could assume your mother's innocence in your father's death and that she had something else to protect in leaving her child behind." Lute's eyes burned into Fern, though she never even raised her head from the rocks.

Fern looked around; people walked past a few meters away. "Please, not so loud."

Kraai's hand squeezed as he whispered in Fern's ear, "None of them could hear her."

"And even if they did, none of them will remember any of this once they leave the veil." Lute tucked her head back and bobbed in the water, soaking her drying hair.

Fern stood in shocked silence. None of *them* would remember. She did not want to give her any more information; she didn't even trust her with the secrets she already knew. Instead, she backtracked in the conversation. "We do not wish to contact the princess. There is someone else who works in the palace whom he wishes to know."

Lute sneered as she fussed with the hair that stuck to her skin. "You are wasting your time. If you are searching for a female, they are likely gone from the palace. If you seek a male, he is under Belle's control and not worth knowing."

This was not Fern's fight, but she was still filled with rage. Kraai deserved to know his father and to know if a shapeshifter could resist a siren's song. "You said the song was my right. Receiving it should not be contingent on your approval of our plans."

Lute backed away from her rock, her arms sweeping the surface of the water to hold herself in place. "You are correct." The color and bounce in her voice was gone. "I will tell the males you are ready. Meet them on the place of sacrifice at midday overmorrow." She kept her head still, but her glare shot to Kraai and back. "It is tradition for you to be alone." Then she was gone, sunk below the surface.

Kraai and Fern spent the next day together, Emily giving her granddaughter some time off from training. Strangely enough, they spent all of it—sunup to sundown—inside. They had been out every day navigating crowds, breathing fresh air, feeling the sun on their faces; Fern was growing sick of it. She spent the morning lying in bed, attempting to read her book until Kraai joined her. Still frustrated with her lack of comprehension, she slid the book to Kraai who ate it up, learning what heat could do. His fingertips would rub together when he was concentrating, generating a small ember. Fern was at the ready with some water in case he rested his hand on the bed.

After she grew bored, Fern dove into discussion about the things that Kraai was planning. He lit up when he got to talk about potentially getting to shift, or even just fly, and his nerves about trying to find his father.

"You have no clues as to where he is?" Fern was lying on her belly, resting on her elbows, facing Kraai who was cross-legged on the other side of the bed.

"I will start at the palace, see what I can find out." He was picking at his fingernails, biting at a part that was bothering him.

"So you just walk in and say, 'Hello, I'm looking for my father, crow demon named—'" Fern's jaw dropped. Had she really been so absorbed in her own problems she never even wondered about Kraai's father's name?

Kraai finished her sentence with the side of his nail still pinned between his teeth. "Flight."

Pushing herself up, she pleaded, "I am so sorry, I should have asked by now."

He looked at his nails in satisfaction, then gave a half-smile. "You had your own things to deal with. I knew we would get around to my problems eventually. Besides, yours are more pressing." He shrugged. "And deadly. But no, I will not be asking about my crow demon father because we do not know how much Belle and the palace know. His magic was hidden; he was a sort of spy for Mask. I suppose his name could have a double meaning, as if he ran from something. Almost as unfortunate as a name sounding like *cry*."

"Are you going to go straight there?" Fern's mind shot to the Mountains—to the fresh air and the song of the trees in the wind. To the clearing you can't find unless you know where it is. To the family she resented, but missed all the same.

"I will go home to let everyone know we are still alive and that you are safe, consult with my mother about how to go about finding him—she must know more about him than she has told me. Places he liked to go, where his family lived, things like that. Then I will make my way to the Dark Region."

Fern's heart stopped as the next question left her lips. "When are you going?" She flinched as her voice cracked.

"Not until you are ready." His warmth radiated from his eyes.

Fern bit her lips together, not allowing her thoughts to make it out. What if she was never ready?

Fern and Kraai fell back into their old ways easily—years of finding ways to occupy themselves while trapped in their clearing with only each other for entertainment were very useful when hiding from the world and responsibilities. Except for two excursions to get food and water, they did not leave Fern's room. But night came soon enough, and Kraai left for his own bed.

Between bouts of tossing and turning, Fern had a repeating nightmare. She was running from a large wave, stumbling over her feet, pleading for the water to stop, but it would not listen. The strangest part of it was that she was watching the event— she clearly saw herself, saw her dark aura, and heard her own voice from outside of her body. After watching herself drown multiple times, she couldn't take it anymore. She walked to Kraai's room and, just as she was about to knock, the door opened.

"I am not sleeping well, either. Come in." He moved out of the way and gestured to the bed. "I suppose we have not exhausted *all* topics of conversation just yet."

Fern finally lowered her fist, still poised to knock, surprised that Kraai knew she was coming—but of course he knew. He *always* knew. She looked for the side where the sheets had not been disturbed, but it was all a complete mess of bunched up cloth and bare spaces. She laid down on the side closer to the door, taking the pillow by her feet to rest her head. Kraai took the other. The bed was large enough they could stretch out and not touch, but their arms still found each other, Kraai's fingers resting on Fern's forearm.

"The smell of the soil after a fresh rain," Fern mused.

"Smoking meat after a productive hunt." Kraai's smile, and even his hunger, could be heard in his voice.

"The way filtered sunlight makes the air glow."

"The way my great grandfather looks at my great grandmother when he sees her smile."

"The chorus of birds in the springtime."

"The screams of crows when—"

Fern chimed in to help him finish. "—you get too close to a fledgling." Her eyes were weighted shut, and her voice was drifting. "I will protect you when you're learning to fly. Scream at anyone who dares come close."

Kraai's response was an inaudible mumble, and sleep found Fern shortly after. Again, she saw herself running, the skirt of a dress ballooning out as she fell, and her face of horror as she was enveloped by the wave. She tried to rescue herself, to call the water away from this image, to claw her way through the dream, but when she awoke, she was grasping onto Kraai, her fingers digging into the flesh of his torso, her head pressed to his chest. Had he been shirtless before? She listened to his heartbeat, fast and light, while she waited for her own to slow its pounding. Sunlight reflected off the windows of the building opposite, sending a glare into the room.

Kraai's hand reached up to rub Fern's arm that was still thrown across him. "It was just a dream," he whispered.

"Tell that to my heart," Fern grumbled, her mind and body still on edge, her breathing still ragged.

"Are you nervous about today?" He shifted himself underneath Fern, but made no effort to move her off.

"Wouldn't you be?" Fern propped herself up to look into Kraai's face. "Won't you be when you get your new power?"

"I think I am more excited than nervous." He tucked the wild hair that was dangling in Fern's face behind her ear. "I enjoy learning new things, and this hidden part of me is something I wish to explore."

Fern played with his feathery, dark hair. "Hidden in plain sight," she mocked. "And my hidden part is not a source of pride. If anything, I am afraid of it. What if my song changes who I am?"

Kraai sat up, holding both Fern's hands in his. He held her gaze, inching closer to her face. "You…" he began with a seriousness seldom heard.

Starlings flocked in Fern's stomach. She, too, leaned forward. "Yes?"

Shock flashed across his face before he leaned back onto the headboard. "You are too stubborn to let anything change who you are." He pivoted off the bed, grabbing his shirt from the bedside table and throwing it over himself. He faced the window, doing up the buttons. "It is a big day today, regardless of the feelings you may have about it. We should have a proper breakfast—build up your strength."

Fern sat slack jawed. Had they been about to…? No. Of course not. She shifted off the bed, recollecting her composure through a deep breath before moving to the door. "You're right. I will see you at breakfast."

Upon returning to her room, she found her clothes missing. In their place was a dress. Not nearly as ridiculous as the one set out for her on the first night, but still incredibly unlike Fern. Sure, the green color was lovely—it was the color of the foothills, the canopy of evergreens, but it was still a *dress*. She moved some pieces around, feeling the long sleeves—they would rest off her shoulder, but still cover her arms. Finally, she fiddled with the skirt. It was a slimmer profile, and shorter in the front than the back, probably easier to move in. Fern's eyes popped when underneath she found new brown leather breeches. Perhaps her grandmother did understand her, if only a little. After tying the pants, she pulled on the dress, lost in the folds of fabric when there was a knocking at the door. "Enter!" she yelled, hoping she could get Kraai's help with navigating the cloth maze.

The door creaked and a feminine laugh followed. "Do you require assistance?" her grandmother asked, her footsteps making their way closer.

Fern deflated a little. She wanted to feel the outfit out before agreeing to wear it. Her grandmother might see this scene as an admittance of defeat. She turned her spark of excitement into frustration in her voice. "This ridiculous thing won't go on. You took my clothes, and I couldn't very well run downstairs in my nightclothes to complain."

Two tugs and Fern was free of the tent. She slid her arms through the sleeves and grazed her hands down the fabric.

Emily held up a brown vest. No, not a vest—a stay of some sort. "Just try this over it—it will hold the dress to your body and add"—she moved her hands in the form of an hourglass—"shape."

Fern looked at it suspiciously, then looked down at her dress. It did look a little loose. The stay would make it less likely to snag on anything, at least. She wrapped it around her waist, tightening as well as she could while still being able to bend and breathe—no point in having a dress that didn't impede movement if one extra article did so.

Emily took some leather boots by the door—darker brown leather than the breeches, about the same shade as the stay— and handed them to her granddaughter. They were brand new, a huge improvement on the falling-apart pair that Fern wore in, but they would require some breaking-in. At least now she had an excuse to go explore more of this part of the Light Region. But if she fell into the water during the ceremony, she'd have no use for boots.

For the first time ever, Kraai finished his food faster than Fern. He wasn't eating particularly quickly, but Fern was distracted. The little food she put on her plate went cold by the time she got around to eating it all. The table was silent. Fern was waiting for someone else to start the conversation, but it never happened. Nobody stood until Fern did.

"Do you want to train today? Take your mind off things?" Emily asked.

Fern didn't look up, pretending to fiddle with something in her empty hands. "No, I think I'll just walk around until it's time."

Taking advantage of the tense silence, Emily said, "You don't have to do it."

"I do, though. If Kraai is going to go near that region, he needs to know of any vulnerabilities, and I don't trust any of *them* to help him test it." Fern looked up in time to see a knowing smile on Emily's lips.

The walk took Fern out into the hills, the orange roofs of the white buildings glowing more as the sun rose toward its crest. She walked around the edge of the main part of the city, steering her way toward the cliffs. Although she mostly accepted what she was about to do, she still had the fear it would change something deep within her—awaken a darkness that swam below the surface. Most of the walk was spent searching herself for this evil so she could squash it before accepting the gift of her siren ancestry. By the time she got to the climb, she had given up and accepted that Kraai would help subdue her siren side while they explored her new power together.

The sun was high over the water, its glare a streak bouncing on the gentle waves. Fern came to the end of the path and sat, her legs dangling off the side. She looked behind her, half-expecting someone to shove her in, and tucked her feet back to sit cross-legged instead. She looked out at nothing in particular, letting her eyes lose focus over the contrast of the blue of the sky with the blue of the water.

A slap broke her escape—the sound of something wet smacking against another flat object. She looked down and found a small island not far from the cliff. Three tailed men sat there, looking up, each of them so different in appearance from the other. One was a muscular siren with no hair, another was even larger with enough hair for them both in long curls down his back, and the third looked a bit like Father with his short, dark hair. Their tails were all different shades of blue.

"Are you ready?" the bald one called up.

Fern didn't dare lean any further, already being so precariously placed at the edge. "Will I lose composure? I do not wish to fall."

All three smiled warmly and the bald one hollered again, "You do not need to see us. Lean back and just listen."

Fern gave a hasty nod before shoving herself back a full body's length. She stayed seated, but rested on her hands behind her, the sun warming the front of her body. She sat there for a few seconds, eyes closed, enjoying the moment, readying herself to put her trust in these strangers. It did not take long, though, as their warmth could be seen in their faces, heard in their voices. She shouted, "Ready!"

A song rose from the island, a harmony Fern could not place, but knew somewhere deep inside of her. The voices blended—a deep rumble and two dancing melodies—to speak directly to Fern's heart.

"A siren leaves the ocean
With dreams to go ashore
Her legs are now beneath her
And fins she has no more.
May a song be on her lips
As far away she roams
With salt water in her veins
To remind her of her home."

Fern felt something rise in her throat. She panicked, doubling over and turning so she would not vomit on herself, but instead of bile, a song came from her lips in a voice she had never heard before. "Of all the songs that come to end, and all those just begun, I sing a song to lure my prey, this voice will be the one." She couldn't move. The words did not awaken something inside her, but rather broke something. Everything in her chest shattered around a stone heart. Lure my prey. *Lure my prey.* The sound of splashing rose from the water. Fern crawled to the edge and barely breathed, "Lure my prey?" as the sun glinted off the blue tails swimming just below the surface. The sun was behind a cloud, yet they still glowed. Their whole bodies were radiating, not just their tails. She found her own voice once more and screamed, "Lure my prey?"

One of the males, the one with the dark hair and small eyes, surfaced, still backstroking in the water. His voice was at a conversational tone, but Fern could hear him as if he were right next to her. "They are traditional words. We have tried to rewrite them, but to no avail. We are not our ancestors."

Fern rolled away from the edge, lying in the dirt of the path and the grass beside it. Staring up at the sky, she spoke to herself, hearing her own voice—her normal voice. "This is who I am. This is me. This is where my human voice, my demonic voice is." She reached her hand to her throat, touching it lightly with her fingertips. Her lips parted, and she sang in a whisper, "And this is my siren tone." It was airy, melodious, murderous. She pulled her hand from her throat, snapping it as far away as it could go. "And this is me. Right here." Her voice was back to normal. She raised a hand in front of her face and used her other to imaginarily write on her palm. "Don't touch throat," she mumbled to herself. She emphasized the period she placed at the end.

She stomped back down the hill, Kraai coming into view as she neared where the land flattened out. He was hunched over the rocks that broke the waves, placing something into his pocket. Closer still, she could see a green glow in front of him.

When she recognized it as an aura, she sped her pace, nearly losing her footing in her haste. She saw his lips moving, smiling. She saw him nod, laugh. She broke into a sprint—no siren was going to seduce her friend and get away with it. When he noticed her coming, he gave a cordial wave and the glow disappeared before Fern could see who it was, but based on the color she thought Carnyx could be the culprit.

A greeting, a joke, anything would have been better than what Fern said first. "What did she give you?" It came off incredibly accusatory.

"Just a rock, a trinket." Kraai shrugged it off. "How was it?"

She refused to let him change the topic. "Why did she give you a rock?"

His brow furrowed as he took far too long to respond. "A good luck charm."

"Let me see." She held out her hand. If there was some kind of weird siren magic embedded in the rock, she wanted to know.

Kraai tucked his left side, the side where the gift was in his pocket, away from Fern. "No, I do not believe I will." He gave a sly smile, then his eyes widened.

Fern found her hand reaching for her throat. She threw it back down and pursed her lips. "Fine. The ceremony was fine. I just want to be myself for a little while before I practice with the tone, if that's alright with you."

His shoulders fell. "Yes. Whatever makes you comfortable."

Chapter 14

Kraai was gone the following morning. After some panicked searching on Fern's part, Emily entered the dining room and reassured her that he was only meeting with the elves.

"Mountain elves, in fact. Well, the Light Region's version. They live further toward the Mountains where the land rises, but they are still within the veil." Just as Emily sat down, James arrived with her chalice.

Fern ignored the drink and began piling food onto her plate to make up for her lack of appetite the day prior. "Do they really think they can get him to shift?"

Emily shrugged as she raised her cup to her lips. "They can try, and that is all we can ask." They sat in silence for a bit before she asked, "Are we training today?"

Through a full mouth, Fern asked, "When will Kraai return?"

"Not for a while. We would get back with plenty of time to spare."

Fern did not want to risk it. She wanted to be here the moment he returned to ask him all about it—she already felt so guilty not knowing that today was the day. "Could we train here?" She dropped her voice, embarrassed to say the next piece, but still feeling it was important to admit. "Perhaps you can guide me through what you'd like me to know from the books, because I am hopelessly lost. I am afraid my parents might have missed some pieces of my schooling if I am supposed to be able to understand all of that and use it." She waited for scolding, for mockery, for contempt.

Instead, Emily smiled with a warmth Fern had never expected from a vampire. "Of course, my dear. Forget the books—I'll teach you how I've learned to apply it."

And so, after breakfast, Emily and Fern practiced their magic in the house. Emily showed how a slight charge in two objects could make them repel each other, how charges move through different materials. The vampire gushed about all of it with the excitement of a small child recounting their favorite story. As the last of the cold exterior melted, Fern almost found herself liking her grandmother. Almost.

After nearly two straight hours of experimenting and explanations, Emily called for James. "A large container of water, if you please, with some cups." Emily cleared space on the table, then reconsidered and sat on her knees on a fur rug on the ground. "I think you will like this one." She held her hands facing each other, then bent her middle fingers to point toward each other. A charge flowed between them, a thin, bright stream of light that buzzed and cracked in the air. "It flows easily through the air, but it takes a lot more effort to get it to run through water. More focus, more energy." James placed a tub of water in front of them, four glass cups bobbing around inside. "Perfect, thank you." Emily removed two of the cups, turned the two remaining upside-down, placed her thumbs inside them, and once again created the arc between her fingers, the entire system completely submerged. Emily's eyes burned with intensity as she stared at the faint light glowing in the water.

Fern shifted her focus from her grandmother's strained face to her hands. She saw nothing special. Only...bubbles? Tiny bubbles formed on the tips of Emily's fingers. After some time, they began to collect and rise in the overturned cups, becoming trapped on the bottoms.

Through gritted teeth, Emily mumbled, "It will not go willingly—the cleaner the water, the less it will conduct—but if you force it through, it *will* break."

Fern held her hand toward the water, not daring to touch it, but hovering over. She felt a trace of her grandmother's charge, but what pushed stronger was a disappearance. Water that connected with her, held her notice, then was *gone*. "What are—?" Her words were lost in her stunned mouth.

The cups filled further with the gases that now streamed up from Emily's thumbs. One container was filling at about twice the rate of the other. But where did it come from? They were completely submerged. It was not water becoming vapor, she would still feel the water present if that were the case.

The arc disappeared, and Emily lifted one of the glasses, leaving it upside-down, the remaining water spilling free as it broke the surface. "Do you know what's in here?"

"Not water," Fern whispered.

"Not water," Emily repeated as she raised her fingers next to the cup. A snap of her fingers, a spark flying from them, and a flash of fire causing a popping sound.

Fern flinched, but as she opened her eyes, she felt something she had never felt before. Something so very familiar, but brand new and unadulterated. "You—" Her eyes felt like they would pop out of her sockets just staring at her grandmother. "You *created* water. That vapor in the air didn't exist before."

"I broke the water in the tub into two pieces. This cup," she shook the empty glass in her hand, "held hydrogen gas. Combine it with heat, it finds the oxygen in the air, creates a reaction, and becomes water. It was a science experiment we did when I had probably thirteen years. I stayed after class that day and convinced my teacher to let me do it at least five or six more times. We used batteries." She held up an imaginary object between her fingers. "They were little boxes that held electricity, which we hooked up to metal wires. We sent the charge through water with stuff in it to make it more conductive. Electrolysis, it was called. Closest thing to magic I thought existed back then, making a fireball out of what looked like thin air." She stared at nothing in particular, a faint smile gracing her lips. "Little did I know…"

"This is a magic that is not harnessed by any water demon—to *create* water. Demons with fire magic can create fire, but water cannot be created or destroyed by a water demon." Fern grabbed the cup, turning it around in her hand as if to search for a better explanation. "You not only did that, but you also made fire from water." She looked at her grandmother, waiting for her to return her gaze. "I want to try."

Emily helped her replicate the setup—hands submerged with cups over the thumbs, creating an arc between points on each hand. It took focus to pull the charge with one hand and push it with the other—the only way it would go through the water. Her arc was stronger and brighter than Emily's, and it took less time to accumulate the bubbles she was looking for. Having her hands in the water, though, she could better sense the water ceasing to exist as she knew it. There was no urgency, no fear from the water—it resisted for a moment, then broke. When the cup had enough gas inside, she picked it up, tilted it to the side and snapped a small charge. *Pop.* The puff of fire showed she had succeeded, and the feeling of new water wafted in the air. She immediately returned her hands to the water. There was one more thing she had to see.

This time, after she ignited the hydrogen, she kept her snapping hand up, threading her fingers through the vapor before it dispersed through the room. It was pristine—cleaner than the water from a glacial stream for a few moments before it mingled with the air around them. It was malleable—not in the helpless way, but in a way in which it was solely bonded with her—she would alone have influence over these droplets of water. She did the process again, this time flipping the cup over and clasping her hand, calming the water from the air, letting it fall in droplets into the cup.

"You can condense water vapor?" Emily asked in a whisper.

Fern kept her eyes fixed on the drops of water on the bottom of the glass. "I've been working with the moisture in the air recently, trying to connect to water without having easy access to a source. I can only do this when I know the water very well, and this new water only knows me. You just have to take some of its energy, like a small child settling down."

Emily reached out to touch the glass, as well. "Hone that talent. I have known few water demons who can do it, and it is a good skill to have."

A voice from behind startled them both. "I will be sure to put it on the list of things to practice."

Fern nearly dropped the glass, but instead shoved it into Emily's hand as she turned to sprint toward Kraai. She couldn't keep her hands to herself, rubbing them up and down his arms as her eyes scanned him from head to toe. "Did it work? Are you basically a bird now?"

He smiled as he unbuttoned his sleeve, pulling up to reveal a black mark on the side of his forearm. Upon closer inspection, it was a spot of miniature feathers. Seeing Fern's hand hovering over them, he said, "Yes, you can touch them." He pulled back, glaring. "Gently, though. It is terribly sensitive."

Fern rubbed one finger along the feathers. They were real and they were attached to her friend, growing from his arm. "Come," she demanded, grabbing his hand and pulling him toward the stairs. "I need to know *everything*."

She dragged him until she was confident that he would follow of his own accord. Closing the door to her room behind him, she leaned against it, her eyes pleading for a story.

"Do not look at me like that. I cannot shift just yet; I am still growing my feathers. They told me to wait a few days before trying."

"Are you going to have feathers all the time?" Fern rubbed her own arm. She hated goose skin—she imagined permanent feathers would be the same sensation day and night. Just the thought of it conjured the bumps.

"No. They'll grow and disappear under the skin, only to come out when I transform." He rolled his sleeve down, buttoning it on his wrist.

Fern took the hint. "How did they do it? Did they lay you down on an altar and"—she wiggled her fingers in the air— "cast a little spell?"

"A potion, actually." His shoulders met his ears in a cringe. "A disgusting potion. It was thick like resin, but tasted like smoke." His face deformed with the memory. "Sitting, waiting for it to come out of the container was torture. The smell was pleasant enough, but once it hit my tongue, I wanted to spit it out, instead I had to wait what felt like an eternity for every drop to make it past my lips and down my throat."

Fern had stopped comprehending when he said the word "tasted." Something felt wrong about it. It was a potion, of course it had a taste. When you consume things, you taste them. When you drink… Fear flooded Fern's mind. Her first instinct was to run to Kraai. She threw her arms around him, pressing him to her, holding her lips by his ears. In a shuddered whisper she managed to say, "You drank something."

His arms hugged back, but instead of the shaking of a terrible realization, they proved calm, steady. "I know." His whisper was warm on her ear.

She held him tighter, unsure of if it should be in anger or pity. "Did you ask how they made it? What was in it?"

"You know how much I want this." He ran his fingers over her hair. "Even if I did not know what it was, I knew it was something I craved. I have felt its absence for so long, just a step away but completely out of reach. It was finally in my grasp, in my hand, and I had to take the chance."

As badly as she wanted to yell at him, scream about him not being careful, about risking his recollection of their last weeks together, she *did* know how badly he wanted this. He had never expressed it verbally, but he had always been frustrated by his weaker powers. It was attributable to being human, but he never truly *was* human. Something must have been trying to claw its way out this whole time. But he chose this over *her*—over possibly the last memories they will ever have together. She pulled out of the embrace, turning away to wipe tears from her cheeks before she faced him, red-eyed. "I suppose we'll find out if there was water in it when you leave."

He reached out to hold her. "You know I would never want to—"

"We should go eat," Fern interrupted, pushing his arms away. "It's been a long day for both of us." She managed to keep her voice steady, but the moment she turned to leave, her chin quivered.

After a meal filled with relative silence, Fern decided not to bring it up again. She couldn't change his decision when it had already been made, and they would find out soon enough if he was going to forget his time here.

Most of Kraai's time was spent in bed, his body recovering and changing. Fern did not come to him, even when her nightmares resumed. One night she was able to sleep long enough to see the bodies left by the immense wave, floating in the shallow water. Her own dead eyes looked up at her, the green of them turned a clouded blue, water lapping over the face. Another figure in the darkness caught her eye. She would not have bothered to approach it if she hadn't seen red gems in its hand, glinting in the moonlight. Her father's empty expression nearly shocked her out of her sleep, but another body dragged her back in. The body was face-down, but Fern clutched an arm to turn it over. It was swollen, waterlogged. Bits of the flesh had been eaten away, as if it had been here long before the wave came for Fern, and it was completely unrecognizable save for the hair—the tight curls that bounced in the lapping water. She backed away from her mother's body, bumping into more behind her.

None of the faces or features were familiar, but she could glimpse parts of their stories: the piercing eyes of a beautiful young woman, the blue-tinged skin of a sea elf, the hair of a horned demon so short she could have sworn he was bald in the darkness, and a demon with locked hair clutching a book in his hands. The last thing she saw before she woke was dust floating on top of the water, a red dress sinking to the bottom beneath it.

Chapter 15

"Want to see something fascinating?" was all Kraai had to say to get Fern to follow him into the hills. His giddy smile dismantled all of her anger about his silence the past week. He sprinted, but she was able to keep up with him easily after all of the runs with her grandmother. She probably could have passed him, but why steal his thunder when he was so excited?

They fled deep into an apple orchard, far from anyone who could see or hear them. His chest heaving, but his smile still bright, Kraai asked, "Are you ready?"

Fern matched his energy. "Yes! Show me!" She laughed her words out, thrilled to finally get to see if his risk paid off. She felt a tingle crawl on her skin, but leaned over to discharge the spark on a nearby tree, never breaking eye contact or losing her smile.

Kraai nodded, took a steadying breath, and lowered his head. His entire form shrank into his clothing, which settled into a pile on the ground. A feathered head and dark eyes peeked out from the neck of the shirt, then the dark bird hopped out.

Fern's hands reached up to her open mouth, but nothing could hide the sheer joy in her eyes. She tucked her fingers away to reveal a smile so wide it was almost painful. "You can shift!" She dragged her fingers through her hair, holding it at the back of her head so she had a clear view of the crow that now hopped in a half-fly up and down the row of trees. "Change back so I can hug you properly!"

The bird faced away and held still, its feathers shaking before they shrank into tan skin on a growing shape. Wings became arms, claws morphed into feet, the feathers on its head barely seemed to change as they transformed into her friend's hair.

Fern admired the whole process, watching in fascination as his muscles became visible and his skin grew clear of plumage. She wanted to reach out and touch him, but soon realized that she was staring at the back of her friend who was now standing completely naked in an apple orchard. Four confused heartbeats later, Fern was averting her eyes and reaching for Kraai's clothes, handing them out to him. "You might want to try to learn to change back while inside your shirt," she said as she fought the urge to look to see if he noticed the clothes. "Then, at least you'll be somewhat decent and poised to pull up your breeches." The clothes tore from her hand, something falling out of them and landing with a *thud* on the dirt. Fern dared not even look in the direction.

"As if you have never seen me in a state of undress," Kraai scoffed.

"Not to this extent." Fern was glad she was turned so Kraai could not see her face—it was uncomfortably warm. "At least not since we were kids."

"But you will stare at my naked body when I take the form of a crow." His tone was soaked with confidence and jest, it was one of Fern's favorite sounds.

"That is diff—" Her head snapped to look at him, but it was still too soon. He was tying his breeches, but his chest was still completely uncovered. It glowed in the sunlight that filtered in through the trees. Wide-eyed, she turned away once more, pursing her lips and clenching her fists. What was happening?

After a bit more amused laughter from Kraai, he finally said, "It is safe to look now. Completely clothed."

Fern turned to see him hastily dressed and ran to him, leaping to attack him with an embrace. "You shifted!" Her voice was nearly a scream right beside his ear.

He wrapped his arms around her, spinning their joined selves in a circle before lowering Fern to the ground. "I shifted!" He backed away to look her in the eyes. "Your turn."

"My turn?" For half a beat, Fern wondered if she might have some hidden animal demon blood.

"Your new power," Kraai reminded her. "It is your turn to show me your song. That was the deal, was it not? You would get the power and try it on me to see if you would be comfortable using it."

Fern kicked herself for being too caught up in Kraai's excitement to remember. "I was going to try it on you in your crow form to see if you were immune."

"We would first need to see if it works on me to begin with, in my demonic form." He gestured to himself, a right mess with a half-tucked shirt, nothing on his feet, and unkempt hair.

"Are you sure you want me to do this?" Fern asked, her fingers unconsciously finding their way to her neck. She caught them and had them rub along her jawline instead.

"My mind is completely at your disposal." His brow furrowed and he leaned forward, adding in a hushed voice, "Just do not make me kill your grandmother. I know you are not her biggest admirer, but I have grown quite fond of her."

Fern just rolled her eyes; she wasn't about to reveal to him that she was starting to see something good in her grandmother after all their time together. "You just try to stand there and do nothing, alright?"

Kraai held out his arms. "Do your worst."

Fern's fingers trailed from where they were resting behind her ear down to her neck. She had been practicing her songtone in a whisper in her room for the past week. She knew how to access it easily now, singing without the urge to vomit. She even grew to like the sound. It was beautiful, seductive—something Fern had never thought any part of herself to be. "You look hungry. Go eat an apple." Fern decided this to be the perfect test—Kraai should still be wary of taking fruit from a farm in the Light Region after what happened on their journey here. Fern knew this particular field was enchantment-free after picking a late apple blossom after a training session with her grandmother, but Kraai was not privy to this information.

One second, two. Kraai stood in place. But before Fern could sing again, he licked his lip and turned to pull an underripe apple from a nearby tree. With no expression, he bit into it, chewed and swallowed.

"Kraai," Fern said in her own voice.

He did not respond, taking another bite.

"Kraai!" Fern yelled, hoping to break the trance.

Nothing. He continued eating until the entire apple was gone, core and all. When he was finished, he blinked, shaking his head. "Why do I have to be so literal?" He gave Fern a straight-lipped smile. "Next time I suppose you will have to be more specific."

"You remember it?"

"Yes." He narrowed his eyes. "Am I not supposed to?"

"I have no idea." Fern stopped for a moment, wondering if he was just having a laugh, but he knew how important this was to her—he wouldn't. "What was it like?"

Kraai moved toward her, looking her in the eye. "I would have done *anything* for you. All I wanted for that minute was to make you happy."

Fern held his gaze. "And now?"

"I still want you to be happy, of course." His eyes shot a stroke of confusion, wanting to choose his wording carefully. "But it felt like the only reason I was alive was to serve you, that all I could ever want to do was what you asked of me."

"Did it feel"—she paused to search for the word—"violating?"

"Honestly?"

"Please."

"Not with you." He grazed her chin with his finger. "But with anyone else it would have. I am not sure I would be as comfortable having a stranger in my mind—in control." His hand lingered a moment too long.

Fern didn't mind. She reached up her hand and rested it on his. "Are you ready to shift so we can try again?"

Kraai didn't move his hand. "I believe I can only change once more before I risk exhaustion. It is still new to me."

Fern nodded, looking to her feet to break eye contact. "I'll be sure to turn around when it's time for you to change back."

"Are you sure you want to miss the show?" Kraai asked, a smile in his voice.

Fern could only respond in what came out to be a sarcastic smile.

Kraai concentrated, shrinking back into his clothes, transforming slightly slower than he had before. The bird bobbed out of the shirt collar once more, turning its head to the side to watch and wait for Fern's command.

Fern looked around for something to demand. She didn't know if he could fly yet, and she did not want to risk forcing him to try, so she went with something on his level. She held her hand to her throat and sang, "You are upset with the tree. Attack its trunk."

The crow did not move. Its beady eye did not flinch.

Fern smiled as she sang again, "Attack the tree."

Still the bird stayed put, puffing its breast.

Fern turned around. "I get it. You're immune. No need to rub it in."

She waited some time, hearing the sound of clothing being shaken out before Kraai's voice cut in. "Nothing. In fact, your voice sounds rather different through a bird's ears. Not nearly as pleasant as how these ears perceive your songtone." He rested his hands on her shoulders.

The warmth of his hands spread down her arms. Fern hadn't felt cold, but this contrast brought chills down her spine. "You think my tone is pleasant?"

"I do. In fact—" Kraai's hands dropped. "Where is it?"

Fern turned around to find him on the ground searching in the dirt. "Where is what?"

"My..." His eyes were frantic, hands digging through the thin loose layer. "It was..." His hair fell into his face, which was reddening with urgency.

"Your what?" Fern demanded, falling to the ground beside him, helping him search for the mystery object. A glint of green caught her eye and she grabbed at it. A green pendant, about the size of a sparrow's egg, set on a golden chain. Half-mystified, she asked, "Is this it?"

Kraai's hand snatched it from hers. "Yes. Yes." He brought it around his neck and clasped it without looking. "It must have fallen from my pocket when I was without my clothes."

"What is it?" Fern had never seen him wear jewelry before, and no item would have been important enough to cause such worry.

Kraai pressed his eyes shut, heaving as if he were about to be sick. After a long pause and a breath, he managed to say, "Just a rock, a trinket."

Fern had heard that before. "This is what the siren gave you?" A fire lit in her gut. He was accepting gifts from a woman, jewelry he had been hiding from Fern. Was this jealousy? Over what? Kraai was not hers—at least, not in that sense. She sat back on her haunches, mirroring Kraai, whose face showed apprehension. What was he not telling her? What was he not *able* to tell her? Suddenly she was seeing her friend in the way this region was forcing her to see him, this way she was trying so hard not to see him. But now, there was nothing to lose. "Should I try my song once more? See if it sounds pleasant again?"

Kraai looked at her in the way she realized she had been looking at him. "Yes."

She leaned forward, one hand on the ground for balance, the other reaching for her throat. "Kiss me." The song came out not as a demand, but a hope.

He pressed forward, dragging his knees through the dirt until he was inches from her. He held the sides of her face in his hands and kissed her. His lips were as soft as she had imagined.

Fern sunk into herself. A flutter in her chest grew to a charge in her skin, a spark arcing from her lips to his.

Instead of backing away, Kraai pressed himself deeper into the kiss. He stroked her cheek with his thumb. His lips lingered for some time, then pulled away only to come back for more an instant later.

It felt so right, his lips on hers. His gentle caress. The warmth of his breath. No. This was not right. Not like this. Fern shoved herself backward, knocking Kraai off-balance as she did so. "I am so sorry. I didn't— I mean...I shouldn't have done that. You did what I asked, the song should be broken."

Kraai gathered himself as he laughed. "I fulfilled your command the moment our lips touched."

Their entire friendship hung in the balance and these next words were critical. "So that was something you *wanted* to do?"

"It is something I have wanted to do for some time. I never wanted to put you in an awkward situation, what with us being such close friends for so long, but my lips were already there at your command, so I suppose I just"—he shrugged—"kept going."

Fern's breath was shallow, quick. "And I suppose I didn't quite stop you."

"Not right away, at least." He moved toward Fern, taking her hands in his. "I felt it twice. I experienced what I felt, but I also read what you were feeling. I can read you, sense you, trust you in a way I cannot anyone else, and there is a feeling here I have never had for anyone else, either." He reached up and held Fern's face, brushing a tear she hadn't realized was there. "But if this is not what you wanted, we can forget it ever happened."

Fern turned into his hand, kissing the heel of his thumb before reaching to pull it off her face. "Even if it *is* what I wanted, you might still forget anyway."

"But if I do leave with my memories, will these not be wonderful ones to have?"

Fern wanted this. She didn't realize how much until now, but all she could think of was Kraai's lips on hers and how right it felt. "Should we try it again? Make sure you weren't just feeling the effects of the song?"

"It was not the song, but if you want to test it, I will kiss you a hundred times more."

Fern leaned forward, letting her lips creep closer to Kraai's. "Let's start with once…" It seemed impossible, but it was even better this time. Knowing he wanted to kiss her, knowing he cared for her not only as a best friend, but in this way, too. It was more than just *right*, it was *truth*. It was pure honesty without saying a word. Perhaps they did kiss a hundred times, Fern would not have been able to keep count, but they stayed in the orchard until the sun set. They laid together in the dirt, staring up at the blue sky that morphed into darker and darker shades. Fern's head rested on Kraai's chest, keeping her hair from gathering any more debris. "If you forget—"

Kraai cut in before she could finish. "I will not forget."

"But if you do…" This time Kraai was considerate enough to let Fern finish her sentence, but she did not know how to. What would happen if he forgot and she remembered?

"If I forget, you will remind me when we meet again." His hand found her arm, rubbing it in a way that made Fern relax instantly. "But if I remember spending these last weeks with you, knowing that we cared about each other but denying it, that would haunt me every day."

Fern considered this for a moment. Either way, he was leaving and she was staying. Would it matter if he remembered or not if there was a chance they would never see each other again? He could be killed in the Dark Region. He could be killed at any point along the way home. He could be killed by attackers waiting in the clearing who had already found and done away with their families. It was best to pretend this was the end, and if this was the end, she would want them both to be as happy as possible—and if he was feeling anything like how she was feeling, this would be how to accomplish that.

They walked back to Emily's house, each walking slightly slower than the other in turn, drawing these quiet moments out. Fern could feel something flowing between them, through their joined hands. It moved like a charge, but felt warmer, safer.

They entered the house as quietly as they could manage, but Emily was in the foyer waiting. Her reading gloves on, she did not look up from her book to ask, "Was it everything you'd hoped and more?"

Fern was a deer caught unaware. She turned to Kraai, who had a similar panic on his face.

Emily closed her book. "The shifting? I thought that is what you went out to practice."

The tension in Fern's chest snapped. "He did very well."

"I'm glad." She set her book on the table beside her and stood. "Now get to bed, you two. Fern, I would like you to show me what you can do with water tomorrow. I know a lovely stream we can use." She looked down at their laced fingers, gave a half-smile, and left for the study.

Chapter 16

Fern had always known that water was bound by rules, but Emily seemed to know what those rules were, down to what the water was made of and how it behaved on the smallest level. She explained the relationship between energy and heat, and how the energy could not be destroyed. It was with this knowledge she was able to help Fern better manipulate water that trusted her, and to convince water that didn't.

By the end of the first week of water training, Fern could create a sort of small cloud from the water vapor in the air—at least on a humid day—by sending the energy from the water in one area out to the space around it, cooling the vapor enough that it wanted to condense. Emily beamed with pride, though Fern knew it was likely not pride in her. She would be proud that her inclination that Fern had power over more energy than just electricity was right. She *was* able to control the heat energy in water, but only because she could interact with the water in a way only a water demon could.

After morning training, when Fern finally felt she had it right, she and Kraai went back out to the orchards for his own practice. He was finally getting the hang of flying—gliding on a breeze was his favorite, but landing was still a clumsy process.

He could still only shift once or twice per session, but he was able to stay in his crow form longer and do more with every passing day. Fern had one-sided conversations with him as he practiced flying and she kept an eye out for anyone who might disrupt their peace. Nobody ever did, though. The apples were still maturing, far from the reds or pinks they would need to be for harvest, despite growing just a bit closer to ready every day.

Kraai, as a crow, burrowed into his clothes on the ground. He was able to transform back in a crouched position that allowed him to fill out his shirt and pull up his breeches in one motion as he rose. Every time he would hurry to find his emerald necklace trapped somewhere in his clothes and place it around his neck.

"Will you ever tell me what that is?" Fern asked, toying with the gem in her fingers as he adjusted the clasp in the back.

Kraai opened his lips as if to speak, then sighed and shook his head.

"Well, if you *could* tell me"—Fern's eyes inquired to see if the first half of the question was formed correctly, to which she received an encouraging nod to continue—"would it be something I should worry about? Something that would pull you away from me?"

Kraai smiled, closing his eyes, searching inside for an answer. Fern knew this move. It was the same thing she had to do to search and see if words would make her sick; if these were secrets that could not be spoken, or if there was a wording that could skirt the rules. He opened his eyes once more and looked into hers. "Just the opposite."

The jealousy that had been eating at her every time she saw that green glow lost its power in three words. Fern threw her arms around Kraai and kissed him. His hands finished their task behind his neck and returned the embrace, pinning her to him. How she had gone so long with him in her life and never done this before now was beyond Fern's current understanding. She pulled her head back. "Want to see something?"

Kraai bit his lip as his brow raised. "Do I?"

She smacked him in the chest. "Not like that." She fought her rising blush and pulled her hand to the side and stretched out her fingers, coursing the energy outward and away. The air developed a chill that caused Kraai to look around for the source. Fern coughed to regain his attention, then nodded to her hand, which she balled into a fist, encouraging the chilled vapor to condense. Around them, the air clouded as if fog had rolled in unseen. Tiny drops of water tickled her skin, not heavy enough to fall, but not light enough to go unnoticed. It was so thick she could barely see Kraai inches from her face. "And now we have some more privacy." She leaned in to kiss him once more, but he pulled away.

"Is it safe to breathe this?" he asked in an awed whisper.

Fern had never felt the enchantment in vapor, and even if she had, they would have been past the point of no return with the humid air that lingered near the salt water. She couldn't say that, though. The words couldn't rise in her mouth without something to accompany it. All she could whisper was, "Yes," before planting her lips on his once more. Her hand tried to hold the vapor in place, but her concentration dwindled and the mist pulled away.

Lying on the ground, staring up at the sky, as was usual for the end of their day, Kraai's voice broke a pensive silence. "Let us take a tally. I get to become a bird. You get to control lightning, influence men to do your bidding, *and* make clouds. Is it even a fair comparison at this point?"

"Hold on. You were already able to make fire and can now use your bird ears to be invincible to a siren's song. I believe we are square."

Kraai's finger wagged in Fern's face. "But you also had control of water before we got here, and now have all the other skills, *while* being part human."

Fern touched her imaginary pearls. "What can I say? This blood *did* win the throne in the Dark Region. Had to be pretty strong to get there, even if it is diluted now."

Kraai turned onto his side, looking Fern in the face. "Would you want it?"

"Want what? The throne?" Fern's heart beat faster.

"Yes."

She tucked her hands under her head, adjusting her back that was now oddly uncomfortable. "I suppose I've never properly considered it." She had a right to the throne, of course, if she could just go to the Dark Region and be named. It was a dangerous prospect, though, and not one she would want to undertake. "If it didn't have the ramifications for the safety of my family, perhaps. I mean, who wouldn't want that kind of power? But why entertain the idea if it can never become anything real?"

After a lingering silence, Kraai spoke. "Do you remember when I fell from the tree and broke my leg?"

"Do I?" Fern turned onto her side to mirror Kraai. "You were bedridden until we could find a healer we could trust not to reveal our location. None of the adults would go exploring with me so I was stuck in the clearing for the most beautiful weeks of the summer. Such an experience for a child with only eight years stays in your memory."

His face scrunched in apprehension. "Did I ever tell you that I was trying to fly?"

Fern's expression flattened. "You what?"

The apprehension grew into a look that showed he was not sure she would believe what he was going to say. "I had a dream multiple nights in a row where I was flying over the clearing. I took off from a tree—that tree—and just soared. It was the same feeling I have now when I fly."

The floating dead bodies flashed in her mind. "Do you think it was a vision?"

"No." His face contorted. "Perhaps. My point is that I did not think it possi—" His hand shot out to rub Fern's arm. "What is wrong?"

She could not stop seeing the dead eyes, the lifeless bodies. Burying her face in her hands, she shook her head. "I've been having nightmares."

Kraai rolled onto his back, pulling Fern to lay her head on top of him. He rubbed her back. "Like the one you had before?"

Fern had never told Kraai what happened in the dream that brought her into his bed, or the ones she had after. She wasn't sure she wanted him to know the details of it, as if it would somehow keep him safe if he was left without this knowledge. She took a shuddering breath. "Something is coming after me and my family." She thought of the half-eaten corpse and her mouth grimaced, struggling to get out the words. "It might have already gotten my mother."

Kraai sat up, forcing Fern up with him. He wrapped his arms around her. "I am sure your mother is safe in the clearing." He pressed his lips into her hair, kissing the top of her head. "I will go to the clearing before I go to the Dark Region. I will make sure they are safe."

Fern bit her lips together, fighting the impulse to burst into tears. Just a week more. Kraai had made his plan to leave. Fern wanted to beg him to stay, to convince him that he should find safety beyond the veil, too, but there were so many other factors at play. Their families would want to know they were safe. Kraai needed to find his father. Fern wanted to know if Kraai was going to remember any of what had happened here.

And now she needed someone to check on her family, to make sure this nightmare was just that and nothing more.

Kraai placed his lips close to Fern's ear. "You could come with me. Adventure together, as we always have."

Every fiber of her being screamed to agree, to echo their phrase, but instead of a dead corpse, she now saw her mother as a crumpled pile on the ground, grieving the daughter she had already lost. What would become of her if she lost Fern, too? It was safe here, at least until her sister had been named and taken the crown in the Dark Region.

Kraai kissed her head again, speaking into her hair, his breath sending a trickle of warmth down her spine. "I understand. I want it to be just us, too. Once this is all over, it will be."

Fern tucked herself into his chest. *If you remember.*

They stayed there until sunset, when they followed the remaining sunlight toward the water. In what had become the routine, Kraai walked Fern to her bedroom door. She would prepare for sleep there, but inevitably find her way to his bed. Nothing inappropriate—it was just nice to be near him. Besides, she refused to do anything more intimate than what they had already done until she knew what he would remember. Not that he had even asked. Perhaps he had the same reservations.

Dressed in her nightclothes, Fern tucked out of her room only to find someone waiting for her in the hallway.

"I wish to speak with you."

Fern could see her father in Emily's face. Something deep inside her wanted to take flight, foreseeing a scolding in that expression, that body language. Arms crossed, head cocked, brow raised.

Fern gestured down the hall, words not coming to her lips.

Emily followed the gesture, found Kraai's door, and gave a smile. "It'll be quick. I promise." She turned and went into the room across the hall.

Fern followed, but not without one last glance at Kraai's room. The part of her trained to be alert sent up a warning not to be alone in an enclosed space with a vampire, but she was able to override this. This was her grandmother. She trusted her...enough. Fern closed the door behind her. Emily was already seated on the windowsill, darkness flickering on the water visible just over the walled entryway.

"When you arrived, you were adamant on having two rooms. Now you share one." Emily raised her eyebrows, waiting for Fern to continue the train of thought for her.

"It feels safer," was all Fern could manage, looking out the windows instead of making eye contact. It was the truth, in a sense. She did not want to delve into the more private aspects of their relationship with her grandmother.

"Your mother was the same when she arrived at the palace. She and Sway kept the door open between their rooms." Emily stood, fiddling with her fingers as she began to pace. "But Sway moved to another part of the palace, and Wave had to figure out how to sleep alone." Again, she paused, looking to Fern to put together the pieces.

Fern shrugged. "And I suppose she struggled with it for some time and then got over it."

Emily closed her eyes, taking a deep breath. "But she and Sway weren't romantically involved. And Sway moved across the palace, not across the Four Regions."

Fern's lip trembled as she fought to keep her voice steady. "I don't want him to go."

Emily's red dress caught the air and fanned out as she crossed the room. She wrapped her arms around her granddaughter.

The cold embrace sent warmth to Fern's core. She sank to the ground and her grandmother sank with her. Tears rushed from her eyes, confusion and anxiety she didn't realize she had been holding back. A charge flowed between them, Emily absorbing all the energy Fern was letting off.

Emily's hand ran over Fern's hair, brushing it in a rhythmic, calming way. "How long have you felt this way about him?"

After a few more sobs, Fern was able to compose herself enough to say, "I suppose I have for some time, but I knew when I told him to kiss me."

"And he did?"

"Well, I sang it. He had to. But then he didn't stop." Fern was hit with another wave of mixed emotions. She would always remember the way that first kiss felt, but would Kraai?

Emily's hand stopped. Her tone changed, adding a heavy dose of confusion and a dash of disgust. "You used your song on him?"

Fern pushed herself away, wiping at her cheeks before facing her grandmother. "He told me to. We were out testing my song, seeing if I was comfortable using it, and seeing if it worked on him in his crow form." Fern studied Emily's face and found only lingering shock. "He told me to have him do anything but murder."

Emily's eyes dropped to her hands as she fiddled with a ring on her finger. "I suppose he consented in a way, but would this relationship have ever happened if not for your song?" She looked her granddaughter in the eye, almost pleadingly. "Would you have ever asked him to kiss you if you knew he could say no in the moment? Would he have ever kissed you if he didn't have that push?"

Fern's mouth hung open, her mind racing with the questions. Of course it would have happened. Eventually. But would it have been soon enough? The only emotion that surged inside her was anger, either at her grandmother or at herself, she wasn't quite sure. "Are we done here?"

Emily's face lacked any expression—a stone-faced vampire. "Yes."

Fern made her way to Kraai's bed. She curled in next to him, resting her head on his chest, but joining her tonight was a nagging thought that this wasn't real. That Kraai would leave with memories of a love founded on something insincere or with no memories and no way to regain what they had without using her song.

Chapter 17

The bug in the back of her mind could be ignored for the most part, but it came to the forefront whenever Fern was alone. In the moment, Fern and Kraai were happy—there was no way it could be fake. There were no regrets. It happened the way it happened, and there was no changing that. However, as his departure approached and their time together began to draw to a close, Fern became more distracted in her time away from him, wondering if what she did was right. Questioning herself, over and over.

"Watch it!" Emily shouted, dodging an arc from Fern's hand.

Fern's eyes snapped back to focus and she brought her hand down. "I'm sorry. I—"

"You zoned out again." Emily rolled her eyes. "Just talk to him. So many of these things resolve themselves when you just *talk* to the other person."

"How did you know—?" Fern was still half-elsewhere. Kraai would leave the next day.

"You haven't had a good day's practice since I talked to you about your relationship. I'm sorry." She threw out her arms, giving up. "I thought a little doubt would go a long way in helping you cope with him leaving, but it has only made you useless. Go talk to him about it. You'll need to know where you stand before he goes."

They had barely started their session, but it did not seem as if much would get done today. "Now?"

Emily's eyes widened, insistent. "Now. I'll linger here to give you time alone. Go."

Fern ran back to the house, hoping the courage to talk to Kraai about what had been bothering her did not shake loose with each pounding footstep. She did not even acknowledge the folk who attempted to exchange the pleasantries that were now part of Fern's daily life. She had to ask him now.

As she closed the front door, leaning against it to catch her breath, Kraai happened to be walking through the foyer. He gave her a sidelong glance with a slight smile as he continued toward the stairs. "Was she that rough on you today?"

Fern returned his stare through her brow. "Is this right?"

He stopped in his tracks. "What do you mean?"

Fern straightened herself. "Is what we are doing right? Was it right to start what we have with a siren song?"

Kraai put down the book he was carrying and moved toward her. "I told you that you could ask me to do anything."

Fern slid to the side, out of his path. "But you couldn't say no."

Again, Kraai stopped, a pain in his eyes. His hand reached up and pressed against his chest. "I would have kissed you if you had asked, song or no song."

Her voice came out as a whisper soaked in pain. "But we will never know if that's true, will we?"

Kraai forced his face into her field of view. "I love you. I love you as my best friend. I love you in a deeper way, too. I look at you in a way I have never been able to look at another being because I see every part of you, I *know* every part of you. Nobody has ever made me as angry or as happy or as absolutely delirious as you do. I felt this way before the song, and I still feel this way now." He ripped open the top of his shirt and grasped the emerald gem in his hand before repeating, "I would have done it, song or no song."

A wave of sickness came over Fern. She hated that necklace, a gift from another woman. No doubt he would leave Fern behind but keep this reminder of the redheaded siren. Her face turned to a snarl.

Kraai's knuckles whitened as his grip on the jewel tightened. "Use your song on me," his words were slow, but pleading.

"What? No." Fern slid out from against the wall, evading Kraai.

He blocked her path. He seemed to retch once, twice, before begging, "Use your song on me. Please."

"No. I will never use my song on you again. Ever." Fern tried to brush past him, but Kraai moved his body once again to keep her where she was. His eyes were wild, frantic, his hand still clasped on the necklace. A twinge of fear sprouted in the back of Fern's mind, but the instant it appeared, Kraai backed away, his face downcast.

"I am sorry. I just"—he closed his eyes, searching for words that would make it past his lips—"needed you to know."

Fern would have asked what he meant but James entered.

Kraai flagged him with a raised hand. "James, I was wondering if you had any thread. The shirt I am wearing tomorrow could use some mending." His voice gave no hint that he had just been in an absolute panic.

James held out his hand and gave a quizzical expression.

"No," Kraai responded. "I would prefer to fix it on my own. I will be doing my own mending once I leave, may as well start now. My mother was a seamstress, I know what I am doing." After James left to retrieve the thread, Kraai put his attention back to Fern. "Fern, you know I would never…"

"I know. That's why it scared me. It was so"—she glanced down at the pendant and back up to his face—"outside of your character."

Kraai tucked the necklace inside his shirt, closing off the buttons that remained intact. He closed his eyes again, his brow furrowed, his chest heaving as he searched. He shook his head before looking at her again, the face of the boy she'd grown up with, who she now loved, calm and caring. "Will you help me prepare?"

Fern fought back a swell of emotions as she nodded.

Each being who left the veil was allowed to take a single note of what had happened within. This is how Emily was able to send messages to Fern's great-grandmother—she found people who did not wish to remember what happened to them within the veil and sent the messages with them. All notes were inspected upon exit to ensure nobody was able to reveal secrets or risk the safety of anyone in hiding. Though, it would have been impossible to try to write the secrets they could not say— whenever Fern tried to write something out, trying to reveal a secret without vomiting, her hand would cramp and release the quill. She had tried everything to skirt the rules, but they held fast. There would be no way to encapsulate everything that had happened in one note, so Fern continued to brainstorm ways for Kraai to guarantee his complete memory of his time there.

"What if you fly out?" Fern asked, helping Kraai fold some of the clothes her grandmother had gifted him. "Maybe it will be like my song—it won't work in bird form."

"But if I leave in my bird form and I…" He shrugged, allowing Fern to fill in the blanks. "Then I am trapped that way." He pressed another shirt into the case. "Or I *can* transform and wind up naked in the Light Region."

Fern gave a curt chuckle at the thought of her friend stranded, naked, days from home. "Fine." She crumpled up some breeches and threw them on the bed. She would be better able to handle preparations if she knew what she was preparing for. Would he remember any of this? What needed to be in the letter? "I hate this. I hate not knowing."

"We will know tomorrow."

"*You* will know tomorrow," Fern corrected. "I will be stuck here, without you, not knowing." Her eyes widened, causing Kraai to stop his work, as well. "Come back."

"Come back?"

Fern moved closer. "Come back. Right after you leave, come back."

His brow furrowed. "But if I do not…"

Fern gestured with open hands. "Then I will know. One way or the other."

Kraai nodded, though his face was still worried.

"Now let's work on the letter." Fern went to the desk in the corner where two pieces of parchment and a quill were waiting. He would only get one page to put anything he wanted to remember. "What do you want in here?" She leaned over the table, her hands on either side of the blank paper that would hold weeks of memories.

Kraai followed, placing his hands just outside of Fern's, pressing his body behind hers. He tucked his chin onto her shoulder. "We can start with how much I love you, and the fact you love me, too. I will be quite relieved to read that."

A chill went down Fern's spine. Was it pleasure of hearing those warm words from his lips, or guilt over how she put them there? "Shouldn't you start with how to transform? What it feels like? How to access it?"

Kraai pulled away, fussing with the sleeves of his shirt. "Sure." His voice was flat, unemotional. "I need you to write it, though."

"As if you would be able to read my writing…" Fern was not known for her penmanship. In fact, Kraai's hand was more beautiful by far.

"It will let me know that you really are safe and give me proof to show your parents." His voice still flat, he managed a knowing glance that Fern caught out of the corner of her eye. "Nobody would think to forge your chicken scratch."

Fern wanted to snap back, but she knew he was right. Her writing had *personality*, as her father put it. They would all recognize it as hers. She sat in the chair and picked up the quill. "What am I writing?"

After an hour of careful consideration, they came up with:

We found who we were looking for. She was who she claimed to be. Fern is with her and will remain beyond the veil until it is safe to leave.

You now have the power to shift. To do this, feel for the rock in your chest. (Your words, not mine—I am just the scribe.) Collapse yourself into that space. It will hurt.

"Wait." Fern pushed the chair out. "It hurts?"

"Oh, yes." He gave a smile through gritted teeth. "Takes everything in me not to scream."

Fern turned back to the paper, underlining the word "will" before continuing.

Practice takeoff and landing somewhere safe (you are still not too great at it). To change back, press yourself out through that same point. There is no great way to describe it, just feel for it. (And change back while burrowed in your shirt because you will be very naked.) Don't shift too much in one day, it exhausts you. (And you become quite ill-humored.)

Kraai came up behind Fern to look at her work so far. "Really? Is the commentary necessary?"

Fern shot a smile over her shoulder. "How else will you know it was truly me writing it?"

With a raise of his eyebrows, Kraai resumed pacing and dictating.

You are immune to a siren's song when you are in your crow form. (Don't rely too heavily on this, we didn't test on stronger siren songs.)

Wear the emerald necklace any time you are in human form. Do not lose it.

Fern rolled her eyes at the necklace getting a spot in the letter, not even hinting at what was so important about it.

"What should we write about us?" Kraai asked.

Fern's hand clutched the quill tighter in reaction to the ache in her chest. She left a space between the last paragraph and the one she was about to write.

She dictated as she wrote.

Fern loves you. She loves the warmth of your hand in hers. She loves the touch of your lips. She loves how you drive her absolutely mad while simultaneously making her the happiest being in the Four Regions. Come back to her after you've done what you need to do.

The words were beginning to creep toward the bottom of the page. "Is there anything you would like to add?"

"About us?" Kraai placed his hands on Fern's shoulders, the warmth radiating through to her skin. "I think I would die happy just reading that part." He bent down to kiss her cheek. "Especially written in your hand."

Fern dropped the quill and turned to meet Kraai's lips. Her fingers reached to graze his cheek as he kneeled down beside her. She hunched over to keep close to him. "You leave tomorrow," she whispered, sinking off the chair and onto the ground with him.

"I leave tomorrow." His voice wavered as he pressed his forehead against hers. A shudder in his chest shook through them both.

Fern pulled away to see Kraai's eyes watering. "But you'll come back." She forced a smile. "You'll come back right away or you'll come back when you've found your father and told our families we are safe."

His forming tears finally released themselves. "I will come back," he echoed. He turned his face away, wiping his cheeks.

With one hand, Fern led his face back to hers. With the other, she dispelled the heat and created a fog to envelop them. If he didn't want to be seen crying, he wouldn't be, but she would not let him bear the pain alone. Keeping her hand clenched in a fist, she wrapped her arm around his neck, pressing her body against him. She let him feel the heaving of her chest as she broke down, burying her face in his shoulder, her tears soaking into his shirt. His body responded in a violent shake and a sob that tore through Fern. Her tears intensified in response. They cried in each other's arms, hidden in a mist, until Fern had nothing left in her.

Then the room was still and silent, the water around them buffering any noise that might have crept in. Fern looked through stinging eyes, unable to see anything but Kraai, his features fading in and out of view through the haze of water vapor. She dismissed the cloud, barely able to hang on to the last thread of energy she had. Kraai came into view, his face warm and inviting. She never wanted to stop looking at him, but sleep called.

"Bed?" Kraai asked.

Fern nodded, but as she tried to rise, she was interrupted by Kraai scooping her up in his arms, carrying her to her spot. She pawed at the stay that held her shirt, just managing to loosen it. "I have to…" The same force that was weighing down her eyelids stole her voice.

"You have to rest." Kraai kissed her on the forehead before moving to the other side of the bed and taking off his shirt. The heat of the summer was especially oppressive in this region, and the nights did little to cool the air. He tucked in beside Fern, guiding her head onto his chest.

She pulled him close, listening to his rapid heartbeat for what might be the last time. One last whisper left her lips before she succumbed to sleep, "One day we'll be together again."

The echo of Kraai's response rang in her dreamless sleep. "As we always have."

Chapter 18

"They're here," Emily said as she entered the study. When her eyes fell on Kraai and Fern's clasped hands, her sharp tooth bit the edge of her lip while her eyes looked with pity on the two.

Fern took a deep breath and looked to her best friend. She wanted to ask if he was ready, to give him some sign of support, but if she were to try to speak it would only collapse the seawall that held back her tears.

Kraai squeezed her hand and gave a sad smile in understanding.

They went to the door together, the two contrasting fairies with dark hair and glowing eyes staring in through the opening.

Her smile unmoving, the fair one asked, "They are both going?"

Emily countered in a stoic tone, raising her chin. "She wishes to say goodbye at the veil, to see him off safely."

There was a tiny twitch of the fairy's lip and a quick glance up and down Emily before she responded, "Very well." They ushered the duo outside, Kraai carrying his luggage in his free hand, and Fern holding the note in hers. Emily gave a wave just before the world melted around them, the stone of the house fading to the green of the rolling hills and the blue of the sky. When they turned, they saw the road on which they stood leading into the golden haze not twenty feet away.

A voice came from behind, but Fern could not tell which fairy was speaking. "Say your goodbyes quickly."

Fern grabbed Kraai, pulling his lips to hers. She fought the tears even harder, wanting to remember the feel of him, the smell of him—the smell of home, and this feeling of being loved so completely. As she pulled away, she pressed the note into his chest, his hands leaving her waist to hold it to his heart, but his eyes not wanting to look away. That note would tell him all he needed to know.

Fern stepped back, keeping her eyes on his.

He moved back, toward the veil. As Kraai's foot tucked into the golden glow, Fern said one last, "I love you."

Just before he disappeared from view, he responded, "And I you, as we always will."

And Fern waited. She stared at the Golden Veil as it rippled and shone in the light of the morning sun, no indication that someone so important had just crossed through it. One second. Two. Three. Her heart tightened in her chest. *Come back. Remember and come back.* Ten seconds. Twenty. Her lungs tried to force her to breathe, but she refused. A minute. Her face contorted as she fell to the dirt, throwing her face into her hands and letting out a primal scream. When the scene around her melted once again, she cried out, "No! Just a little longer!" But by the time the words left her lips, she saw Emily, cloak billowing as she rushed to Fern, falling to the ground to wrap her in an embrace.

Fern did not fight it, instead she melted into her grandmother and cried. The coolness of her pulled the heat from Fern's cheeks. It was an eerie comfort, but a welcome one. She wanted to explain everything, to tell her grandmother what had just happened, but all she could let out between gasps for air was, "He didn't come back."

They sat in the cobbled courtyard for a length of time before Fern had any semblance of composure. She could not bring herself to say what she had done, but when she was finally down to sniffles, she reached into her shirt and pulled out the parchment that had rested there—the piece she had cut from the bottom of the note while Kraai was saying his goodbyes to Emily.

She opened it to look at the memories that were now lost to Kraai, ones she didn't want him to remember if they were founded on her song.

Fern loves you. She loves the warmth of your hand in hers. She loves the touch of your lips. She loves how you drive her absolutely mad while simultaneously making her the happiest being in the Four Regions. Come back to her after you've done what you need to do.

Fern sat alone in her room the rest of the day, staring at the parchment lying on the bed. Had she done the right thing? She would never know. But at least Kraai would have a fresh start as he went into the Dark Region, not worrying about needing to come back because of an intimacy he didn't know he had with his childhood friend.

Despite the summer heat, Fern shivered in her bed. Every time she grazed the edge of unconsciousness, she was violently awakened by the sense of being completely alone. When she finally did sleep, her nightmare returned. She watched from afar as the wave overtook her. This time, however, the only body in the carnage was one she had not seen before in her nightmares—someone she had only before seen in the best of her dreams and the best of her waking moments. She stood over him, the water soaking her to the waist. She leaned down to kiss him. His lips were cold. He smelled of salt and sulfur. She whispered, "I love you," before leaving Kraai's body to move into the darkness beyond.

Chapter 19

It took months for the fog to leave Fern's mind. The few attempts at training were distracted at best, but explosive at worst. Fern would not conjure mist anymore; Kraai's features always formed in the negative spaces. She wanted to forget him—that would be easiest—but he haunted her nightmares and her daydreams.

When the apples found their way to the table, Fern could only think of their afternoons in the orchards. When the leaves changed colors, she thought of the guarded oak in the Mountains. As the autumnal chill pressed in, she reached for him in her sleep.

One day, she was able to be present for a conversation with Emily during breakfast. Not long after, she was able to focus her lightning the way she had at the height of her practice. There had been no word from Kraai, who surely was not worried about her as much as she was about him. Why would he be? He knew she was safe, and nothing else. If she really wanted to forget about him, she would have to put her focus elsewhere.

And so she did. She trained longer and harder than she had before. She worked herself until she was barely able to make it back to the house under her own power. She threw her frustration and anger into becoming faster, stronger, and more powerful. In the Mountains, she could have never done what she did here—but without having to hide, to hunt, to run, she was able to focus on her powers alone. She spent so much time with her grandmother, she became her closest confidant. Of course she would have preferred *anyone* else, but James did not speak, and she was afraid to reveal too much to someone without a vested interest. But with this closeness came a willingness to ask some of the more sensitive questions.

"Why am I here and not my parents?" Fern was already up and eating when Emily came down from her room.

The question caused Emily to falter and slow her stride to the table. "We are liabilities." She moved to pull out her chair, but instead rested her hands on the high back and remained standing. "We are only here by the permission of The Monarch. If Belle were to find out I was alive, she would do anything she could to get rid of me so I don't pose a risk to her power. If I were to go back, I *would* still be the queen. Her discovering that I was here would create tension between the Light and the Dark—tensions that could turn to war."

"But there has never been war between the regions," Fern pointed out.

"Exactly." Emily finally sat, signaling James to bring out her chalice. "The Light Region wishes it to remain that way. It took lots of convincing for The Monarch to allow me to invite you at all. But now that there are two of us here with claim to the throne, it is ammunition waiting to be set off. If your father came, even more. Not to mention Belle despises your mother to the point she would likely tear down the regions themselves to annihilate her."

Finally, a reason why her mother and father had to stay in the Mountains. Her chest panged with the memory of them.

She returned to the topic at hand to push them from her mind. "The Monarch is the queen, yes?"

"She has been for decades, but that is not always the case. The Monarch is whatever the Light Region needs them to be. They change as the demands of the region do. A strong being in times of conflict, a motherly one in times of internal struggles, a plump one during famine..."

Fern had stopped eating by this point, much more interested in the politics of this region. She had only heard of the Light Region having a queen. She had never inquired even as to what she looked like—why would she, never feeling she would enter this region? "I don't understand—they trade out leaders according to the whims of the citizens? That is not a monarchy, then, is it?"

"They are all the same being—granted immortality in exchange for a life of servitude to the region. As winter begins, they change into what the region will need the coming year— the citizens do not decide, the region itself does." Emily took a sip while Fern soaked in the information. "You will understand more soon enough. The Monarch does a tour of the region after the annual transformation. They have not changed much in recent years, but it is reassuring for the citizens to see them as a sort of prophecy of what the next year will bring."

"How does this work with inter-regional relations, with the reigning being changing all the time? Do the other regions know about it or is it a regional secret?" Fern rubbed her tongue against the roof of her mouth, expecting an all-too-familiar acidic taste. "But we are talking about it, then it is surely not—" She stopped, realizing if she brought up the fact she wasn't vomiting, it might cross the secretive line that would actually make her vomit, and she had just enjoyed a breakfast she wanted to taste only once.

"Everyone in the region knows. Those who do business with The Monarch know. Even some common folk in other regions know, but do they need to? No. If you are not from the Light Region, the form of The Monarch has no bearing over your life. You probably never gave any consideration to the leaders of other regions, except possibly the Dark Region because I assume your father would have wanted you to know the history."

"What does The Monarch look like now?"

"She looks almost human, but with the grace of an elf. Petite, tan, absolutely lovely to look upon. These past years have been good for the Light Region, so I think most hope she will remain the same, as she has for almost a decade."

"And if they don't?" Fern asked, half-knowing the answer.

"Then we will have to see what form they take and prepare for what the region feels is coming."

A silence fell as Emily sipped from her chalice. The red stains on her lips did not affect Fern as much as it had when she first arrived. Nothing did. The chill as her grandmother entered a room, the silence of James, even the incessant sunlight. She had grown accustomed to life in the Light Region. She did not love it, but she didn't hate it; it was more an indifference to her own presence in the Light Region. Soon Fern would be able to choose where she wanted to live, once her sister was named and secured her reign in the Dark Region.

"Why can't you go back now? Surely The Monarch knows a way for you to get out without..." Fern brought her hand to her forehead and let it float away.

"I know too much. I have been here nearly twenty years; she won't let me leave with that much knowledge. If I leave without a way around, I will lose my sister again. I will not leave until I am sure I will keep it all." A small smirk grew on her lips.

Fern caught the sparkle in Emily's eye and responded with a smirk of her own. The woman knew something.

They trained hard again that day, Emily retiring to the house well before Fern felt they were done, but she enjoyed the time alone to push herself harder than her grandmother dared to push. The air was drier now, as the air held less vapor when it was cold. When she could accumulate what was left, however, she could create clouds easily, hardly needing to disperse energy before it willingly condensed. She could create clouds around her without seeing Kraai's face now, though sometimes she wished she still saw him among the vapors. The way he looked was fading from her memory. She could recall him altogether, but each piece in isolation was missing, like a reverse cloaking potion. *No. Don't think about him. Think about training.*

Fern buckled to her task, sending lightning through the cloud, a storm of her own making. She felt the water break apart and reform in the heat of the spark. A laugh escaped her lips, nearly a cackle of joy. Pushing harder, she expanded the cloud with her right hand. The fog began to block more light, refracting the afternoon sun that was blaring down on her. She let the excitement churn within her, charging a new energy that she let out through her left arm. The crack was louder than any charge she had released before. It reverberated within her chest, nearly making her lose her breath. *More.*

Fern conjured her pride, her only source of joy at this time. She could do this, even with diluted blood. She could become more powerful than anyone who might dare threaten her or her family. This was her survival and she could *do* it. The cloud churned around her, the water echoing the chaos of her mind. More light faded as the cloud grew, and the sparks that jumped over her skin were more visible. Her body shook as she took in a breath, then screamed as she let everything within her go. Every ounce of energy was released in a grand arc that bounced throughout the cloud, completely illuminating the tiny droplets like gems in the sunlight. Fern could see each in isolation for the last moment her eyes were open before she collapsed to the ground.

The first time Fern woke up after an episode like this, she was alone in her room. The darkness told her she missed at least six hours.

The second time she collapsed, she was forced awake by a kick to her side. A stern elf stood over Fern, face shadowed by the blinding sun behind her. "You are not welcome to practice your magic here anymore. The thunder scares my animals, and I do not want to hold any responsibility when you finally kill yourself."

Fern moved further into the Light Region's mountains—if you could even call them that. *Hills* would be a more appropriate title. She could see the veil, thin and shimmering on the horizon, from her new vantage. The reminder of what was beyond caused more discord within her, further fueling her ebullitions. She was a little more reserved, though, ensuring she would have just enough energy to walk home, where she would go straight to sleep. That's all she did now—practice and sleep. Eat, too, more than ever, filling herself to the point of near-sickness before being away for twelve, maybe fourteen hours. But she was always home before dark at Emily's request.

But one night she had the dream again, this time with all the bodies she had seen before and more, each face burned into Fern's memory and haunted her throughout the morning. If she had exhausted herself enough, if she had trained hard enough, she would not have had the energy to dream. Her goal every night now was a dreamless sleep. But when she trained on the hill that day, eyes unable to see what was before her and instead looking into the dead eyes of her loved ones and strangers, she made everything churn inside her to its breaking point, then gave up control. As her limp body fell to the ground, she caught sight of a thousand bolts of lightning spreading in every direction, forking to fill in every empty space—a white hot orb with her at the center.

When she could finally open her eyes, before they could even adjust to the space she was now lying in, a voice asked, "Are you done?"

Fern rubbed the spot on her head that felt like it had taken the pointed end of a spike, pressing her head back into a pillow. Her mouth was dry with a tang of copper. How did she even get here? She let out a raspy, "Done with what?"

Emily stood over the bed, staring into Fern's clearing eyes. "This tantrum. It's been months. You need to rein it in, control yourself."

A deep urge in Fern wanted to put up a fight, but when it rose to her mind it signaled another sharp pain. She pressed her eyes and rolled over into the pillow.

"James brought you in yesterday, and it is almost sunset now. I'll give you this one more night of rest and then we are going to talk."

Fern wanted to ask for water, but knew she couldn't purify it in her current state. Instead, she forced her breath through the pillow, waiting for sleep to take her again.

The shaded morning light shone through Fern's door, outlining Emily's form, skirt flowing from her waist. "Get up. You have some water to clean."

The sharp pain in Fern's head was now a dull throb. She sat up and it pressed harder on her skull. The pain was almost worth it for two nights of dreamless sleep and seeing the upper limit of what her power could do. She moved again and felt her brain bounce against her skull. *Almost* worth it. Her limbs were like jelly, she could hardly stand without her legs quaking.

Emily made a face. "And you will bathe, too."

Fern looked down to see she was still wearing the clothes in which she had been training. Grass-stained, sticking to the sweat on her body, and overall an outright mess.

Flatly, Emily said, "I will have James bring your other clothes." She turned and left, not to be seen again while Fern attended to her tasks.

The process of purifying the drinking water was slow and exhausting, so much more than it had ever been before, even when she first entered the veil and had no idea just what she was doing. She was done about midday.

Fern didn't have the stomach for eating much at breakfast, so she ate her first lunch in months. At the table, Emily was waiting, stone-faced, the effect emphasized by her grey hue. Fern piled food onto her plate, but not nearly the amount she had been eating before. It was still more than she would have had available to her in the Mountains, though. Would her family have more food on the table with one less mouth to feed? Perhaps two less if Kraai was not there. Fern swallowed down the lump in her throat that formed whenever she allowed herself to think of him.

"You are to cease training." Emily's voice cut the silence Fern tried to force into her mind.

Fern dropped her plate. Thankfully, she was about to sit down and it fell all of two inches to the table. "What?" She hadn't meant to be so loud.

"For at least one week, in order to recover. You can do small things around the house, but that's it. And once I feel you are ready, we can continue your training with me, but not alone."

Fern hovered over her chair, pressing her hands onto the tabletop. "That's not fair. I can do so much more than you ask me to in training."

Emily's head cocked to the side. "And when you do that, you risk more than you think. You have become too confident in your power and in the thought you will be alright after one of your episodes. But the truth is, you won't always have someone looking out for you when you take it too far. Your body won't always be able to recover." Her free hand rose to touch her cheek. "There will be permanent reminders of temporary stupidity." Her fingers curled, lingering on her chin before her attention snapped to the chalice and she reached for it. "And if I catch you working yourself to exhaustion again, I will stick you in the middle of the salt water on a rickety boat—that should make you think twice about causing a storm."

"You wouldn't." Fern narrowed her eyes in challenge.

Emily responded in kind, adding a smirk on her blood-stained lips as she set down her cup. "Try me."

Fern picked up her plate from the table and stormed to her room, ensuring each footstep pounded as she ascended the stairs. She threw the food on the desk and herself onto the bed. Fern knew the limits to her power now; she wouldn't pass them. Being treated like a child and put on probation would make the dreams come back, would give her mind too much time to linger on things she did not want to think about. Yet being stuck over water that would not obey her, that would change her into a beast if she fell in—she wanted to avoid that fate. Emily gave Fern no reason to doubt the threat. Her only option was to oblige because she was not ready to break her mother's heart by running out of the veil and into danger.

Chapter 20

The dreams returned every night and the ghost of Kraai haunted her. Fern refused to speak to her grandmother for weeks, moping around the house, only using her power to clean her drinking water and spark an occasional flame in the fireplace.

The nights grew cold, but never cold enough for snow. Fern missed the clearing. It was high enough that late fall would bring the first dustings to the area surrounding it, but a short walk would reveal the caps of the taller mountains blanketed in white.

When she was young, she stood at the edge of the clearing, where the artificial warmth gave way to the nip of cold, and asked her father why the snows only came around winter. He wrapped her in his arms, tucking her small form into his coat, his body pressed against her back, providing enough heat for them both. He showed her how the human world had their seasons, using her balled fist to represent the world and his own fingers to represent sunlight. He demonstrated how the angle of the sun changed the intensity of the light, and that the shorter days meant less sunlight overall, cooling and heating the land and oceans.

"But our days and nights are the same length all year," young Fern had pointed out. "How does it get cold enough?"

Her father pressed his cheek against hers and she could feel the muscles in his face smiling. He held up his fingers in a shrinking ring in front of their faces. "The lens through which we get our sunlight is narrowed ever so slightly each day from the end of summer to the end of winter." He opened the circle again. "Then it grows the rest of the year." His arms wrapped around Fern again, filling her with warmth and love.

In glancing through the diagrams in the books in her grandmother's study, Fern found the model of the human world. She had come to find that the day with the least sunlight in that world was the first day of winter, not the last as it was in the Four Regions—something about oceans and heat that she did not care to read into, as she had no interest in salt water in this world or any other.

Where she lived, the first day of winter came at the midpoint between the largest lens and the smallest, and it was on that day that Emily pounded on her door. It startled Fern, who was resting after a supervised training session. "What?"

"The Monarch is starting their tour within the Golden Veil this year. We need to be ready to watch them pass soon."

"I thought they did the veil last." Fern scurried out of bed, glaring at the dress she was required to wear. Not breeches and a shirt with a skirt over, but an actual *dress* that would need considerable navigation. She had yet to try it on.

Emily opened the door, sweeping in like a cool breeze. "Change of plans, apparently. Let's get you dressed. People are already lining the streets." She grabbed the dress, bundling it to be ready to throw over Fern's head.

Emily's haste flustered Fern. It was unlike her grandmother to be anything but poised. She was barely out of her nightdress when she was suddenly buried in a mess of green cloth. Swimming toward the light, she found the top and, after some twisting of arms through sleeves, her torso was appropriately positioned. Before she could admire the black lace along the collar, her breath was squeezed from her lungs in one swift pull. Fern's hands grasped at her chest where the frame of the bodice was preventing her from breathing. She looked over her shoulder with urgent eyes.

Emily held up empty hands. "Sorry. Vampire strength." Two quick tugs and the constrictor loosened its hold. "I don't typically worry about things like *breathing* when I get dressed." She pulled again, this time leaving some room for her lungs to expand, but not nearly as much as Fern would have preferred.

Navigating lower air supply, Fern got some words out. "I don't see why I have to wear this."

"The Monarch is royalty," Emily reminded, tying the ribbon into a bow that rested at the base of Fern's spine.

Fern turned around, her hands rubbing at the inward curve of her waist. "*You're* royalty, I haven't had to wear a dress for you."

"I'm your grandmother. It doesn't matter how I see you—I should have helped change your diapers." A flash of sadness brushed across Emily's face. "But The Monarch is our host and deserves a higher level of effort and respect." She looked her granddaughter up and down. "You look good." After seeing the expression on Fern's face, she added, "You can take it off once we've seen The Monarch." She pushed Fern in the direction of the door with one hand and fussed with Fern's hair with the other. It was a mess of loose curls—there was nothing that could be done in the minutes it would take to get to the road, but the grandmother still attempted.

The roar of the crowd could be heard the moment the door opened. The cool bite of the air stung Fern's nose. Her hands grasped her arms, wishing for a coat. Perhaps her grandmother did not need to bother with taking ambient temperatures into consideration, either. She powered forward, headed toward the gate that James opened as they approached. The wall of bodies on the other side parted slightly, just enough to let Fern and Emily through to stand on the edge of the road.

The buzz of excitement was palpable. Children sat atop their parents' shoulders. Friends and neighbors attempted to whisper their own predictions about what they would see, but ended up yelling to be heard over the competing noise. Women waved small pieces of cloth held in the tips of their fingers, mostly gold but some in white, yellow, green, or pink. Everyone Fern had met in this town was here, as well as many she had never before seen—likely those travelling in from smaller nearby towns, all adding to the rich mosaic of different beings that called this region home and each other neighbor. It had been a strange realization when Fern found she could see an aura radiating from some beings in this region—bits of siren blood were weaved through the population.

Fern was so engrossed in the sights and sounds, she almost did not notice that the crowd to her left was growing quieter. The hush travelled like a wave, keeping pace just before the single-participant procession. When the silence finally reached Fern, her eyes fell upon one man walking alone down the road. His face stern, he did not look to the crowd that wanted to celebrate, keeping his eyes forward. His stiff stride only emphasized his immense height and overall mass. This was a far cry from the petite woman that Fern—that everyone—was expecting. The only thing that had remained from Emily's description was the tan skin.

Fern's mind put together the puzzle pieces, trying to figure out what this form meant. His muscles were barely contained in his coat. His bald head shone in the light that made it through the thick layer of clouds overhead. He looked almost demonic: strong, powerful, and ready to erupt at any time. His expression did not change, but his head turned to Fern, eyes burning into her. After a surge of nervous energy flowed through her, she realized he was not actually looking at her. She followed The Monarch's gaze and found Emily staring right back at him, horror on her face. Her grandmother gave a single nod and The Monarch faced forward once more, continuing the procession through town.

Fern's shallow breaths quickened and she suddenly realized just how tight her dress was. Her grandmother's face had gone back to stone, but her eyes were screaming. Fern scanned the crowd. Nobody's feet budged, nobody's lips moved, but their faces searched desperately for an answer from someone around them. Children whispered in their parents' ears, only to be met with shaking heads. Even after The Monarch had disappeared from view, there was a stunned silence, everyone waiting for a cue from someone else. Finally, Emily cleared her throat, getting Fern's attention, and turned back toward the gate. As the gate closed behind them, people began to move again, the loud, excited roar from before replaced with hushed whispers and mumbling.

The moment they were alone in the foyer, Emily's hands reached for her head, pulling at her hair. The panic was contained in her eyes, the rest of her face remaining still. A sharp breath rushed through her nose as she dropped into a fetal position, let out a small yelp, and lunged back upright. At some point during this motion, the fear had spread across her face. "James, The Monarch will return sometime next week. Please be sure the house is prepared for such a guest." The unease had entered her tone now, too. She held a hand to her head, closing her eyes. "Fern, I know there is much to discuss, but I need some time alone." Her hand reached out to stop any protest that might come.

Fern was unsure how she would even begin any rebuttal or line of questioning. To have heard such a large crowd go so quiet, it was an experience that removed any words from her mind and left only a chilled fear in her core. After her grandmother made her way silently up the stairs, Fern found the nearest chair and just...sat. When her mind finally found space to think, she noticed that James was doing the same thing—his eyes stuck to an unimportant part of the wall, unconcerned about anything around him. Had she just had the same vacant expression on her face? Fern didn't want to interrupt, so she remained in her seat to process. The citizens must have seen The Monarch as a man before, but something was particularly shocking. Fern thought of the men in her life. Her father, the sap that held the family together. Kraai's great-grandfather, quiet and uncommonly understanding. Kraai, the person whose presence made Fern better. Perhaps The Monarch being a man was a good omen—a new era of care and stability, of—

"War." Emily was standing at the top of the stairs.

Fern jumped in her seat, but her heart continued to sink even after she had overcome the surprise. James was similarly alert in his seat, the both of them watching Emily descend the stairs.

"James, you saw what I saw." Emily's statement had a twinge of a question to it.

James only nodded.

Emily sat in a chair near Fern. Her eyes shone, dark streaks staining the whites. Could vampires cry? Her face was once again stoic, but still held an uneasiness. "The Monarch has never looked like this. They can skew anything to the positive, but his expression today shows something bad is coming." She pressed her eyes closed and shook off a ghost. "I've seen that face before. It looks eerily similar to the face of the first Champion of the Dark Region—he was much paler, though. The Light Region would never rally behind someone who looked deprived of sunlight, so the change makes sense."

Fern was still unsure how this amounted to war. "What was the first Champion like?"

Emily's eyes sharpened, pressing emphasis through her eye contact. "Nearly invincible. The first Grand Trial had some of the strongest demons, vampires, elves, and dwarves that ever lived, and he took them all down in a matter of days. He was a master of strategy and combat. He didn't just kill his opponents—he ripped them apart, limb from limb. Hunted those who tried to hide. Instilled a fear so strong that most of those who came face to face with him would leave the trial instead of taking him on. He created an alliance that he honored until they were the only ones left, then took them out by their weaknesses he'd learned in working with them. When it was all over, the Dark Region had sworn an oath of loyalty to him. He had no need to keep guards. None from his region would dare try to kill him and assassins from other regions were dead the moment he could grasp them. His power inspired and united the region."

"And now the Light Region needs to be inspired and united?" Fern asked.

"Exactly. Behind someone powerful, someone who looks like they could take on the world and win."

Fern grabbed at her chest. She should have taken the dress off the moment she came inside. Was its tightness making her breathless or the weight of the conversation? "How do you know he will be here next week?"

Emily's focus was on her hands, as if the process of her thumbs massaging her fingers was the most important thing in the room. "He will want information on the Dark Region. After he finishes the tour, this will be his next stop."

"But why would…?" Fern began, but as she looked at her grandmother once again meeting her gaze, she remembered the counterparts to them both. The other grandmother, so hungry for power she would destroy her own family. The other granddaughter, readying herself for the throne.

He was so much larger than Fern remembered from the parade. Perhaps her memory changed itself to make him seem smaller, less intimidating, but there he was nearly needing to duck through the immense doorway, at least two heads taller than Fern. His intense eyes looked her up and down. Fern's feet, hidden under the skirt of her dress, tensed to run in response. Even as her body wanted to shrink into itself, she forced her eyes to meet his when they came back to her face. She set her jaw, emulating her grandmother's stone visage.

His voice was a deep growl that vibrated in Fern's chest. "Your family tends to cause trouble for me."

Fern wanted a witty retort, to use words to cut him down just one branch. That wasn't her, though. That was her father and her grandmother. Instead, she allowed one corner of her mouth to rise in the smirk Kraai would give her.

One breath, then two. The Monarch mirrored the smirk. "I suppose it is in your blood. Join us." It was not a request. He walked to the study door, his guards staying behind.

Emily had requested that Fern be the one to meet him when he arrived. She did not want to seem too eager and thought the inclusion or exclusion of Fern from the conversation would say much about his intentions.

When they entered, Emily's face was expressionless, but her eyes shot to Fern and back. Her eyebrows crept up. "Does she need to be here?"

"Yes." Despite his mumbling, his voice shook the room.

Emily gestured to the four leather chairs in the middle of the room. Fern sat beside her grandmother, both facing The Monarch, who filled out his entire seat.

"Tea?" Emily asked as James stepped through the doorway.

"No. Privacy," The Monarch demanded.

Emily waved her hand and James disappeared, closing the study door.

"Information, then?" Emily leaned forward, bringing her voice down with her body.

"No. My spies give me all the information I need."

Emily's eyes narrowed. "Yet you still seemed shocked to be in your current form."

The Monarch's stare intensified. "I knew they were planning on taking the Region of the Seas. There was no indication they would move on from there."

"Then what do you need from me?" Emily developed a snarl, her sharp teeth peeking out with each enunciated word.

The Monarch turned his gaze to Fern. "Her."

Before Fern's jaw could fall completely to the floor, her line of sight was blocked by the red velvet of Emily's dress. She forgot how fast her grandmother could be.

"Absolutely not," Emily hissed. "She is here for safety. If you want someone to contest the crown, send me. Send me with my memories and we will be done with all of this."

"Do you think I would let you go knowing what you do?" His voice boomed, rattling the empty tea cups on the table.

Fern felt the hair on her arms stand in response to the sparks beneath her grandmother's skin as the vampire's hands clenched.

The Monarch lowered his volume, but kept his firm tone. "Sit down. You are making a fool of yourself. I am not about to kidnap her from this room." He waited for Emily to reluctantly return to her seat before continuing. "She has a choice if she would like to help, of course. Will you hear my plan, young one?"

Fern started to turn toward her grandmother for confirmation, but abandoned that to watch The Monarch instead, giving him a sharp nod. Any war in the Seas and the

Light Region would surely trickle into the Mountains. Perhaps his plan would keep all four regions safe.

The Monarch raised his chin, further looking down at Fern. "You must have heard the tale of Mask. Perhaps it was a story of a lowly human finding power in a new world." He did not hide his disdain as he stole a glance at Emily. "But how did she secure that power? She stole it from her sister. Pretended to be the chosen heir and took over her sister's entire life, down to her fiancé. She banished her sister to another world, unable to return."

A flash of confusion crossed Fern's face. Did he not know that she was aware of the sister's return? She played off her confusion as not knowing the story, turning to Emily with a look of bewildered betrayal before looking back to The Monarch.

His eyes lit with smug satisfaction. "I would like you to follow in your dear grandmother's footsteps. Impersonate your sister, dispose of her, and take the crown for yourself." He gave a short chuckle. "You can even take her fiancé if you wish."

Fern couldn't help but laugh. "You want me to go to the Dark Region, into the home of the people I have been running from my entire life, and kill my sister. *Why* would I do that willingly?"

"Because your sister's death will prevent many others. Do you see my form?" The Monarch stood, outstretching his massive arms. "In my hundreds of years, I have never looked like this. Never *sounded* like this." The windows quaked as he lowered his voice to a barely audible rumble. "I will protect my people no matter the cost."

Emily stood to match him, not coming anywhere close to him in size, yet almost his equal in intensity. "The cost will not be Fern's life. Send another assassin to do your bidding."

"Are you under the impression that I have not *already* sent other assassins? No being is allowed near the princess except her personal guard and Belle. Even palace staff are required to give her a wide berth. Belle has a considerable hold on the guard, to the point she was able to sniff out someone using his semblance immediately. If anyone tries to impersonate Belle or the princess, other sirens notice the missing aura. This girl is the only one whose aura will match that of the princess, because she has the same one, if I am not mistaken." He gave Fern a once-over, as if trying to see the glow. "She can get access to her private quarters and poison her water, slit her throat in her sleep, however she wants to do it."

The passion with which the two royals stared each other down was hard to read. In the next seconds, The Monarch could lean down to kiss Emily or Emily could send a bolt of lightning through The Monarch's chest—either seemed plausible based on their intensity. Fern cleared her throat to get their attention. They did not turn, but stopped to let her speak. "Then I become the only heir. I do not *want* to be queen."

"Fern, I need you to leave," Emily demanded through gritted teeth.

The words didn't process quickly enough. Fern stood, waiting to see what would happen next.

Emily turned, her face reminding Fern that she had been part demon in her first life. But instead of fire in her eyes, they burned with a white spark. "Go. *Now.*"

Not wanting to be a witness to regicide, Fern scurried to the door. She found James on the other side and he directed her away from the main foyer. He pointed to his eyes, then gestured to the bit of wall that hid the main door from view. The Monarch's guards couldn't see this door. James stood at his post and covertly rubbed his fingers along the doorframe.

Not needing to be told twice, Fern pressed her ear to the edge of the door. It was not too hard to pick up on their shouting.

"Of course you would need to take someone from the Mountains to do your dirty work—your Light Region assassins couldn't even take *me* out." Her grandmother's voice shook with rage.

"They disposed of your husband well enough."

Fern felt a surge of energy from the room, barely contained. Was this the other memory she wanted to keep—the knowledge of who was responsible for Will's death?

"You will *not* take her. She is staying with me."

"She *will* do this and you will be the one to convince her to do so. You forget that you are both here through my charity alone. I have the power to throw you both out of the veil and leave you at the border of the Light Region with no memory of how much danger you are both in. If she does not agree to this, I will do just that and tell Belle exactly where her men can find you."

"You wouldn't."

After a silence, Fern could barely hear The Monarch rumble, "You know I would. I will return in two days and she will agree to do this."

The ground-shaking footsteps were her cue to pretend to be busy elsewhere in the room. James went to the overflow bookshelf and handed a book to Fern.

Fern took it without looking at the title. As the door opened, she said, "Oh, thank you, James. I have been looking for this." She did her best to seem surprised by The Monarch's appearance. "Are you leaving already?"

He did not even look her way, just growled, "I will be back," as he pounded to the front door.

As Emily left the study to watch her guest leave, Fern set the book, *The Art of War*, on a nearby table, watching The

Monarch disappear from view. She crept up next to her grandmother. The moment the door closed, she whispered into her ear, "Should I do it?"

Emily turned, intensity barely veiling the fear in her eyes. "I will not allow my granddaughter to die in someone else's war. I am finding a way out. I will reclaim the throne."

"I am powerful. I can do it." Fern wished for her grandmother to have some confidence in her.

"One twin always has more power than the other. I am fairly confident that you are that twin." Emily leaned in closer. "But if he sends you over there, and you kill your sister, I am still losing a granddaughter in someone else's war."

Fern wanted to zap sense into her grandmother. "She was raised by Belle, completely under her influence. She is likely one of the driving forces behind this war."

The vampire's eyes left for a distant thought. "I knew a girl who was raised by Belle. She was smart and good, and she disobeyed her mother when the time came." She brushed the hair from Fern's eyes. "And now I must hope that your sister is the same—that she hasn't inherited the desire for power and that she has had some other influence on her character."

There wasn't time for hope, though. There were only two days before The Monarch would return for an answer. As much as Fern wanted to discuss it with someone, there was only her grandmother. She needed someone neutral, who could help her navigate the truth of the situation while also understanding her feelings. She needed Kraai, and Kraai was somewhere outside the veil.

That night her dream was even more vivid than it had ever been before. She could feel the bite of the water on her calves as she waded through it. She did not make it far, though, before she was stopped in her tracks. The entire surface of the water was littered with dead bodies. Dwarves, elves, sirens, demons, fairies, the dusty remains of vampires—none were spared. Panic set in as she scanned the faces—beings she knew, beings she didn't, but none of her loved ones; they were out there somewhere, in the sea of the dead. The eerie stillness of lapping water was cut by a sound. Fern raised her head to hear more clearly—a song that sounded like gold.

Chapter 21

Fern's bags were already packed. She skipped breakfast in order to wait outside for The Monarch. Time passed slowly, so Fern watched those who walked on the main road. The overall attitude was much less jovial, less alive. Smiling greetings were short, and the expressions shot back to uneasiness soon after. Was it the winter chill encouraging residents to go about their business quickly? Or was The Monarch's reveal too much for them to bear?

Fern wouldn't have noticed the cold if it weren't for her hands. Most of her body was overheated from nerves, but her fingers were like ice. She held them to her neck, letting them warm on her skin, sending the chill down her spine.

Hinges creaked, but the gate that stood before her stayed put. Fern turned to see her grandmother standing in the doorway. A flash of confusion crossed her face before her brow furrowed and her lip tucked under her teeth. Fern waited for a scolding or a plea to change her mind, but Emily just lowered her eyes to the ground and shut the door.

Once Fern realized she would not be stopped, she paced the courtyard, no longer worried about those inside hearing her footsteps. She practiced what she would say under her breath, trying to remember her talking points, looking quite mad to passers-by. The minutes were dragging on, but she still felt there would never be enough time to prepare fully.

He arrived alone, dressed appropriately for the bit of warmth that had crept in since Fern had begun waiting. He had to be staying close by—otherwise, he would be wearing warmer clothes. His eyes scanned Fern with an uncomfortable air of possession. "Are you ready to leave?" His voice rumbled through the metal gate that Fern was holding.

She stepped back, raising her chin to meet his eyes. "I have some demands." Her brain screamed to run, but she held firm, breathing through the shaking in her chest.

The Monarch stepped forward, his face creeping through the gap in the bars, his eyes narrowed. "You forget where you are. I do not hear your demands. You cater to mine."

"Questions, then." Fern acquiesced. "I deserve to know what I am getting myself into." Her breaths were shallow, her mouth barely open, as she waited for the response.

"You are acting on your own in this. I am not involved in any way. Nobody from the Light Region is." He pushed forward, his body passing through the bars unhindered, as if he were a mist creeping around the solid metal.

Fern took short, quick steps back, the soles of her shoes scraping against the stone below her. She had never thought to consider what power he held. "But how—" Her voice caught as she realized he might not even be there, simply an image to trick the mind. She wanted to reach out and touch him, to see if he was solid. "But how will I remember what I have to do when I leave the veil?"

He reached into his coat pocket, pulling out a small vial filled with an amber liquid. He held it out, cupped in his large hands.

Fern's hand grazed The Monarch's warm, firm fingers as she delicately picked up the glass. She held it to the light.

Flecks of gold swirled inside the viscous potion. "What is it?" she asked in a whisper, half to herself and half to the royalty beside her.

"It allows you to keep your memories when you pass through the veil." He admired the vial with a sincere reverence.

The trance broke, and Fern looked up to The Monarch. "And that is the whole of it? Just drink and I am immune to the veil's magic?"

He took his eyes off the vial and looked down at Fern, towering over her. "It is liquid made from the Golden Veil itself. So long as it courses through your veins, your memories will linger, but if the need arises, a simple spell will remove it from you—taking all of your memories from the moment you entered the veil up to the moment of the spell's casting."

Fern tried to keep eye contact, but shot to look at the container in her hand when it became too much. "Why would I need to forget?"

"Belle is not to know I have been harboring you and your grandmother." His words were not a warning, but a demand.

"I wouldn't tell her." Fern still could not look up, again mesmerized by the golden particles dancing inside.

"And when was the last time you were tortured by a demon, fire licking your skin, boiling the moisture in your body until you gave up any useful information?" There was a slight caring in The Monarch's voice, but was it caring for Fern or for his own people?

Never. She hadn't even considered the possibility. She was about to dive into political intrigue head-first with no preparation. A single mistake and it would be over. She would have one shot at this. One shot to save all of the regions. "I understand."

The Monarch turned and phased through the gate once again. He adjusted his shirt sleeve on the other side, not turning around to speak to her. "Say your goodbyes quickly.

The tailor down the way has a dress for you just like one your sister wears. A carriage is waiting by the veil with a man who can bring you to the Dark Region. I will be back tomorrow to be sure you have gone. I would like everything wrapped up by midwinter."

Fern wrapped her fingers around the vial and watched as the king strode down the road. Still hard, his face at least showed some attempt at connecting with those he encountered. Their reactions were more rooted in fear than reverence, however. When he was out of eyesight, Fern hurried inside, finding her grandmother waiting in a chair in the foyer.

Her face showed worry, and the orange light cast by the fire gave her a warmth that made her look almost human. Fern waited for the expression to change, to harden, to push past any emotion she might feel, but it never did. Emily started with a whisper. "You're going, then?"

Fern placed the potion on the mantel, feeling the warmth of the fire warming the deep chill that crept into her bones while she was outside. She watched the yellow flame dance on top of the orange blaze. "Yes. Unless you have a plan you are going to act on immediately, it's our only choice." The silence behind her was palpable. Fern's hand rested on the mantle, lightly touching the glass. She looked at it again, realizing. "Or if you want to drink this." She turned around, handing the vial to Emily.

Emily reached out, her cold fingers pulling heat from the air around Fern's. "What did he tell you this was?" She clearly recognized it, but still had an air of surprise as she took it.

"It lets you—" Fern's voice halted as bile churned. She bit her lips together as she internally cursed The Monarch for not being susceptible to this magic. With a pointed look at her grandmother, she gestured in the general direction of the veil. "But it—" This time she put too much trust in her words, doubling over while trying to keep her stomach acid down.

Once she regained control, she shouted, "Damn this stupid region!"

"Agreed." The disdain was thick in the vampire's voice. "Were you trying to say this potion works until it doesn't?"

Fern was finally able to right herself, but did so slowly as to not aggravate her abdomen. "How did you know?"

"One pieces things together over time." Emily caressed the vial, looking at it the same way Fern would look at the ripped parchment from Kraai's departure—something she wanted more than anything, but not in the way it was offered.

But if Fern was successful, she would need Emily out, too. Not Emily, she would need Mask. She was not about to be a queen or a princess, but the only way out of that would be death or the miraculous reappearance of someone higher in the royal lineage. She crossed her arms. "How is your plan coming along?"

"Weeks to months. Not quickly enough to help you, unfortunately, but once you leave, I will be back to it in full force. I'm sure there is a way." She stood, placing the vial back on the mantel. She lingered next to Fern, not bringing her eyes to meet her granddaughter's. "You know I do not want you to go, but you would have been named by now if you were raised in the Dark Region, so I will treat you as an adult. This is your decision to make. All I ask is that if there is any way to accomplish what you need to without killing your sister, then please make it happen."

Fern had thought of a way—to banish her sister to the human world, just like Emily had once done. Portal magic was a difficult study, though. There was no way she would be able to learn how to travel to another realm of existence and return safely soon enough to prevent Belle and her sister from declaring war on any of the other regions. That didn't even take into consideration the dangers of placing a siren in the human world. She had to change the subject. "Do I take it?" She gestured her head toward the potion.

"You are taking a risk either way." Emily grabbed Fern's hand. The icy touch was a comfort. "But you will know what the veil can take and when it will be taken, you don't get the same from The Monarch." She squeezed her hand before letting go. "Is there anything you need from me?"

Fern wanted to go write the note to herself. She would leave with the hope that she managed to avoid the enchantment in the water, but it was no guarantee. She gave her grandmother a task she thought the vampire would appreciate. "I need a dress from the tailor."

The sun was falling in the sky and Fern had gone through four pages of parchment before she finally had a draft she could live with. It was enough to know what she had to do, and nothing more. There was so much that she wanted to forget—perhaps if the veil took her memories, it wouldn't be such a bad thing.

Emily entered Fern's room with a bundle wrapped in wool. "Personally, I love the style of it. You might not be as big of a fan, though."

Fern stood to accept the delivery, unwrapping the wool to reveal a rich green fabric. Her fingers ran along the lace. It felt as beautiful as it looked. She still hated dresses, but if she had to wear one, this would be the least disagreeable. "But I thought green was forbidden in the Dark Region."

Emily took the dress and shook it out, showing it in its entirety. "I had the tailor place an enchantment on it. It's actually a black dress, but it will appear green until you go through the mist of the Dark Region." She shrugged. "I know you don't really like black, I figured we could keep you in the green of the Mountains as long as possible."

Fern couldn't pinpoint when she started feeling amicable toward her grandmother, but it was at this moment she felt a twinge of love. She rolled her eyes at how ridiculous it was to feel this about the color of a dress before she sighed and said, "Thank you."

Emily gave a soft smile. "I know you were listening the other day. You doing this is giving me a chance to remember my sister, to remember the truth of my husband's death, and to keep the last seventeen years of my life. Thank *you*."

Fern's face hardened. "If I make it out unscathed, I will be sure you never forget who was responsible for Will's death and who trapped you here."

Sparks shot in Emily's eyes, mirrored by the electricity in Fern's. Devious smiles crept onto both of their lips. The vampire's sharp teeth peeked through, but Fern was not scared. In fact, she was emboldened. She had a vampire on her side who would break free of her prison soon enough.

"I've called the fairies to bring you to the veil. They will be here soon." Emily rolled up the dress, stuffing it into one of the two travelling bags. Bits of fabric stuck out even after she cinched the top. She took the bags, holding open the strap to help Fern put them on. "You have the Seas in your veins, the Mountains in your heart, and Darkness in your ancestry. You are a child of the best of the Four Regions. It is up to you to protect them."

Fern gave her bravest smile and nodded. There was a rock in her chest. Perhaps she could collapse into it and become someone else—someone who cared nothing for those dead bodies in her dreams, someone who did not have this responsibility. But she couldn't. She was the siren who shared the same aura as the princess. She was the one who shared her visage. She was the only one who could get close enough to stop all of this.

The two fairies were waiting outside. Their plastered-on smiles did not reach their eyes. Fern took her place between them and took one last look toward the door. She was looking at her grandmother, but she couldn't help but see her mother—was it the face of guilt? Helplessness?

The world melted, giving way to a vibrant green. The sky was a cloudy grey, but the golden wall still shimmered as if the sun was striking it directly. Fern shifted both bags on her shoulders, patted the pocket where she kept her parchment, and walked through the Golden Veil.

The veil swam like honey pouring through her head. The weight within her lightened in the first step. Fern wanted to let go, to allow the veil to give her the false ecstasy she had felt the last time, but she pushed it away. She kept her worries in her mind and trepidation in her heart. Perhaps these would block the veil from stealing everything from within her. With her second step she smiled as if lost in a dream, trying to recreate her expression from the first time on the other side for whoever might be waiting for her. Sound returned as her foot crunched on the ground outside the veil.

A guard approached from her left. "I will need your bags and your papers." He held out his hand, waiting.

Fern swung one of her bags off her shoulder, but was stopped by a voice from the other side of the road. "This one is mine. Order of The Monarch."

Fern held the strap of her bag tighter as a man crossed the road, handing parchment to the guard.

He took it, broke the seal, unrolled it, and read silently. He looked the man who interrupted up and down. "*You* have the permission of The Monarch?"

The man no longer acknowledged the guard, grabbing Fern's wrist as he pulled her toward a waiting carriage.

Fern fought back, planting her feet as she wriggled her hand free of his grasp. She looked pleadingly at the guard, who only shrugged off his responsibility for her.

The man stepped closer, whispering into Fern's ear, "Monarch's orders." His voice caused the hairs on her arm to stand on end. He smelled like salt and ash, but with the warmth of new leather. A foreign smell, to be sure, but a hint of it felt familiar.

Fern whispered back through gritted teeth, "I can walk myself." Her feet crunched on the gravel with purpose. She threw open the carriage door, hoisted herself in, and slammed it closed. Not long after, the carriage jolted forward. Fern took in her surroundings, noting the materials the carriage was made of. No gold, no wood, just black metal with leather-upholstered seats. A dark region carriage. A wave of panic rushed over her—had she just been handed over to the enemy directly? Before she could think too long, the carriage pulled to the side of the road. The driver jumped down and opened the door.

He shot his hand into the cabin. "Your bags and parchment." When Fern didn't respond immediately, he closed and opened his hand for emphasis.

Fern handed over one of her bags—the one she would have handed the guard first. He opened the top and dumped everything out onto the carriage floor, rifling through the pile of clothes. He shook out the dress. "Correct style, but not the color." He threw the green dress at Fern. "You cannot bring this."

Fern removed the cloth from where it landed on her head. "It is a black dress. It will be fine when we cross the border into the Dark Region."

He looked up at her, surprised. "Good. You do remember why you are here." There was a warmth in the brown hue of his eyes. Why was she so drawn to them?

Fern scooped up her bag and the rest of her clothes from the floor. "I do. And I know you are to bring me there, but I have a stop to make first." She shoved everything back in, not worrying about creasing the fabric.

He was busy with the note he found, but Fern was not concerned. Thankfully she didn't need it, but it still said what she needed to know. She kept it vague, telling herself she had to "take care" of her sister, that she had "her song," and that "her friend" was either in the Dark Region or at home, and that he could shift now. Yet when Fern watched the man's face, she saw his head tilt slightly to one side. When he returned the letter to Fern, his eyes glared at her with suspicion. How much was he supposed to know?

"May we leave?" Fern asked. She wanted the interaction over.

He didn't even ask, just hoisted himself into the carriage, reached over Fern, and took her other bag from beside her. Before she could protest, the contents were spilling onto the ground, a second piece of parchment, folded and sealed, falling out last.

"Another note?" He growled with shock. "You are only allowed—" His voice fell when he examined the word written on the outside. Was it anger or curiosity in his eyes? "Where did you get this?"

Fern leaned over and tried to rip it from his hands, but he gripped tighter.

"Why is my son's name written on this parchment?" His voice was strained, holding back from screaming.

It all made sense. His eyes were Kraai's eyes. The undertones of his scent reminded Fern of her friend. "Flight?"

He repeated himself, louder this time. "Why is my son's name written on this parchment?"

Fern wasn't really sure why. She had taken the piece of parchment that she had cut off of Kraai's note, folded it, and sealed it. It felt wrong to leave it behind, wrong to burn it. So she wrote his name on the outside and hid it in the folds of some of her clothes, hoping the guard wouldn't find it. But how much should she reveal? "It's a note for a friend. Just in case something happens to me." Not the complete truth—she had no intention of it ever falling into his hands, but it sounded good as she said it. Kraai said he would die happy reading those words, and remembering that threw a sharp pain into Fern's chest.

His jaw slack, he leaned in to examine Fern closer. "Of course you two would know each other. Your mothers escaped together."

"Did he find you?" Fern asked, placing her hand on the parchment, poised so she could take it from his hand the moment he stopped thinking about it.

"My mother flew to the palace to convince me to make a trip home to spend time with her." He let a smile crack. "She neglected to tell me that my son was there waiting; it was a pleasant surprise."

Fern snapped her wrist, pulling the parchment from his hands. "And where is he now?"

"He went home." Flight shook his head. "We agreed it is best if I did not know where that was, just in case."

"Are you often under their influence?" Fern asked. She wasn't sure it was an appropriate question, but she also needed to know how much she could trust him.

Flight climbed inside the carriage, sitting on the bench opposite Fern before closing the door and lowering his voice to a near-whisper. "Never the girl's. She only uses her song when her grandmother tells her. I have been under Belle's song a handful of times. I now know how to avoid her, to hide when I hear she is looking for me or interrogating house staff, but she does not often concern herself with us. She does not find us to be a threat."

"Yet you've been working for the Light Region." Fern loved the idea that Flight had been undermining Belle right under her nose.

He leaned forward, making it clear where Kraai got his giddy, conspiratorial grin. "There are many of us inside the palace. Belle destroyed everyone that she thought knew about you, about the fact there were twins, but some of us remained. We have only recently been in dealings with the Light Region—we thought alliances in the Seas would be beneficial, as that is where Belle has her sights set first. Nobody is willing to fight, though. There was a pirate crew who showed some interest, but they are wary of Belle. They won't fight until they know their side will win or their hand is forced."

So she wasn't alone in this. She had a team of "many" inside the palace. She might have Kraai if he had made it home safely. "Why are you trusting me with all of this information?"

"You are an heir." He was visibly confused by the question. "We want you in the palace in place of your sister. We want you to take the throne out from under Belle and her young puppet. Is that not why you are here?"

It was why she was there, but not why she *wanted* to be there. "I am here to keep my family safe." She closed her eyes and shook her head. "And I need to see them before I go to the Dark Region. I need to say goodbye, just in case."

Flight stared. It took Fern some time to realize he was waiting for direction.

Fern channeled her grandmother, stone-faced, chin up, as if she knew her own importance. But she took something from The Monarch, too—a fire in her eyes that demanded obedience. "You will take me to the midpoint of the road between the Light Region and the Dark Region, then you will leave. You will not look back. You will keep your eyes forward. You will wait on the other side of the mist and take me to the palace when I arrive."

His eyes lit up. This seemed to be the heir he had been waiting for. "Of course, your Highness."

And she didn't even have to use her songtone.

Chapter 22

It was a long day's hike to the clearing, even longer since Fern hadn't slept the entire night; she hadn't tried. She was hypnotized by the fields racing by, accented with fairy lights, but she would not let her eyes close. Once again, she had thrown herself blindly into the protection of someone she had never met, who might or might not have her safety in their interest. Sure, she trusted Flight, but not *that* much.

The moisture left in the night was burning off the foothills as the sun rose over the taller peaks. She took a deep breath in through her nose. The sting of cold air and the scent of pine fueled her in the final burst. She found the trees she had learned to recognize as a child—two towering spruces with a never-growing sapling just off-center, blocking the path between them. It was not a hindrance to Fern, though, as she knew the tree was only an illusion. She walked through it, the sky above opening up to let in light and the artificial warmth slowly encapsulating her. Her skin prickled with the feel of home. Her face contorted as she fought back an avalanche of tears.

She was barely two steps in when the cabin door opened. She dropped her bags.

"Fern!" Her mother's frantic cry barely had time to reach her before the woman had her daughter in an embrace. "Fern. You are alright." She kissed the side of her face again and again, holding Fern's head in her hands. She stood back to look at her, checking her up and down.

Fern got a good look at her mother and she couldn't fight the tears anymore. She radiated the most beautiful shade of purple and a love she had never let herself feel before. "I'm alright."

Her father followed, biting his lip as his eyes welled with tears. His arms wrapped around the two women, pulling them closer together.

Fern stood in the embrace, knowing this wouldn't last long. She reached up to her shoulder to touch her father's hand, letting a gentle spark arc between them. His hand grabbed hers, squeezing. "I'm alright," she repeated.

Wave took in a long breath and stepped away. Based on the pain on her face, she clearly did not want to say the next words. "Why have you come home?"

Fern stepped away from her parents, her hands finding each other to massage her fingers. When her eyes found the ground, she remembered who she was and who she had to be right now. She raised her head, clearing her eyes of worry. "I—" Movement caught her attention from the corner of her vision. She turned toward it and all the confidence faltered. "Kraai," she whispered, her voice cracking.

He had just entered the clearing from another access point. His face showed worry, but morphed into a grand smile. "I knew it." He rushed toward her. "I knew you were back. I could sense it."

Fern stepped forward to meet him partway, but what would that matter? The embrace she wanted to give him would be out of character for what their relationship would have to revert to. A deep inhale stuttered halfway, the sight of him unlocking memories she wished had stayed within the veil. She rubbed her arms, trying to pass off her quaking as her adjustment to the warmth.

He stopped short, pain on his face. What was he picking up on?

Sneak's small voice hollered from the doorway of Kraai's cabin. "I put on some tea! Come tell us all about your travels!"

Fern gave one more glance at Kraai before she followed her parents in. She forced a smile on her face as she greeted Kraai's family, but Lathron could see through it; the slight raise of his brow made it clear. He said nothing, though. He never would.

"Stories are best told by a fire," Sneak said as she threw flame into the hearth, causing the logs to combust. She led Fern to the chair closest and sat opposite, her eyes wide. "Now, Journey got you there safely, that much Kraai could tell us. What about your trip out of the veil?"

Fern glanced to the doorway where Kraai was leaning against the frame, arms crossed. Did he even remember that there was a plan to leave the veil with their memories? Or was that only discussed within the veil? She looked back and smiled. "Someone arranged transport for me. Not a very exciting drive, I'm afraid." She neglected to mention *who* transported her—that could open up an entire conversation Fern was not ready for just yet.

Wave leaned forward, her face still unsure if she wanted answers. "And what did your note say?"

"A few things, but I didn't need it." Fern bit the inside of her lip as she waited for a response.

It took some time for the realization to hit. Eyes widened or brows furrowed in succession, starting with Strike, Sneak, Lathron, Iris, and finally Wave.

Kraai shifted, starting to creep forward. "You figured it out, then?"

Fern gave a sheepish smile. "I think we both did. We just couldn't say it out loud."

Gesturing to himself, Kraai scoffed, "Clearly not, as I remember absolutely nothing from the time we walked in together to the time I walked out alone."

Fire burned in Fern's nostrils as she tried to speak without crying. "You made a choice and that choice made it so you wouldn't remember."

Kraai chuckled, "So it was that bad, huh?"

That knife to Fern's heart twisted. She wouldn't be able to keep her composure much longer.

"It has been a long journey," Lathron interrupted. "We can ask all of our questions after you get some rest."

Fern had an internal burst of gratitude she hoped Lathron would sense and left the cabin for her own. As she passed Kraai, his scent filled her nose. Thankfully she had already passed him as the tears welled in her eyes. Rain began to fall, striking her head as she made her way across the clearing to her own cabin. The wooden door gave its familiar creak, revealing the room in which most of Fern's life had been lived. It was so small, so insignificant compared to the world she had just travelled and the world she would enter next, but it was exactly where she wanted to be. Her sleeping space was right where it had been, except her blanket had been neatly folded in the corner.

Fern curled up into it. She used her emotion to send a small charge into the fireplace, exhausting the last of her energy. The ensuing flame was nowhere near as impressive as Sneak's, but it grew into a sturdy fire before Fern was fully asleep.

The dreamless slumber was interrupted by a whispered argument.

"You had no right to open that." Her father's voice, harsh but understanding.

"I needed answers," her mother's voice snapped. "I could not just wait until she told us. *If* she even told us."

Her father's tone took an angrier turn. "A note from the veil is private."

Fern's eyes shot open and she hoisted herself off the ground in one smooth motion. The last of the fog still clearing from her mind, she found her way to her mother, trying to snap the note from her grasp.

Wave pulled it away, tucking it behind her back, leaning onto the wall. "Not until you explain yourself."

"Which note is that?" Fern asked as calmly as she could manage.

"A note you wrote in the veil. Explain to me why—"

Fern clawed at her mother's shoulder, trying to rip her arm out from behind her. "Which note?" Her voice was frantic now. She finally managed to get the note with the tips of her fingers, grasping as hard as she could, tearing it from her mother's hands. There were no words written on the outside. There was no seal. It was not the one to Kraai. She took a steadying breath as she realized what her mother had read. "Has Father read it?"

"No." Wave looked her husband up and down. "He refused, even though its contents concern this whole family."

Fern thought about how to explain, but instead just held the note out to Strike. "Go ahead. You might as well."

He took the note and opened it. Fern watched his face, anticipating where he was based on his facial expression: "*You must take care of your sister for the sake of the Four Regions.*" Alarm. "*You wouldn't have left if it wasn't urgent.*" Concern. "*You have your song.*" A flash of something unpleasant. "*Your friend is either home or in the Dark Region. He can shift now. You don't think you do, but you need him.*" A warm understanding that did not quite override the initial unease. His eyes met Fern's over the top of the note. "And by 'take care of,' you mean…"

Fern nodded. It was an old human phrase her father used to use. Her mother knew the meaning, too, but always hated when it was used. It was the perfect way to tell herself what she had to do without outright writing about an assassination plot.

Strike scowled. "Burn this." He handed his daughter the parchment. "Now."

"But nobody will understand—" Fern started.

"My mother used to use this phrase frequently. Any holdovers in staff from the palace will know exactly what it implies."

Flight. If he wasn't in on the plan before, he was now. And now he was waiting for her at the border. Fern threw it on the fire, watching it until the edges caught. When she turned around, she realized the contents of both her bags were piled on the dining table. "Where is the other parchment?"

"The one for Kraai?" Her mother asked. "I left it with his parents."

The only sound Fern could hear was the blood rushing through her head. She tried to run for the door, but it felt like her feet were trudging through a pool of sap. Her parents were saying something behind her, but the only thing she could focus on was getting a hold of the letter. She didn't even notice that Kraai entered the clearing until she passed directly in front of him. He was carrying firewood. He had been out. It was a good sign.

Lathron was opening the door before Fern could even knock. "What do you need?" He was always so warm and understanding. It must have been exhausting.

"The note my mother gave you," Fern panted.

His brow furrowed. "That note is for Kraai."

Pulling all of her pleading into her eyes, Fern said, "It is, but not yet." She hoped he wouldn't sense the truth that "not yet" meant "never."

He disappeared behind the door and returned with the note. He held it out, but drew it back when Fern reached. "Things will be easier if you just tell him."

Fern froze. With a harsh whisper, she asked, "You read it?"

He placed the parchment in Fern's waiting hand. "No." His eyes glanced behind Fern as he closed the door in her face.

"What did you do to make him so upset?" Kraai's voice asked from behind her.

Fern moved to hide the parchment, but Kraai's hand shot out and grabbed her wrist playfully.

Kraai saw the seal and rotated Fern's wrist to find his name written on the other side. His jovial attitude shifted. "What is this?"

"It's nothing," Fern lied. "Nothing with which you need to concern yourself."

His tone was flat. "It has my name on it."

Fern pulled her arm toward herself, dragging Kraai in with it. "Written in my hand, so I get to choose when you receive it."

He drew his face close to hers, loosening his grip on her. "My note was also written in your hand. My note was missing a piece that would be about this size."

Part of Fern wanted to hand it over, to be done with this, to fall back into the lie that made her so happy. But what if it was truly a lie? How would he react if he didn't feel that way at all, and it was actually all sparked by her song? "It was and it is, but I need you to trust me. Let me give this to you when it is right to do so."

Kraai looked her dead in the eye, searching for something. Fern held his gaze, hoping the urgency would convince him. After a few heartbeats, he let go, allowing Fern's hand to fall. "Of course I trust you." His lips remained parted, some words held back on his tongue, but he remained silent.

Fern tucked the parchment into her vest. "Do you trust me enough to do something completely stupid and dangerous together?"

There were few things that would have lifted Fern's spirit in that moment, but the conspiratorial smile that crept onto Kraai's face was one of them. "As we always have."

"Let's take a walk." Fern led Kraai out of the clearing. She told him some of what happened within the veil, filling in the multiple month gap in his memories. He truly remembered none of it. One moment they were venturing in, hand in hand, and the next he was stepping out backward alone. If his clothing hadn't changed, and a guard not been waiting upon his exit, he would have assumed he just got bumped back out.

She told him about her grandmother and how the vampire was determined to leave with her memories, about living out in the open and getting to walk through a city in plain sight, about the week he spent in bed when he took the potion that would allow him to shift—he was somewhat relieved he got to forget that part. When she spoke of meeting sirens, Kraai tucked his hand into his shirt, grasping something hanging from his neck—that damned necklace.

Fern stopped in her tracks. "How did you know?"

Kraai attempted to keep walking, but slowed when he saw Fern wasn't going to budge. "How did I know what?"

She looked at him sidelong. "That you got the necklace from the sirens."

He removed his hand and matched Fern's expression, mirroring the hint of distrust. "I need you to trust me to give you that information when it is right to do so."

Fern closed her eyes. It was only fair he got to keep a secret if she was going to, too. It was unfortunate that it had to be this one. "Fine." She walked again, Kraai falling into step beside her. She still hated that necklace, though.

The next topic of conversation was the period of time after Kraai left. Fern left out the parts about her agony and self-destructive behavior, glossing it over with an, "it was strange to be without you for the first time." In order to change the subject as quickly as possible, she then let Kraai talk about what he did after he left—going back to the clearing to assure the families that he and Fern were safe, venturing into the Dark Region to find his grandmother, meeting and getting to know his father, then returning home.

After the conversation hit a lull, Fern finally felt it was time to reveal the reason she came back. "I need to know that you will be on my side no matter what, that you know I would never ask you to do something like this if it wasn't absolutely necessary."

Kraai grabbed Fern's hand and stopped walking, jolting her back. He turned her around to look deep into her eyes once again.

It wasn't the look she had known so well within the veil. It penetrated just as deep, but did not hold the longing Fern wished she would see. "Why do you keep looking at me like that?"

His gaze shot back and forth from one of her eyes to the other. "I need to be sure that you are still you. You feel different; something about you has changed. I am just searching for the person I know in there." He jabbed his finger above her brow.

Fern winced, rubbing her forehead. "And am I still there?"

Kraai turned and began to walk away with an animated strut, calling out behind him, "You sure are. Now what mischief are we getting into?"

Fern remained rooted to her spot. She swallowed hard and spoke just loudly enough that Kraai would be able to hear her. "We are going to murder my sister."

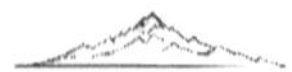

When they arrived back at the clearing, Wave and Strike were waiting outside. Kraai and Fern were already making jokes about who would get to the princess first, how the other would mess up in an extraordinary fashion and get them caught. If they couldn't joke about it, how would they ever live with the weight of what they were about to do? But the look on Fern's mother's face brought the reality of it crashing back onto her.

"You are not going." Wave's eyes churned, turbulent. She must have just finished crying, her mind at its most clear.

"I am." Fern channeled her grandmother, raising her chin, narrowing her eyes with assuredness. "I must."

"Why? Why you?" Her mother was clearly fighting back emotion, but remained somewhat composed.

"Because we are running out of time and I am part of the only plan that has a chance of working." Fern could not hold her fortitude. Her voice cracked with impatience.

"Running out of time? There is plenty of time." Wave flicked the idea away with her hand. "Your sister is far from being named."

"You still think I have a sister? You truly believe that person over there is still your daughter?" Fern leaned in close to her mother, an ominous spark to her voice. "She is a puppet. She is doing nothing to prevent the war Belle wishes to start. The Light Region will be attacked within the year, the Seas even sooner. I know you've read about wars in the human world. Think of the destruction a war between the regions would cause—a war fought with magic, with fire, with chaos and blood. How many more families must be destroyed to satisfy Belle's lust for power?"

Tears streaked down Wave's face. "But why does she have to destroy what is left of mine?"

Strike held his wife, bringing his body between her and their daughter. He looked over his shoulder and gave Fern the faintest of nods, enough to acknowledge that Fern knew her own path and he would not stand in her way. At least, that's what Fern took from it.

Fern walked past them, signaling Kraai to come with her. Inside her cabin, she threw the clothes back into her bags, but Kraai took the dress before she could grab it.

"Really?" he asked, trying to make sense of the folds and folds of green cloth.

Fern snatched it from his hands. "Really. I wore dresses within the veil." She rolled her eyes. "They're not *that* bad. Besides, I am impersonating the princess to get into the palace. A dress is a requirement."

Kraai's brow raised. "Did I ever see you in a dress?"

Fern glared. "No."

His smile rose as he sang, "But I get to soon."

She shoved her sheathed hunting blade into the bag, along with the rest of what she might need for the trek to the Dark Region. "We're leaving before nightfall."

"Today?" His voice was incredulous.

"You saw my mother. The sooner we're gone, the sooner she can cope with my departure." She slung the bag over her shoulder. "And I wasn't lying to her. We *are* running out of time." It was still a long way from midwinter, but Fern knew she would lose her nerve if she waited. The human side of her was emboldened by the recklessness of diving in head-first.

"I will say my goodbyes." There was a hurt to his voice, perhaps a regret for agreeing to go with Fern now that he knew he was leaving immediately.

Once he was gone, Fern had no idea what to do with herself. She stood, leaning on the table, not wanting to go outside and be confronted by her mother again. Taking the dress back out, she laid it over her body, giving it a spin as she pressed it to her chest. Something about the way the skirt flew out, the way the green popped in the light of the crests and hid in the shadows of the troughs, sent a small ripple of joy through her. She folded the dress neatly, putting it at the top of her bag. She would need it before leaving the Mountains, but did not want to put it on now as it would be nearly impossible to navigate the undergrowth in it.

Fern sat alone at the table, her eyes surveying the room where most of her childhood took place. This was where she learned to walk, where her father would tend to her wounds, where she and Kraai would play games on winter nights that grew so cold not even the enchantment of the clearing was warm enough. It was the room where she learned to read and do sums, where she listened to her mother suffer through her fits on the other side of the door, where she thought she would live the rest of her life in hiding. But now she would leave, to kill the princess and claim the throne for herself. *For now. Please let it be just for now.*

A knock on the door broke her mind's wandering. It creaked open, the cool air dispersing the ghosts.

"Are you ready?" Kraai asked, his voice still pained.

"Are you sure you want to come?" Fern asked as she stood, slinging her bag over her shoulder. "There is no shame if you want to stay here and take care of our families." She needed to be sure of him. She needed to give him this one more chance to get out.

He tucked through the small opening and closed the door behind him. His face serious, his eyes found hers. "Where you go is where I want to be. We will do this together."

A flutter rose in Fern's chest. "As we always have." She couldn't help it, she ran and wrapped her arms around his neck, holding him close.

Kraai stood stunned for a moment, then wrapped his arms around her. "As we always have," he repeated with a hint of surprise to his words, but weaved with joy.

The embrace felt right. It was completely out of character for their relationship prior to the veil, but warmed a part of Fern that had been left cold since Kraai left. She let the hug linger longer than she should have, but when she disengaged, she topped it off by hitting him in the chest with the back of her hand for good measure. "Let's go."

Kraai opened the door and gestured for Fern to lead, giving an exaggerated bow. "Royalty first."

Fern scrunched her face, holding back her retort, but hoping he could sense it somehow. She left the cabin ready to face the regions, but her mother was waiting, her father standing behind her with his hands on her shoulders. Fern let out a sigh. "I'm going."

"I know. I have just one more thing to say." Wave's voice was eerily quiet.

Fern said nothing, waiting for her mother to plead or cry.

"When you see her—when you see the dark aura, the radiant cloud of ash—know that is what I see when I look at you." Wave's eyes misted over. "If it is possible for you to both survive this, make it happen. Let me see both my girls alive and well." She took in a gasp. "But if she tries anything, if she even suggests she might hurt you, you kill her with no second thought."

Fern's jaw dropped. Why was her mother no longer fighting it? "Mother…"

Wave grit her teeth. "I had a chance to kill Belle. I stood before her, weapon in my hand"—she looked down at her hand, grasping an invisible object—"but shock prevented me from moving. You must let nothing stop you from protecting yourself and Kraai."

Fern looked to her father. "And you agree?"

"I thought Belle being family meant we could trust her, regardless of her original intentions. I thought she would have your and your sister's best interest at heart." His jaw set, his eyes dimming. "But I was wrong and our whole family suffered because of it. Sometimes blood means nothing."

Fern shot forward, wrapping both parents in her arms. This was goodbye, for now or forever. Sometimes blood means nothing, but sometimes it means the world. Her world. The demonic siren and the human with a spark. These were pieces of her. They would be two of a handful of people who would remember her when she was gone.

Fern and Kraai walked to the edge of the clearing—the same spot her father had taught her about seasons so long ago—and stood, facing their future. Fern reached to take Kraai's hand and he squeezed. Together, the two left the clearing for what might be the final time.

Chapter 23

It was just warm enough at these low elevations that the water falling from the sky was still liquid, however, the cold still bit at their faces and settled in their bones. Fern assumed her cloak would have been soaked through by now, but her mother must have placed a water protection spell on it when she wasn't looking—her mother was incredibly skilled when it came to those spells. The evergreens also provided some protection from the elements. Instead of walking directly to the road, they decided to get most of the way to the border through the trees, obscuring where they were coming from to protect the clearing and its inhabitants. The terrain became more craggily, though, and the rocky faces were slick with dead leaves and rain. It was a miserable trek, but Kraai being there was enough to motivate Fern to keep moving forward. They challenged each other on occasion, seeing who could conquer a difficult obstacle first, making the worst parts of the journey into the best.

"Why don't you just fly down and I'll meet you at the border?" Fern asked as she tended a scrape received when she lost traction on a descent down a rock face into a small crevice.

Kraai bent over her, cupping her hand in his. "It would not be as fun that way." His hand warmed, the temperature change feeling like needles in Fern's numbed fingers. He met her gaze with a smile as his other hand touched the wound.

Fern flinched at the discomfort of healing, but held his gaze. She wanted so badly to be within the veil again, to not let this physical closeness go to waste, but she needed to focus on other things—they were off to kill someone, or kill themselves in trying. She pulled her hand away, trying to force a smile of gratitude.

"What did I do?" Kraai asked.

Fern looked down, shaking her head. "You healed me. Pretty well, actually. Has Lathron been teaching you—"

"Beyond the veil," he interrupted. "What did I do that makes you so sad when you look at me?"

"It wasn't something you did. You were…"—she searched for the right word, but could only find one—"perfect. I was the one who messed up." The last words rushed from her lips as she turned to climb the other side of the fissure. There was a pulsing of magic in the area, no doubt they were near another clan's hiding place.

Kraai placed his hand under her foot, hoisting her halfway up and holding her until she found a proper grip. Even with that disadvantage, he still managed to scale the wall before her. "Looks like that princess lifestyle in the Light Region really messed with your physical abilities." His teasing was a welcome sound.

When Fern met him at the top, she scoffed, "Not many mountains to climb over there, but get us in an open field and I will best you on foot any day."

His face scrunched. "But who would ever want to be in an open field?"

With a brow raise and sidelong glance, Fern noted, "Then I suppose it's good to get across one quickly." She bolted forward, trying to get the advantage on the foot race she was starting.

They set up camp for the night. Fern wanted to walk through the dark, but Kraai convinced her that impersonating a princess would be easier with adequate rest. They found a rocky overhang and Kraai made a small fire by igniting a piece of smokeless coal. It wasn't as comforting as a night by the hearth, but it kept away the worst of the winter chill. Barely able to keep their eyes open, they laid down just inches apart, but Fern was sure to keep a buffer between them. When she awoke in the middle of the night, she noticed that Kraai had moved closer—or she did, she wasn't sure which. Regardless, his warmth helped lull her back to sleep.

Fern awoke to morning light and a sudden cold where Kraai had been pressed. Her arm grabbed at the air—he was gone. She sat bolt upright, scanning the surroundings for him. The panic of believing him to be kidnapped was quickly abated when she saw him approaching with a cupped hand.

He bent down, presenting a few dozen sad winter berries to Fern. "Not much, but at least the bush did not try to kill me."

Fern took the berries happily. They may be the last fresh fruit she would have until spring. Then she remembered, they may be the last fresh fruit she would have *ever*. She savored them, spitting out the seeds as she went.

They trekked for one more day in the miserable, unrelenting drizzle, camping out near the edge of the tree line. There were no berries here, and the trees appeared almost sickly, growing against all odds out of the rock itself. The air carried a sulfuric tang that wafted over from the volcanic peaks of the Dark Region. The dismal grey of the sky was indistinguishable from the dismal grey of the mist that made up the border.

By the morning, all of the moisture had been pulled from the sky. They awoke before dawn, neither able to go back to sleep after an ominous howl accompanying the setting moon. It was time to face the darkness.

Fern sent Kraai away so she could change into her dress in private, but had to call him back to help secure it—she did not want to exhaust herself by using magic for the intricate lacing that hid itself within the bodice. His breath, a fog on the cold morning, wrapped around her exposed shoulders. She could feel the moisture lick her skin, closing her eyes and biting her lip in response. A ribbon secured her hair off her shoulders. As usual, it was in tangles, but it would look more presentable if it seemed as if it were intended to be that way.

Fern shoved her old clothes into the bag. She wouldn't need them, but it felt wrong to leave them. Out of the corner of her eye, she noticed Kraai hadn't moved. His eyes were fixed on her, his lips parted ever so slightly. Fern asked, "Are you sufficiently amused?"

Kraai's lips snapped shut as he blinked back to attention, shaking his head to clear whatever was on his mind. "You look… I mean, the dress is…" He stopped, taking a quick breath. "Beautiful."

Fern rubbed her free hand over the dress. It hugged her torso and arms with a heavy green lace, while a silken skirt fell from the hips. It felt as if every curve was on display, while her shoulders were left completely bare. She was to be completely exposed in this new place. Biting her lips together, she went back to shoving her clothes in the bag.

"Will you hold onto mine, too?" Kraai asked.

Fern's shoulders fell. "Are you shifting now?" If he were a crow, she wouldn't have anyone to talk to for the last leg of the journey to the border.

"I will need to fly into the Dark Region. Anyone on the road or at the border that recognizes your face would be suspicious if the princess was seen with a stranger. And I don't want to shift in the open—it feels too"—he winced—"vulnerable."

She nodded. "Shift and I'll throw your clothes in."

Kraai's head tilted forward. "And the necklace."

Fern groaned. "And the necklace." Her eyes rolled so hard they hurt.

Kraai collapsed into himself, visibly more dramatic than his graceful shifting he had done beyond the veil. He had to teach himself out here, though, and this must be how he interpreted his own instructions. He did a few hops out of his clothes, then flew to perch on a branch to watch Fern pick up his stuff.

She made a production of picking up the necklace and chucking it into the bag before turning for the open field that hugged the tree line. There were few obstacles between her and the road, so she pressed forward as quickly as she could without sweating too much or tripping over the gown. Kraai flew overhead, zig-zagging across her path to keep pace despite his clear advantage in speed.

When he drew near enough that he might hear her, Fern yelled, keeping her eyes forward, "I said I could best you *on foot*!"

By the time they reached the border with the Null, the sun had long passed its highest point and now illuminated a cloudless blue sky. There were quite a few carts on the road—it must be a market day; Fern had no idea exactly what day it was, just that it was closer to midwinter than it had been the day before. She threw her cloak over the dress, staying at the bottom of the road's embankment to draw as little attention as possible. Still, she couldn't help but feel stares as carts slowed when they approached her. She kept her eyes forward, walking with purpose toward the border. When the steady stream of carts slowed, she climbed up to the road, the dust of the path adhering to the dew of the grass that had collected on the hem during her walk.

The wall of cloud, a light grey mass from afar, was now just before her, churning like a storm behind a pane of glass. It was taller than she had expected, too, reaching so far into the sky that she had to crane her neck and lower her hood to even see what might be the top. Kraai zoomed beside her, diving through the cloud without hesitation. Fern turned to look over her right shoulder—back toward the mountains, toward home. She would die or become the sole heir to the Dark Region. This wouldn't be home anymore. She took one last deep breath of Mountain air and walked forward, through a foreign moisture that seemed to know her too well. It guided her through a wall thicker than the veil, one that did not give a sense of weightlessness and joy, but fear. The silence made it all the more eerie. The light was fading with each step, the grey that surrounded her growing darker and darker. But she continued, for her family, for the Four Regions.

Suddenly her ears and eyes were engaged again—the bustle of a town, its buildings dark and quaint compared to the opulence of the Light Region. Torches illuminated stone streets and buildings. The night was warm, so Fern unfastened her cloak, revealing the now-black dress. She looked around for Kraai or his father, but could find neither. She could still run, and a piece of her screamed to, but before she could react, a hand held her wrist.

"Princess, come with me." Flight's voice was firm.

Fern was frozen to the spot, eyes wide. No more chance of escape.

Flight stood in front of her, bringing his eyes to hers. "Princess, let us get you back to the palace."

Fern shook her arm free of his grip and squared her jaw. "Yes. Let's." She moved in the direction he led, no longer looking around to take in her surroundings. The princess would have been here before, right? She would know her region. A crow landed on her shoulder. She nudged him with her head.

As Flight opened the door of the parked carriage, he noticed the new arrival, worry immediately clear on his brow. "What is he doing here?"

"He's come to help."

Flight's voice lowered to almost a growl. "Get in the carriage. Both of you."

Fern climbed in, Kraai swooping onto one seat as Fern made her way onto the other. Flight followed, closing the door behind him and reaching over to close the curtains. Fern pulled Kraai's clothes from the bag and threw them onto his chair. He burrowed inside, shifting his form awkwardly in the confined space.

Once his son was clothed, Flight turned in the seat to put his face close to Kraai. "What are you doing?"

Kraai continued buttoning his shirt, not even looking at his father. "I am helping a friend."

He had only known his son was alive for a few months, but his concern for Kraai rivaled Strike's for Fern. "And you know what she is to do?"

Kraai's eyes locked on Fern's in a way that made Fern more sure of his loyalty than ever. "What *we* are to do."

The elder crow shot a glance at Fern so quick she almost didn't catch it. "And you are doing this of your own will?"

Kraai finally turned to face his father. "Yes. I am. Now please refrain from suggesting she would use her song to manipulate me. I trust her, and if you truly believed in your cause, you would, too."

With a bow of his head, Flight finally addressed Fern. "My apologies, Highness, but he is my son. I fear losing him so soon after finding him."

After hearing the pain in his voice, Fern could not fault him. The tension in her shoulders fell and she spoke softly, still holding Kraai's gaze. "And he is my"—her blink lingered, her mind reliving the feeling of Kraai's lips on hers—"dearest friend. If you don't trust me, then trust him. I do." Her breath was shallow, having looked into his eyes for so long. It reminded her of what it once was, when he—

"You need to stop doing that." Flight gruffed.

The thread holding Fern's mind snapped and she finally managed to look at Flight. Was he an empath, too? "Stop what?"

His eyes narrowed under his furrowed brow. "Cramming your words together. It might have been common in the palace when Mask and Strike were alive, but Belle has seen the end of it. It would raise suspicions instantly."

Fern couldn't help but feel like a child receiving a scolding. She shifted in her seat, crossing her arms. "I *do not* intend to speak until *it is* necessary." She emphasized the split words. "You will take me directly to the princess' room, leading me under the guise of carrying luggage, and I will wait for her there." A wave of nausea came over her, which she forced down with a deep breath. "That is the first task we will complete. Then we can decide what to do about Belle."

Flight covered his ears. "Do not tell me of your plans. If Belle senses something amiss, she may force me to divulge information. Just be careful of the princess' personal guard. He will not enter her room, but—" He paused abruptly, then asked Fern, "Do you know anything of her guardian?"

"No, just that he is always with her."

Flight's eyes aimlessly scanned over the ground as he mumbled, "Yes. Yes, it is better you do not know."

"Know what?" Fern demanded.

His eyes continued their mad search for clarity. "All you need to know of him is not to challenge him physically and to have your water magic ready." He looked her up and down. "You clearly have not begun to exhibit any vampiric traits, being so comfortable in the sunlight, so I hope you have honed the other skills at your disposal." His voice began to quake and Fern started to wonder which of them was more worried about what was to come.

Kraai placed his hand on his father's back. "We should go." Only three words in his calm tone and the tension in the carriage seemed to vanish.

Flight nodded and wrapped his arms around Kraai. He whispered something in his ear before patting him on the back and releasing him. "This is the last I will be able to speak to you both. Kraai, you fly out before we reach the palace. If we make good time and they stick to their usual schedule, Daughter of Strike and Belle will still be out when we arrive. Highness, your role begins now. Those of us who support you will be throughout the palace—call on us once you have secured yourself as the only heir." With that he left the carriage, pausing for a weak smile before closing the door.

Kraai instantly kicked his feet up. "Best get comfortable. It is a long drive to the palace." Of course he would know, having gotten a literal bird's-eye view of the road to Capital.

Fern wasn't ready to rest. It was all too real now. They were in the Dark Region, the plan set in motion. She needed to know her every move from here on out. "Do you think I can trust those in the palace to come to my aid? Won't Belle have some sort of hold on them?"

He closed his eyes, resting his hands behind his head. "Perhaps not the princess' guard, as he is known to be completely under Belle's influence, but not *every* man is susceptible to a siren's song. If they are not attracted to women, if they are deaf, if they—" He shot forward, eyes wide, his hand clutching his chest. "Do you have the necklace?"

Fern glared as she felt for her bag. Without looking, she reached in, wrapping her fingers around the smooth, cold stone.

Kraai's body relaxed as his eyes scanned Fern. "Actually, keep it for now. I will not need it until we are in the palace."

Fern released her grip, letting the heavy pendant sink back into the pile of clothes, glad she would not have to lay eyes on it just yet. The frustration still stuck in her gut, that rock of uneasiness growing so large that she wanted to ask questions, but she didn't want Kraai to doubt her faith in him. She didn't want to doubt that faith, either. There was just so much resting on their shoulders. She threw her face into her palms, pressing on her eyelids; it was a means by which she calmed herself many times as a child. Colors swirled in the darkness she created, pulling up the left side of her vision and crashing down over the center. Fern's hands broke from her eyes as she gasped. *The wave.* As much as she hated being in this place, risking her life, assuming a title she had no desire to have, it was all better than the destruction she would see in her sleep. To kill two people to save the Four Regions seemed an appropriate sacrifice, but why did she still feel so unsure of this plan?

"Let us play a game." Kraai moved to share a bench with Fern, turning to face her, and held out his hands in front of him, palms down.

Fern smiled, shifting to sit cross-legged, facing her friend. It was a game they'd been playing for ages, one of the games that passed the time on the way into the Light Region. She placed her hands below his, palms up, close enough she could feel his warmth. She held his gaze, twitching her right hand to make him flinch. He didn't move, only raising his eyebrows in a dare. Fern brought her hand halfway up the side of his. Still no reaction. As she reset, the carriage hit a bump in the road, slamming her hands into Kraai's and threatening to jolt her off the seat.

Kraai's hands clasped onto hers, tension in his arms helping stabilize her before she fell. Excitement pumped through her body, first the fear, then the realization that Kraai was holding her, just inches from her face. The pang of sadness threatened to overtake her mind, but what took its place was the realization that Kraai was here. It might not be the same Kraai she knew in the veil, but it was her friend, the one who would play games to cheer her up when on their way to kill her sister. This is who she needed right now.

"Fern, I…" Kraai began.

With those two words, everything Fern had just thought about only needing a friend went out the window. A glimmer of hope flickered within her. "Yes?"

"I think we can make it out of this alive." He looked down at their joined hands and squeezed. "I can stay in the Dark Region with you until you have everything figured out. Until you feel safe. If you want me to."

Not quite what she wanted to hear, but she took it. "Please don't go back to the Mountains without me." She rubbed her thumb along his knuckles. "I won't be stuck here forever, but I'll need you with me while I am."

He watched their hands, a furrow forming in his brow. After a long pause, he finally raised his head and said, "I will be by your side until you tell me to go." He glanced at her bag. "How do you plan on doing the deed?"

"I've gotten quite good at—" Fern's eyes widened, suddenly realizing any of her training might be moot—her sister could be similarly skilled with water and electricity, possibly able to use her own magic against her. She shrugged. "I suppose it would have to include the element of surprise."

"You brought your hunting knife, right?" he asked.

"I did, but I don't see—" Her face sank. "Oh."

"You just have to get behind her and slit her throat."

Fern was taken aback by his matter-of-fact demeanor. But it was exactly what had to be done, there was no way to gloss over it anymore. She needed to look at it like a task, keep her emotions out of it. "At least it will be quick." Her eyes lost themselves, her mind envisioning the blood on her hands.

Kraai let go of Fern and held his hands hovering over hers again. "You still have yet to get me."

Chapter 24

Kraai sensed when they drew near to the palace—he made sure to learn the lay of the city when he went to find his grandmother and father. "Put my clothes in the bag," he instructed as he slid out of some of the outer layers.

"I might have more pressing things to think about than keeping track of the bag," Fern warned as she handed the bag to him.

He moved to stuff his coat inside, but paused. "In that case"—he reached in and pulled out the sheathed hunting knife—"I think you should keep this on you." He handed it to her, hilt first.

Fern was thankful she opted for wearing her boots, otherwise she might have had to tie it on her thigh. She tucked the blade into the cuff, the extra bulk making the leather snug on her calf. She threw the skirt of her dress back down over it, but not before catching Kraai watching her movement. "Can I help you with something?" she asked, heavy on the sarcasm.

Kraai's hand was in the bag again. "Actually, yes." He removed it, revealing the pendant of the necklace between his thumb and forefinger. "Keep this on you, as well." He held it out, balanced on the tips of his fingers.

Fern knew time was running out. She reached out gingerly. "And if I don't?"

He stared at the green gem, nearly whispering, "Then your chances of losing me increase greatly."

Fern snatched the necklace from him. If he believed it would help him stay alive, then Fern would guard it, even if she still did not know what exactly it did and still did not particularly *like* the object. Her eyes were fixed on it, as if looking at it just a little longer would force it to reveal its secrets.

"Fern." The sad warmth in Kraai's voice signaled that this was goodbye.

She looked up, fighting the pain in her nose that signaled she could cry at any moment. "Listen, if we don't—"

"We will," he interrupted, taking her empty hand. "And we will do it together."

"As we always have." She bit back the words she wanted to add as Kraai transformed before her, his hand receding from her grasp and flapping as a wing moments later. He dove out the window, a black blur in the darkness as the carriage slowed in its approach.

They stopped to listen to the stress of the metal gate's overworked hinges. The sound reverberated in Fern's chest, throwing off the rapid beat of her heart. The jolt forward made it steady once again, but did nothing for the speed, as they entered a massive courtyard. Fern rubbed her palms on the fabric of her dress as she waited for the door to open. When it finally did, a travelling trunk slid in. Fern opened it and placed her tattered bag inside, contrasting the immaculate velvet lining.

Flight reached inside, closing the trunk and securing the clasps. "Your Highness, if you will allow me." He moved to pull it from the carriage, but instead froze, locking his eyes on the emerald pendant still sitting in Fern's hand.

Fern looked, too. It seemed out of place here. So...*green.* Fern's breath halted as she rushed to stuff it down the front of her dress, letting it rest where the bodice hugged her skin.

With that, Flight pulled the trunk from the carriage with one hand, and held out the other to help Fern down the stairs. As she ducked out of the door, a tall building stood before her, the grey stone made even colder by the silver of the moonlight. Despite the surprising warmth of the air, Fern had to hold back a shiver.

She took Flight's hand, even though she didn't need his help, and descended, inches closer to her fate with each step. He took off in a hurried pace, Fern keeping on his tail as best she could. The tall doors opened for them, the two guards standing outside not so much as glancing their way. The entryway led to a tall main room, three stories of balconies visible from her vantage, but Fern kept her eyes forward, glued on Flight's heels. Voices from her left caused Fern's eyes to flick in their direction. The glows of red and blue and green signaled what they were—and these would be nothing like the sirens of the Light Region; they were the ones who tried to annihilate that shoal. She pressed forward, nearly tiptoeing to avoid stares, yet nobody cared to—or perhaps nobody dared to—look at her.

As Fern ascended the stairs, she kept her breath steady, thinking lighter thoughts in case an empath was nearby. She imagined her mother and father here in happier times, imagined Mask in the height of her power. When they reached the third story, she glanced over the balcony, noticing the emptiness. Even a vampire had tapestries, paintings, but this immense room was barren. Beings were absent from anywhere Fern had stepped foot. A wave of pity washed over her, having lived only moments in her sister's shoes—what a lonely, cold life she must lead. *That life will be over soon enough.* She nearly flinched at her own thoughts.

Flight opened a door, disappeared inside, and returned without the trunk. He bowed to Fern and left, walking around the third floor balcony instead of passing by her to return to the stairs. She ran her fingers along the railing, wondering who from her dreams had walked here, had touched these same surfaces, and if she could save them. The friction of the coarse stone tickled her fingertips. When she reached the room, she entered, shutting the door behind her. It was as barren and cold, but at least there was a fire made up to cast its orange glow. Unfortunately, it made the air incredibly dry, a stark contrast from the humidity outside. Fern rushed to the window, pushing it open to let in her dearest companions—the hint of water on the night air and the crow that was circling the building. She knew that, as darkness fell in the other regions, the breeze would switch. The air would no longer be coming from the Seas, but from the Mountains, and with it would come the water that used to know her. Would it be willing to answer her call?

Kraai landed on the window ledge, frantically bobbing his head toward the gate, moonlight catching on his feathers each time he lowered himself. Fern wanted to lean out to look, but realized what he meant when he began to peck her away. *It's time.* She retrieved her cloak from the trunk and moved to the corner of the room, face shrouded, blade in hand. Her focus was on the door, which would hide her when it opened. She bounced on her toes, unable to keep still, picking at the leather on the hilt with her thumbnail. Voices and footsteps passed by, but none stopped. After some time, the tension in her shoulders eased, but the strain in her chest remained. She dared not move, dared not look at Kraai. Waiting was always her least favorite activity.

Finally, the handle turned. The door opened soundlessly on its hinges. The first glimpse Fern got was of the ashen aura, like the bits of debris that fly from a roaring fire, radiating from the being. As she entered the room, she saw her own untamable hair, her own tan skin. She was watching herself from outside of her own body. The arm holding the knife slackened. Fern could not move, could do nothing but watch as this young woman took jewelry from her neck and reached to begin untying the laces of her dress.

A gust of wind from the open window cut the trance. Fern shot a glance to Kraai, who seemed to be similarly awestruck, but noticed his friend's movement. He clicked his beak against the window frame. The princess jumped, then smiled lightly before wandering over to see the bird. This was the time. On ghost's feet, Fern crept behind her sister. A chant resonated in her ears with each beat of her human heart. *Do it. Do it. Do it.* If the voice was silenced, she would lose her nerve. *Do it. Do it.* The hunting knife was heavy in her hand as she brought it up and around the body that was so like hers. She pressed the blade onto her throat, inhaling sharply to bind her courage. Just a flick of the wrist and it was over, but her mother's plea forced its way into her head. *Let me see both my girls alive and well.* She hesitated—just one moment too long.

Two hands grasped her wrist, then hips thrust into her own as her target folded over, bringing Fern over the top of her. A flap of wings, a clattering of metal on stone, and the slap of Fern's back falling onto the floor. She looked up to see her own face, inverted above her, and felt the cold metal of a blade on her own neck. Dark, tangled curls fell into her face.

"How did you replicate my aura?" she asked, anger seething in her voice.

Fern moved just an inch to the left—an inch too far. She felt the blade press closer to her skin, on the verge of breaking it. She froze, too afraid to swallow.

Her sister, Daughter of Strike, grit her teeth as she asked again, more slowly, "How did you replicate my aura?"

Fern's lips started, then stopped. Would the vibration in her vocal cords push the tension on her skin too far? Sure, it would be just a nick to her neck, but once the blood starts flowing, the hunter's mind calls for more. She moved her eyes down in the direction of her sister's wrist.

Daughter of Strike took the hint and loosened the blade, still against the skin, but now with a little more breathing room.

"I replicated nothing. This is my aura," Fern explained.

Fern could feel the blade wobble on her throat as her sister regripped it, bringing her face closer. "I will not go with you if you lie to me."

Why would she think the plan was to bring her with us? Fern's mouth remained open while her eyes searched for a response. The truth might kill her, but a lie would be seen through immediately. Her gaze rested on what she could see of the bed, where a familiar figure was taking shape.

"So you will go with us?" Kraai asked.

No. Oh, no. What was he doing?

The distraction was exactly what was needed. Daughter of Strike looked over at him, straightening her body ever so slightly. Fern was able to roll out from under the blade, which just barely skimmed the side of her neck on the way out. She stood to look at her friend—exactly what she imagined. He was naked, legs tucked under the sheets, relaxing against the headboard. Fern couldn't help but stare.

"You do not both have to look at me like that." He chuckled, sitting up. "It is actually quite eerie, both of you having the same expression on your faces." His face flattened. "Please stop." He pulled the top blanket from the bed, covering his lower half as he slid out, tying it around him. "Now, if you come with us, we can answer all of your questions when we get to our destination."

Daughter of Strike finally caught on that Fern was no longer where she had left her. She looked back, then shrugged it off, her attention captured by the shirtless young man who had just left her bed. "Where will you take me?"

"Somewhere safe." Kraai's smile warmed the room, but chilled Fern's heart. That was the smile he used with her, the smile that brought Fern comfort so many times before, now given to someone else—to this mimic.

"We must hurry, then." Daughter of Strike ran to the window. "What is the plan?"

Fern locked eyes with Kraai, urgency beaming. She mouthed the words "there's a plan?"

His eyes widened for a half-second, a plea to trust him. "Run, fast and far, until you reach the dark side of the dock district." Kraai looked away, back at their now-captive. "Follow the bird. Do not get caught. My associate will provide cover." He looked back to Fern and raised his eyebrows.

Fern made a noise, a sort of half-sigh, half-grunt as she, too, went to the window. Now she had to come up with an escape plan for three—fantastic.

There were four guards in the courtyard, unmoving. The air was not dry, yet not particularly humid, either. She would have to be strategic—a cloud just around their eyes, thicker in the area around the building's facade and outer walls. She would have to hold four of them in place while climbing, running. If any of the sentries caught on and moved even a step away, she would have to adjust.

"There are fewer guards around back." At first Fern thought the voice was her own, in her head, but it only came through her left ear. She looked at her sister, firelight bouncing off of her own likeness. "I can bring us to another room, one whose window opens to the back of the building. Just a few yards to the wall. There are some footholds. They are small, but with enough motivation you can make it up. We have to move quickly."

Fern stared. Her sister had planned an escape before. She *wanted* to flee. They were her way out. "You go first, princess. I will follow with my"—she gave Kraai a look—"associate."

Daughter of Strike threw a cloak under her arm as she walked out the door, head held high. She cut across the wide hall to another door, opened it, and slipped inside.

As Fern readied herself, she whispered over her shoulder, "How are you so calm about this? She is supposed to be dead already." She saw no point in taking her sister somewhere else if it didn't change the end goal.

Kraai stood right behind Fern, looking out the open door. "Well, you royally messed up that plan, so let us see how this new one plays out." He shifted, hopping onto her shoulder, ending the conversation.

Fern put on her princess face, raising her head, squaring her shoulders, giving herself an air of grace absent in her everyday life. She meant to keep her eyes straight on the door, but movement in her peripheral startled her. A horned demon, his hair short, his stature burly, and his face shocked. Had he seen Daughter of Strike? Fern picked up her pace. It was only a dozen or so steps, but it felt like a mile. What if the princess had locked the door? What if it was a trap? She continued anyway, holding her breath the entire time. The door opened as she pushed it. "Go!" Fern said, jaw set, as she continued her pace, moving toward the window. "*Now.*"

With those words, Kraai took off from Fern's shoulder, his wing beating against her cheek. A quick glance down the outside wall showed one sentry. Fern held out her hand, and clasped it tightly. The water behind him condensed and Fern pulled it to envelop him slowly. "Oh, no," she sang to herself. "Looks like the fog is rolling in." She kept one hand clenched to hold the water steady as she used her other to hold tight to the ledge as she threw herself out of the window. Her grip was not very strong, but it held long enough to find the next ledge she would grasp. She fell ten feet to the next window, her fingertips barely taking hold, the skin peeling from the friction. She looked up to see her sister leap from the window, arms flailing to keep herself upright down the two stories between the room and the ground. She landed like a cat, the gravel barely stirring under her feet, as she shifted to fall onto her side, rolling out the impact. Fern, dangling from a second story window, pushed off with a foot and let go, twisting to try and reach the top of the stone wall that surrounded the palace. The arm of her clenched fist looped over the top, her shoulder nearly tearing from the jolt when gravity continued to pull on her body. She winced, letting out a small yelp.

Kraai was sitting on the wall, head pointed at the guard's position. Fern pulled the cloud closer so it would act as a buffer between them.

Daughter of Strike began to scale the wall, taking a running jump and reaching for hidden hand holds. When Fern finally pulled her body over, she held her free hand down for her sister. The face looking up at Fern was filled with excitement and apprehension. It could have been Fern's own face when she was going to the market for the first time, but the eyes— they weren't green, rather a cloudy blue. Three swift pulls upward and the princess was reaching for Fern's hand. Just before they met, a spark flashed between them. Fern almost flinched away, but the spark was warm, welcoming. Instead, she brought her other hand to join in pulling her sister up.

The cloud barrier disappeared just as Daughter of Strike pulled her body over, but Fern took one last glance at the window from which they had escaped. The horned demon seemed to fill the entire opening. The shock in his eyes was still present, but he nodded at the girls just before they dropped down to the ground and ran. Mid-stride, Daughter of Strike whipped the cloak around her, hiding her face from curious onlookers. Fern knew where the docks were—she just had to follow the water's call—but Kraai still led the way, soaring overhead.

They pounded over the cobbled streets, Daughter of Strike matching Fern step for step, two cloaks whipping the wind behind them. The buildings grew smaller, more pressed together, the roads tighter between them. They were moving away from the palace, clearly, but what was the ultimate destination? They crossed a bridge over the river. The vapors that rose from it made Fern slow—it was Mountain water. True, it was dirtied and dark, but the essence of it was still there. She was even familiar with the glacier some of the water had melted from. She smiled, recognizing an old friend, then regained her momentum to catch up to the other two.

They slipped between buildings, Kraai's attempt to throw off anyone in pursuit, left, right, right again—did Kraai have any idea where he was going? They lost sight of him and stopped in an alleyway. Daughter of Strike leaned against a wall to gasp for breath, fanning the cloak. Sweat dripped from her hairline.

Fern rested her hands on knees, trying to compose herself. "I didn't...expect you...to be able to...run like that."

Instead of replying in labored bursts, Daughter of Strike took one long breath and answered in an airy, calm voice, "Grandmother has me train daily." She stopped for another long breath. "She was convinced I would be kidnapped by my mother." She looked both ways down the street. "Where is your man?"

As if on cue, clothing fell from an open window above them, followed by a crow swooping down and burrowing into them. He shifted back into his demonic form, facing away from the ladies, his hands pulling the breeches up as he stood. He turned to look at them, adjusting the shirt over his frame, his hair an outright mess. He stood beside Fern and nudged her, holding out his hand.

Fern's first reaction was to take it, but as her hand raised, she realized his intention. She shoved her hand into her bosom, fishing around for a moment until she hooked her finger on the chain. She dangled it in front of his face, it seemed to glow from within.

Kraai secured it around his neck, tucking the gem into the shirt he was wearing. "Shall we continue?" He smiled as he looked between the young women.

Daughter of Strike was busy looking between Fern and Kraai. "Is that…?" Her words were lost somewhere in her airy breath.

Kraai gave her his knowing look, the sly glance that Fern now realized she hated seeing being given to anyone but her. "It is." He patted the shirt, his hand covering the pendant and his heart. "But questions are best saved for when we are no longer in the open."

Chapter 25

Kraai turned and weaved through the city, navigating the maze with confidence. Hundreds, possibly thousands of hurried steps later, Kraai tucked into a doorway, pulling hard at a heavy metal door. He tugged a few times, only getting it to move after bracing his foot against the frame, clumps of rust falling from the seal. He gestured for Fern and Daughter of Strike to enter first.

The air was stale in the nearly-empty room. Once the door was closed, Fern created an arc between her fingers for light, only to reveal two toppled-over chairs and a collection of spider webs. There were no windows to the street, only on the opposite wall, but the glow from the spark made them mirrors. "What is this place?" Fern asked.

Kraai lifted the chairs, brushing off a thick layer of dust before setting them upright. "I found it when I was flying over Capital a while back, getting a feel for the layout. Thought a hideout might prove useful at some point, and it looked like nobody had been here for ages." He moved toward the wall of exposed windows, their dressings torn or eaten away, mostly in a pile of fabric on the ground.

Fern moved toward a chair. Between the running, the dress, and the stuffiness of the room, she needed a breath. Kraai caught her arm as she tried to sit, pulling her back to stand.

"I would not shut you two up in a room like this." He placed his hand in the small of her back, the pressure of it guiding Fern toward the door opposite the one they entered. He opened it for her, bowing at both the sisters as they moved through.

The night air hit Fern, but not the noise that the city made. It was a beautiful silence, so still that the air itself seemed not to move. She looked up at the stars—none of the symbols or constellations that were painted in the Mountains, no forecasts or warnings she could ascertain, but the light seemed to make the space glow. It bounced off of colored tiles that surrounded a central feature, an empty pool. Though the floor was chipped and worn from countless feet, it was nearly pristine—as if the idle time that had haunted the indoor space could not touch this courtyard. Kraai lit a torch that was hanging on the wall by the door, casting even more light, giving movement to the patterns of blue, orange, and white that surrounded them.

Daughter of Strike sat on the edge of the pool, her eyes taking in the entirety of the space. "It is lovely," she mused, mouth agape. As she came to the place where Fern was standing, she fixed her eyes, closing her lips in a stern expression before asking, "Am I allowed to know your names?"

Fern shot a look at Kraai, who gave a wide-eyed shrug in return. She faced her mirror. "I am"—lies escaped her and the only word allowed from her mouth was the truth—"Fern." She lowered her head and gestured to her companion. "And this is Kraai."

The brow over the captive's blue eyes furrowed. "No. What are your names in the Dark Region?" Each word came out slowly, as if explaining this concept to a small child.

"We have none." Once the words left her lips, Fern realized this was a lie. She was Daughter of Strike, just like her sister, but she was not quite ready for that revelation yet.

Daughter of Strike gave a nervous laugh. "Guards stop everyone without a name on their way in. If your blood is new to the region, they are summoned immediately to your entrance point." She looked somewhat like a trapped animal, eyes darting from Kraai to Fern and back. "Please tell me your names."

Kraai moved forward slowly, hands out before him. His voice was equally paced. "I entered in my crow form—the magic must have overlooked me. Fern, however…" He trailed off, gesturing for Fern to finish.

The voice that came next was not Fern's, though. "Carries my blood." Daughter of Strike stood slowly, awe painted on her face. "I thought you were a clever mimic at first—the hair, the form, everything but the eyes." She crept closer, one hand out to hover over the skin of Fern's cheeks as she looked into her eyes. "I did not kill you because I was curious about the eyes."

The blue of the princess' eyes seemed to swirl as Fern watched, more alive than when she had first seen them—not while running, not in the palace, but in her dreams. Fern hadn't been watching herself run from the wave at all. "My eyes have always been green. We believed it was because my father was part snake demon."

"A small part of me always wished for a story like Mask's— that I would come to find I had a sister." Daughter of Strike's eyes looked away, watching a dream somewhere in the open sky. "What young girl does not wish for a companion growing up?"

Fern felt Kraai's hand on her back again. She never wished for a companion, she never needed to.

The princess continued, almost in a trance, "I told myself you were a mimic, but why would you have changed my eyes? Then I saw the aura—it is near impossible to copy a siren's aura, but not completely unheard of. It gave me enough pause to realize that if you truly wanted me dead, I would have been dead. Then I saw you manipulate water with more skill than I could ever hope to possess, and the spark in your hand when we entered this building—I knew it might not be a childish dream, after all." Her eyes finally focused as she looked down at her hands, which were taking Fern's. "Was I a twin? Are you my sister?"

The buzz of current where their skin met caused Fern to pull her hands away. "I am." It came out as a mumble as Fern took a step back. There was still a job to be done. To satisfy The Monarch, she needed to secure herself as the heir, to be rid of her sister in some way, and there was only one that came to mind. Walking to a counter on the side of the courtyard, she glanced over what was stored on the shelves inside. Glasses, bottles, and tucked far back, a knife. How fortuitous. She took a bottle and sat on a stair, swirling the liquid inside around as she avoided her sister. Delaying the inevitable would just make it harder, but she needed to see if there was a way to avoid it altogether. She had promised.

Kraai sat beside Daughter of Strike on the edge of the pool. Fern ignored their closeness as they spoke in hushed tones, low enough she could make out nothing but her own name being said every so often. Each time that happened, Kraai looked up, as if to check she hadn't heard what they were discussing. Fern suffered through the burning in her gut when he placed his arm around her. He wasn't hers, so she had no right to feel possessive of his affections. When she leaned in close to him, Fern's ears felt like they had caught on fire, but she held her emotion in.

Of course the princess would be his main focus—she had a grace that Fern could never replicate. Her bearing was reserved, it drew people in while maintaining mystery. It was only when he gave her that warm smile, the smile that had assured Fern that all was well on countless occasions, that the churning within her reached a breaking point. The bottle she clutched in her hand fought the current, heating until it shattered. The liquid caught fire, spreading across the tiles in a graceful blue blaze that extinguished itself before Fern even realized what happened.

Kraai hurried to her, but Fern noted that he lingered to say something to Daughter of Strike before doing so. Kneeling in the shattered glass, his hands moved to pick fragments from Fern's palm—she hadn't even noticed they were there, but the blood was already creeping out around the tiny pieces.

"This courtyard is enchanted to not let noise escape. You can scream if you need to," he said as he dug his nails into her skin to pull out the deeper pieces.

Fern was still processing what had happened, she still had no feeling in her hand. "I'm fine. Get as much out as you can before the shock wears off. There's a knife over on those shelves."

Kraai studied Fern's face. "Are you sure? I could have sworn I picked up on you being in some sort of pain."

Yes, the pain of having to share you. Fern shook the thought and pointed at the shelves with the glasses and bottles. "The knife, hurry. There are some deep ones."

Kraai found the blade quickly, heating it with fire as he returned to his friend. He made swift work of it, using the tip to slide under the skin and pull out each tiny blood-soaked piece. Fern never felt the pain of what was happening beneath her skin, only the warmth of Kraai's hand holding hers. When he finished fishing out the pieces, he held his hand over hers, the skin healing enough to stop the blood before Fern stopped him.

"Save your energy. I will be fine for now." Fern noticed how close his face was, those features that haunted her. Her eyes happened over his shoulder and she saw her sister looking over their way. Fern brought her voice to a whisper. "Why are you being so kind to her?"

"I was curious about her story. I wanted to know why she was so eager to run. She was trapped in that palace her entire life, closely guarded if she ever got to leave, never interacting with anyone." Kraai tore a piece of the shirt he was wearing and wrapped it around Fern's hand.

"I was trapped, too. Never allowed out on my own, never allowed to meet others." Fern squeezed her hand. She felt the pain now, just a sting, nothing compared to what she should have felt.

Kraai glanced over his shoulder at the pool, then back to Fern. "She had nobody. You had me."

"Yes, I *had* you." Fern's voice started to grow louder, but she dropped back to an angered whisper. "And now she will."

"You are being ridiculous," he scoffed, grabbing her wrist and pulling her through the door, back into the dark entry room. When the door closed, he continued, still keeping his voice low. "You sound like a child who will not share."

Anger bubbled inside. "I have been sharing with her my entire life." It came out louder than expected, but Fern could not care less. "My mother has never been a true mother. Why? Because her mind has been here, constantly thinking of the daughter who was not in the Mountains. My father was always caring for my mother. Who did I have? You. I had you. Having you was enough."

He stood straighter, bringing his head away from Fern. "You still have me. I am here in the Dark Region because you asked me to be here, tending your wounds, fighting this fight—"

"Consoling the person we were to do away with." Fern's face held no amusement.

"What more do you want of me?" The question was asked in frustration, but even in the darkness, Fern could see that he truly wanted to know.

Things will be easier if you just tell him. Lathron's advice was hardly ever wrong. "I want all of you." She wanted to sound warm, but emotions were still crashing within her, leading to a frantic near-yell.

"All of me?" Kraai repeated.

"Yes." Fern took a shaking breath, trying to calm herself well enough to explain. "I had all of you beyond the veil and I want it again, but I know I can't have it."

"Why can you not have it?" He stepped forward, his hand reaching for Fern's.

Fern stepped back, pulling her hand away. Why was everyone trying to touch her tonight? "Because it wasn't real." She had finally gotten the anger under control, but now the sadness came creeping in. Kraai would be able to see her well in the dark, so she fiddled with her hands to avoid having to look at him. "We were practicing my song. I told you to kiss me, and you did. And it was the most wonderful thing. It felt *so* right until I realized it wasn't real." Sparks began to crawl on her skin, casting flickers of light on Kraai's face as she looked at him again. "I would ask you to kiss me now if I wasn't worried some part of you was still under my influence."

"And if I told you I wanted to kiss you, would that mean nothing?"

"It might mean you were still under the song's influence." She pushed aside the thought of what else it might mean.

They stood in silence, Fern back to messing with her fingers and Kraai's eyes searching for thoughts in the dark.

Kraai's sudden intake of air cued Fern to look at him. His hand was grasping inside his shirt. "Was I wearing this when I kissed you?" He rested the pendant outside the cloth. The green seemed to have a glow of its own, almost pulsing in the darkness.

Fern remembered the day. Kraai ate the apple, he turned into a crow and was not affected, then when she was handing him his clothes, he was searching frantically for the pendant. She furrowed her brow. "You were."

Kraai's face lit up. He grabbed Fern's hand, not even flinching when a spark discharged on him. "Tell me to kiss you. Use your song."

Fern wanted to pull away again, but she needed the comfort of physical touch right now. "No. I won't use my song again." She squeezed his hand, hoping to bring his gaze away from the tear running down her cheek.

He looked away, but not to their hands—to the door. He rushed to the entry to the courtyard, Fern struggling to keep up with his sudden change of velocity. She barely had stable footing in the open space before Kraai let go and walked over to Daughter of Strike.

"Tell me to kiss you. Use your song." The words were the same, but the emotion was pure excitement now.

"What?" Fern shrieked.

"What?" Daughter of Strike asked, in a slightly more confused tone. Her eyes flicked down to his chest and her face grew into a smile. "She does not know?"

Fern could only see the back of Kraai's head as he shook it.

"With pleasure." Daughter of Strike made eye contact with Fern as she reached for her throat, then as she began her song, she looked into Kraai's eyes. "Kiss me."

Fern watched in horror, more nauseous than she had ever been from a Light Region secret. She was watching her own sister use her song on the person she loved. Was Kraai trying to help her not feel bad about killing her? She turned to look for the blade they were using earlier, but stopped when she heard Kraai's response.

"No." It was short, clear, and sweet to Fern's ears. Kraai was still facing Daughter of Strike. "Are you able to tell her? Apparently, I am still held to keeping the secret I learned in the Light Region, despite not actually remembering learning it."

Daughter of Strike looked to Fern, but then back to Kraai in confusion. "The Light Region? Who would have given this to you in the Light Region?"

Kraai shrugged. "Again, no recollection."

The sister cocked her head, but accepted the answer, turning back to Fern. "It is a siren ward. The wearer is immune to siren songs"—she bobbed her head side to side, scrunching up one side of her face and letting out a small giggle—"if certain conditions are met." Her hand shielded her lips as she let out another nervous laugh. After she'd had her moment, her eyes looked Kraai up and down. "Do you require that I tell her that part, as well?"

Kraai searched for words, his face sour. He closed his eyes, letting out a defeated sigh before nodding.

Daughter of Strike bit her lip, her smile too giddy to come from someone who should be mature enough to rule a region. "The pendant only works if the wearer has loved a siren. *Truly* loved—without a song." She let out another laugh. Fern was having fewer and fewer reservations about killing her. When the sister made eye contact with Fern, her joviality lessened, and she continued, "They were created by the ancient sirens to protect the humans they cherished from the songs of other sirens. Very few were created, and even fewer found their way to the Four Regions."

Fern did not comprehend immediately what this meant. Her mind was fixated on love being a condition for something to work—how would the pendant know? How do you create conditional magic? Kraai crept into the corner of her vision. Fern's brow furrowed as her eyes found him. "So all of it—*all* of it was real?"

Kraai squared himself in front of Fern, his chest puffed. "Tell me to kiss you."

Fern tucked her arms behind her back, interlacing the fingers to prove to herself they were nowhere near her throat. Raising her chin, she mimicked his stance, daring him. "Kiss me." As the words left her, Kraai's hand reached for the nape of her neck, pulling her into the lips she had missed for so long. Her fingers unclasped, finding their way into Kraai's hair. For this moment, everything was right in the regions. That is, until another giggle cut the ambiance. Stone-faced, Fern turned to the noise, then raised her eyebrows, daring the princess to say something.

"I did not intend to ruin the moment." She shrunk down into a shrug. "I was simply going to ask what the plan is."

"The plan?" Fern did not even attempt to hide her annoyance.

"Do you intend to keep me here until day so I burn in the sun? Will you take me to another region for torture? Banish me to the human world?" Each option was listed with sick enthusiasm.

Fern's jaw fell as she listened. "Burn in the sun? Were...were you bitten by a vampire?"

Daughter of Strike's head tilted again. "No. My father was a vampire." Her eyes narrowed. "Are you not vampiric, too?"

"No. Neither of us are. Our father is—" Fern gave a light cough. "Our father was human."

Fern could see Daughter of Strike's world come to a halt, her eyes looking back on a million memories. She looked up, as if to start speaking, but her gaze retreated to the floor when she couldn't find the words.

Kraai whispered in Fern's ear, "She is going to need a moment, but you and I will continue our...conversation later." He squeezed her arm, then moved to help Daughter of Strike sit safely.

Daughter of Strike continued scanning the ground, her chest heaving in panic. "All of the blood I have forced down my throat, all of the days spent hiding indoors, all of the pacts based on vampiric bonds, all of the bloodletting to remove the demonic magic stifling my vampiric power." She looked at Fern, tears welling in her eyes, her voice strained. "It was all for nothing?"

Fern's lips hung open. It was completely by chance that she had been saved from this fate—she could have easily been the child left behind, the one in the turned demon's arms. A perfect change of subject. "Daughter of Strike..." The name felt so bulky on her tongue. "Princess, you wouldn't remember, but perhaps you have heard something about it. The night our mother escaped, you were being held by a demon. Do you know what has become of him?"

Daughter of Strike lifted her head, a small spark of joy flashing in her watery eyes while a light smile graced her lips. "Stalworth. He remains my protector."

Kraai and Fern met each other's surprised glance before both looking back to Daughter of Strike. Fern stepped in closer, reaching out to touch her sister's shoulder, discharging the current that she could feel building up. "And what has he told you about that night?"

Daughter of Strike wiped the last remaining tear with her sleeve. With a slow, sporadic cadence, she said, "He has no memory of that night. Grandmother said he did not want to remember it, so she used her song on him, commanding him to forget." She took a long breath before continuing, "If I loved someone and they tried to kill me, I would want to forget, too."

As Daughter of Strike again hung her head, Fern and Kraai exchanged a series of looks. First Kraai's sympathetic plea to tell Daughter of Strike everything, followed by Fern urging him to keep his mouth shut with pursed lips and raised eyebrows, then Kraai's flat expression of insistence, and finally Fern rolling her eyes and throwing up her hands in defeat.

Before either could speak, however, the princess' voice chimed in. "Please tell me what you intend to do with me."

Kraai rubbed his hand on her back. "We intended to kill you."

The grey-blue eyes shot up, burning into Fern's. "But you did not."

Fern raised her chin, looking down at her sister. "I did not. There are parties that requested you be kept alive if it were possible."

"For torture? Ransom?" The ease with which her twin was asking about this sent a chill down Fern's spine.

"For a mother's love." Fern could see her mother in her sister's face. Her father, too, but it was still too much of a risk to even think about him here.

"But is she not the one who sent you to kill me?"

Frustration churned within Fern's core, having to explain all of this to someone who should be dead already. She felt the charge building up, arcing on her skin, as she near-yelled, "There is a war coming. There are beings in every region who want you dead to take away Belle's hold on the throne, to stop her from sparking the conflict. Stalworth wasn't *defending* you that night, he was keeping you from fleeing with our mother, from running away from the woman who stabbed our father in the chest and threatened to kill one of us to keep the lineage tidy."

Seeing Kraai's concerned face, Fern realized she was nearing her breaking point, that her charge was searching for somewhere to ground itself. She closed her eyes, reaching down to the ground to allow the electricity out gently through her fingertips. When she rose, a still calm held within her. "I hold no ill will toward you; I only wish to keep the people I love safe and to prevent the war. Agree to give up your claim to the throne, allow me to be named first, and you can live."

Without missing a beat, Daughter of Strike said in a clear voice, "I renounce my claim to the throne."

Fern took a moment to register what had just been said, convinced her ears had played a trick on her. "Just like that?"

"When I was granted my song, I fell in love with the Region of the Seas. I cannot live a true life anywhere else. The silence under the water, the openness, the songs of the sailors." She bit her lip, lost in a thought, before beaming a smile at Fern. "I have undergone the transformation countless times. It does not hurt me anymore. I can live above or below as I wish. It is a region of opportunity. I want that."

Kraai held her hands, bringing his face close. "What of all you would be giving up? Are you not engaged? Will you not miss the power?"

Fern wanted to smack him. She was giving it up so easily—why let her second guess any of it, especially when her other option is death?

Daughter of Strike gave a nervous chuckle. "My engagement is to my uncle. Grandmother wishes for us to mate to ensure the next heir is fully siren. I had no say in the decision. And I do not wish for power over the Dark Region, I wish to take my own power from the Seas—to earn it. The salt water in my blood calls me back." She turned to Fern. "Do you not hear it, too?"

Fern pulled her sleeve back, looking at the vein in the base of her hand. She caressed it with her fingertips. "I do feel the salt water"—she pulled the cloth back down—"but I hear a different call."

"A call to the Dark Region?" Daughter of Strike asked.

Fern looked at Kraai, her symbol of home, her demon of the Mountains. "For now."

The rest of the night was spent telling the true history to Daughter of Strike. At times, she would become vacant, reconciling what she thought she knew with this new information, but she never fought any of it. Apparently, all of the accusations against Belle were completely within her understanding of what her grandmother was capable of.

"You know we have to get rid of her, as well, right?" Fern asked.

"That is not possible," Daughter of Strike said, confused. "She is the de facto queen regent. She holds power until you are named."

"I can think of at least one way to make her not the queen regent anymore."

Daughter of Strike laughed until she realized Fern was not jesting, then her face fell to a deathly seriousness. "You cannot kill our grandmother."

Fern turned her head, hiding her absolute shock at the response. Rolling her eyes, she returned to stare down her sister, static needles tickling the back of her neck. "Did you not hear a word we just told you? She destroyed our family."

"What family?" Disgust coated Daughter of Strike's face and voice. "Do you not realize who raised me? Who told me stories when I was a child? Who trained me? It was not our mother, and not anyone in your"—she shot a glance at Kraai—"*family*. You want to come in here and take the throne, be my guest, but you will *not* take the only family I have ever known."

"Then what do you suggest? If we don't take her from power"—Fern gave Kraai her own glance, sad and desperate—"someone we love will die."

Daughter of Strike's demeanor shifted, calming considerably with one thought. "The being who sent you took a hostage." It wasn't a question.

Fern gave a slow nod, and in her peripheral vision, she could see Kraai doing the same.

Daughter of Strike mirrored the nods. "Clever." Her eyes shot back toward the ground, again searching for thoughts, before she raised her head, a slight sadness in her eyes. "I will ask her to step down."

"You truly believe that will work?" Fern asked, astounded it could be that easy.

"If the alternative is her death, then I sincerely hope so."

Chapter 26

They spent the day in the courtyard, Daughter of Strike basking in the sun for the first time in her life. She pressed her cheek to the sun-baked tiles, soaking in the heat. Fern had to convince her to move to the shade when she began to doze off.

Fern was sleeping, too, when the commotion came from the entry room. The sun was no longer beating down into their space, but the sky was still alight. Nobody should be out during the day. She flipped over, poising herself on fingertips and toes, seeing her sister doing the same across the courtyard. Fern scanned the space—no sign of Kraai. She bolted toward the noise, her hands charged. She pulled the door open to find Kraai lying on the ground, a dark figure standing over him. Her heart stopped as her dream came back to haunt her, fixating on his limp body. The stranger turned around, the last of the daylight coming from the windows to illuminate the same face that she had seen as they were leaving the palace.

Upon seeing Fern, he pressed forward, grabbing her upper arm firmly. "Princess, we must go."

Fern struggled to pull away, but was nowhere near strong enough. She pressed her charged hand onto his arm, but he did not even flinch. Her eyes bounced between the hand on her arm and her friend on the ground. Was he breathing? Bleeding? She couldn't see in the shadows.

"Stalworth." The voice came from behind them, stern but shaky. "Let her go."

He did not turn, did not even move, but his grip loosened enough that Fern could pry his fingers open with her free hand. She backed away as the demon stood nearly stone-still, save for his shoulders rising and falling with his heavy breath. When she was a handful of steps away, she dove for Kraai. Under her hands, his chest rose and fell, his heartbeat pounding at its usual rapid rate. Fern shook him, pleading, "Kraai, wake up," as she glanced over her shoulder. The demon was turning slowly, his eyes locked on Fern. She placed her body between Kraai and the massive being, trying her best to build a new charge from her fear but also knowing it likely wouldn't stop him.

"Stalworth," Daughter of Strike repeated.

The fire in his eyes roared as he moved to look upon Daughter of Strike. His hand reached for something in his sleeve. No, not something *in* his sleeve, but his sleeve itself. He unbuttoned the cuff and pulled, revealing his forearm, which he stared at in slow confusion.

Daughter of Strike's hand was on her neck, a song on her lips. "I will go with you, but there are some things you must first understand. Wait here with me as long as you can."

His fists clenched, body shaking. Something inside him was fighting hard against her song, but after nearly a breathless minute, he nodded.

She turned her attention toward the unconscious Kraai and Fern who dared not move. "I can only hold him for a short time. He is under the command of our grandmother's song—I must go with him when it once again takes his mind." She looked with pity on Kraai. "Wake him. I will need you there when I tell our grandmother to leave the palace."

Fern saw the drastic contrast between the tiny princess and the enormous guard. If he wanted her to go somewhere, there would be no fighting it. They were about to go to the palace—whatever was going to happen was going to happen tonight. Fern turned back to Kraai. If he hadn't been awkwardly contorted by his fall, she could almost swear he was just sleeping. She looked at her hands, still charged in preparation for an oncoming attack. It was worth a try. Pulling her face away, she shoved her hands onto his chest, sending a charge through him.

His body surged upward, his muscles all contracting at once. His mouth and eyes flew open, taking in a gasp of air that was let out in a half-shout, half-moan. There were two more deep, panicked breaths before his eyes focused on Fern. "Are you alright?"

"You were knocked senseless to the point I woke you up with an electric charge and you are asking if *I* am alright?"

"There was someone—a demon—" His eyes found Stalworth and he immediately shifted to place himself between the demon and Fern.

Daughter of Strike was still watching and held out her hand to reassure Kraai. "He will not hurt anyone for now." She looked back up into Stalworth's eyes. "Kraai is helping to protect me. We do not need to hurt him. And Fern is…" She trailed off, her brow scrunched.

"The other princess," Stalworth finished, still not taking his eyes off his charge.

Daughter of Strike's eyes widened. "How did you know?"

Stalworth held out the arm that he had looked at before, turning it toward Daughter of Strike.

"Your blood oath?" The princess took it, running her fingertips over the underside of his forearm.

Emboldened by curiosity, Fern pushed herself past Kraai to see. The scars on his arm looked old, but there was still a faint tinge of red in the very center of each marking—a sign of an oath made in blood. It read "PROTECT THE PRINCESS" in all uppercase letters.

"I was told he made the oath before he forgot everything." Daughter of Strike smiled as she traced along the letters. "The magic is so strong that no spell could overpower his promise. He swore to protect me above everything, and even when his memory left him, he remembered his duty."

Stalworth snapped his fingers, fire hugging his thumb and index finger after he did so. He held the flame up to his wrist, where the words ended, revealing that they, in fact, did not end. Right along the vein in his wrist, shone an "E" and an "S" that had faded over nearly two decades, just as typical scars would.

Fern looked up at this demon, this friend of her parents, the one who turned on the woman he loved under the song of a siren. From the pain of that night, he found a way to be sure he would never hurt his friends' daughters. "You've known about me."

He closed his eyes and shook his head. His words came out with a great deal of effort, as if he was still struggling internally just to function. "I did not know what it meant. Not until last night."

"How did you find us?" Kraai's voice asked from his spot on the floor.

Fern shot daggers at her companion.

He slowly got to his feet, his hand grabbing at the side of his head. "If he found us, others might, too. We need to know if we are safe here."

Stalworth fought for words. "The door, in the sunlight. It laughed with a beautiful voice." His eyes welled with a haunted sadness. "Heard with the mind, not the ears."

With the mind? Was it a memory? "Stalworth, have you been here before?" Fern asked.

He looked at Fern with the clarity she had seen back at the palace. "I hope so." His words came out with ease, and a smile found its way to the corner of his lip, but with a blink, his calm was gone, fire raging in his eyes as he grabbed for Daughter of Strike.

Daughter of Strike did not pull back, she did not fight. Instead, she walked with him, taking two delicate steps for each of his booming ones. She yelled over her shoulder. "It appears we are leaving."

Kraai moved to help her, but Fern placed her hand on his chest. She whispered into his ear, "We know where they're going. He won't hurt her. We will follow from a distance—not bring attention to ourselves." She went to get her cloak from where she had been sleeping, only a slight hurry to her steps. By the time they left through the rusty door, the sun had dipped below the horizon and the city was waking up. They joined a swarm of beings making their way to the docks, which were closer than Fern had realized in their scattered journey here. As they pushed and weaved through the crowd, Kraai grabbed Fern's hand, interlacing their fingers. Fern smiled, despite knowing what she was about to face. They had no view of Stalworth and Daughter of Strike, but they knew their way to the palace, crossing over the same bridge as before.

As the buildings got bigger and more elegant, Fern pulled Kraai off to the side of the road in front of a large brick manor with turrets on each side. In daylight, or with proper torches to light the facade, it would have been a beautiful structure, but in the darkness of dusk it felt cold and empty. Panting from the excitement and exertion, Fern smiled as she faced her best friend. "I love you." She'd said it so many times, but this time he would remember.

Kraai leaned toward Fern, resting his forehead on hers. "I love you." He pushed forward, kissing her.

Fern wanted to continue, but pulled away. "We are about to face Belle, and I don't think she will simply *give up* power. This is the most dangerous thing we've ever done."

Kraai's brow raised. "Do you not remember that oak tree on the dwarven lands?"

"We discussed this beyond the veil, and I feel as if we have very different recollections of the event. This is clearly more dangerous." She couldn't help but laugh. "Besides, *you* were the one who dared *me* to get the acorn in the first place."

"And now *you* dare *me* to face a power-hungry siren." Kraai gave her another quick kiss before saying, "It will be dangerous, but we will do it together, as we always have."

Fern wrapped her arms around him, pulling him into a tight embrace, whispering into his shoulder, "As we always have." She wanted to tell him to run at any sign of trouble, to fly far and fast in order to leave one of them alive to care for their families—but she did not want him to go. She wanted him by her side and, if she was to die tonight, she wanted him with her when it happened. And if Kraai died? Then Fern would get to see what her limits truly were when she crossed them in order to destroy whoever hurt him. She kissed him on the cheek, lingering so she could breathe in the trace of the scent of the Mountains still trapped in his hair. When she finally pushed away, she forced a grin onto her face and a chipperness into her voice when she said, "Let's go claim a throne."

Kraai took her hand, leading her the remaining blocks to the palace. Its black, iron gates were closed, but when Fern pulled down the hood of her cloak, they opened, their screech echoing the screaming in her mind. Her breaths were shallow, but she paced them so as to seem calm. The murmurs from the nearby guards caught her attention, and she soon realized they were looking frantically between Fern and Daughter of Strike, who was pacing the courtyard with Stalworth. When their eyes were on Fern, she gave a single firm nod, hoping these were some of the palace staff on her side.

The princess paused her hurried steps when she saw Fern and pivoted to meet her with Stalworth on her tail. "Are you ready?"

Kraai looked Stalworth up and down. "Is he with us now?"

"Yes, he brought me back to the palace. That is all she asked him to do." Daughter of Strike pulled her protector beside her. "Besides, he will not hurt Fern or me, even under a song."

Kraai's brow shot up. "So he is with *you two*. Noted."

Meanwhile, the guards had disappeared. Not just the two from the gate, but the entire courtyard was empty—the four stood alone in the eerie quiet, a dramatic change from the chaos by the river. Fern scanned the faces of her companions—her dearest friend, her lost sister, and her mother's friend who could turn on them at any moment—four beings ready to stand up against the most powerful woman in the Four Regions.

A voice, taunting in tone but clear in intent, rang out. "You should not have come."

Chapter 27

Fern could feel it on her skin—the cool Mountain breeze, pulled through the Dark Region by the warmth of the Seas. The vapor bouncing off her skin sent a familiar chill to her core. She hoped she would not need it, but the water was on her side. She turned to her sister, whose wide eyes were fixed on the woman moving toward them. A knot formed in Fern's stomach.

A golden aura radiated from the blonde who took her place in the center of the cavity created by the two wings of the palace. Even from afar, her beauty made her immediately recognizable. "That disgusting half-breed had you so well hidden, but now you willingly give yourself up."

Fern needed a moment to find her voice, but when she did, it was clear and firm. "If you didn't have your sights set outside the borders of the Dark Region, I could have stayed away." She gestured to her sister. "I could have hidden until she was named. But I cannot stand by and watch you tear apart the Four Regions."

Belle seemed to float with an eerie grace, a cold smirk on her lips that somehow made her even more attractive. "And what will you do to me? One song and Daughter of Strike is named. Better yet, one song and you are dead. I will not have you take what I"—she glanced at Daughter of Strike—"what *we* have worked so hard for." Her hand went for her neck, her eyes to Stalworth. "Stalworth, there is an imposter who wishes to kill the princess," she sang. "Kill her before she can harm your ward."

Stalworth turned to Fern, jaw set, nostrils flaring as he refrained from laying a finger on her. After standing, staring, visibly uncomfortable for some time, he turned back to Belle, waiting for something.

"Stalworth, *kill her*," Belle urged. But when he made no motion to obey, she rolled her eyes. "So much for poetic justice." Her eyes scanned Fern, noticing how closely she was standing to another in their party. With a golden glow in her eyes, Belle moved her hand to her neck again and sang sweetly, "Stalworth, kill her friend."

Fern turned, placing herself in front of Stalworth and pressing her back against Kraai as the brutish demon locked fiery eyes on him. She wanted to try to talk him down, to beg him to turn his attention elsewhere, but she knew that would be a losing battle. Speaking over her shoulder, she assured Kraai, "He won't hurt me. Fly. See if you can find anyone else on our side." The resistance against her back fell away, and Fern stumbled to keep her balance as a crow took flight, an emerald pendant dangling from a golden chain in his claws. She never would have imagined the relief it would bring her to see that despicable object in his possession.

Stalworth followed the black bird with his gaze, raising his hand slowly, fire readied to strike Kraai down from the sky.

Fern could only watch in horror, knowing what was about to happen, before Daughter of Strike took the ignited hand in hers and pulled down with the full weight of her body. She screamed in pain, the smell of burning flesh permeating the fresh air. Stalworth dropped his hand, the fire disappearing as something within him realized what he had done. For this moment, his attention was completely on the princess, allowing Kraai time to hide from view.

Belle's aura glowed even brighter, her hair rising off of her neck to create almost a halo around her. Her fingertips grazed her throat as she sang in feigned fear, "There is an imposter, one who wishes to steal the throne. Kill the green-eyed mimic to protect the true princess." The song was loud enough that Fern and Daughter of Strike both instinctively covered their ears, while Fern tried to calculate how far it would be heard and how many might fall under the influence of her song. The numbers were not looking favorable.

Dozens of guards poured out from the palace doors, weapons in hand, flanking the group from a distance. Swords glinted in the light of the rising moon, while arrows were pointed at the three of them. Could they see the subtle difference between Fern and her sister?

Fern moved closer to the other two, realizing they would not loose an arrow until they had a clear shot that would not hurt the princess.

Daughter of Strike still held tight to Stalworth's hand as she screamed to Belle and anyone who would listen, "I renounce my claim to the throne! My sister is now the sole heir in the Dark Region!"

At that, some of the guards turned their attention to the guard standing closest to Belle. In response, he gave Fern a slow bow, rising with a satisfied grin on his face. "Gentlemen, we serve the heir."

Fern scanned the scene—perhaps six or seven of the guards, in addition to this lead guard, were no longer staring them down like animals about to attack. Instead, they watched Fern as if awaiting orders. These were her allies in the palace, somehow immune. But would they be enough? She counted, three, six, nine, ten, eleven arrows still aimed directly at them, but the bows… Something was strange about the bows. A wide grin spread across her face as she realized it: *metal.* She looked her grandmother directly in the eyes and said, "Belle, you are no longer welcome in the palace or in the Dark Region. Leave now or you will be removed by force."

Belle's eyes narrowed; she shifted the hand resting on her clavicle to access her songtone once again. "Stalworth, pull the blue-eyed princess away. Guards, take your shot."

In one moment, Daughter of Strike was being dragged backward, the guards still under Belle's influence drew their bows, and Fern sent a surge of fork lightning in eleven directions, striking the metal bows of the archers. Most of them collapsed, but some of the arrows were still loosed. Most flew upward as their owners fell to the ground, but one made its way directly toward Fern.

While her body could not move fast enough to evade it, her mind flashed through her options. It would not respond to a song, a charge could not deflect it, nor could she summon enough water to do so. All she could manage was a flinch, but the arrow never struck her. She opened her eyes to see why and saw Stalworth standing there, eyes pressed shut in pain. He took a heavy breath before ripping the arrow from his shoulder and saying, "Protect the princesses."

As her senses finally returned to the present, she heard the chaos of swords clashing—those who were immune to Belle's song were actively fighting those who were not so fortunate. Red shone off the blades, but the puppets remained standing, none of their injuries enough to take them down. Part of Fern was relieved—these beings had no control over what they were doing, they shouldn't have to die for Belle—but at the same time, they were not holding their blows like their unaffected counterparts were.

The song rang out again, "Stalworth, kill the bird."

Fern's eyes shot to the sky. There he was, his feathers shining in the silver glow of the moon. Why would he come back when Belle was set on destroying him?

A rumble from the ground brought her attention back to the chaos. The lead guard was kneeling beside a fallen demon, pressing their foreheads together, crying out in agony. His body shook as he wept, but within moments his demeanor changed. Grabbing for his sword, he swung around and attacked the nearest guard under Belle's influence, cutting him down in one swift motion, blood spattering across his enraged face.

"Stalworth, no!" Daughter of Strike screamed as an orb of fire shot to the sky.

Fern might have screamed, too, but the world went silent as she saw black feathers erupt into flame and fall to the ground behind the line of guards. She rushed toward him, shooting a charge at the three beings in her way, knocking two off their feet. The third charged her, but she ducked out of the way of a clumsy swing of his sword. She retched when she saw what lay on the ground—a crow, burned to a crisp, undeniably dead. In an instant, she knew exactly what the guard was feeling, the fire of revenge burning within her. It wasn't burning for Stalworth, though. It was never his fault. It was *hers*. Fern turned, snarling, sparks arcing over her skin.

More of the household were filing out of the palace doors, weapons or magic at the ready—guards, footmen, even maids—and there was no way to tell which side they were on. Making her way to the open center of the turmoil, Fern realized that only one person needed to die for this to be over, and there was nobody standing between them.

Arms outstretched, Fern's fingers clenched, pulling the heat energy from the Mountainous air around them. The water responded like an old friend, like Kraai, asking no questions in this time of need. A thick mist seemed to creep from her hands, spreading across the entire courtyard. The sounds were dampened by the water, then stopped altogether as visibility decreased; if they couldn't see, they couldn't fight. The only space left cloudless was the direct line from Stalworth and Daughter of Strike to Fern to Belle. Their eyes locked as pure rage filled Fern's core, churning into a storm that she was waiting to release. If she struck too soon, Belle might somehow survive. She wanted to be sure her charge was strong enough to destroy Belle so completely that there would be nothing left of her.

A stroke of black crossed the top of her vision. Perhaps Fern wouldn't have noticed if not for the flash of green that accompanied it. The stutter in her breath came out as nearly a laugh of relief. She watched as Kraai flew down and, before Stalworth could process that his target was so close, the crow wrapped the chain around the demon's neck. Daughter of Strike immediately picked up on what was happening and secured the clasp in the back.

Stalworth's hands reached for his head, pulling at his horns as his clearing eyes looked at the ground in horror. He knelt down to caress the gravel with his hands, tears falling harder than an autumnal rain. Daughter of Strike's words came back to Fern's mind—*so she used her song on him, commanding him to forget*. Because he loved Sway, he now remembered what he did to her.

Belle's flash of confusion was replaced by terror as Stalworth rose, disgust and anger masking a deep sorrow that could still be seen through his tears. She brought her hand to her neck and sang, panic evident, "Guards, find me. Push through the fog and defend me."

Feet pivoted on gravel within the haze, but the only sure steps were Stalworth's, pressing past Fern toward Belle. Fire licked his hands and forearms as he flexed his fingers in and out of white-knuckled fists. One guard appeared from the fog, placing himself between Belle and Stalworth. Barely noticing the slice of the sword into the flesh of his arm, Stalworth picked the defender up by the shoulder and threw him back into the cloud.

Belle stumbled backward, the mist parting as she moved to keep her in sight. Her hand grasped at her neck. "Stalworth, you do not want—"

Stalworth ripped Belle's hand from her neck, replacing it with his own. Fire licked up the sides of her face as she clawed at the strong hand that now held her a good distance off the ground.

"Stalworth, no!" The frantic scream came from behind Fern. Daughter of Strike ran up, threatening to pass her sister, but instead using her to shield part of her view of the scene. "Please! Do not kill her!" It was not a command, not a song, but a desperate plea from a young woman about to watch her protector destroy the only family she'd ever known.

Stalworth froze, keeping his body completely still despite the flailing body in his right hand, the blood from his wounds spreading down the arm and across the shoulder of his shirt. The fire slowly flickered out, leaving Belle only struggling for breath. His shoulders rose and fell with one long breath before he brought her back to the ground, keeping his hand tight on her neck while wrapping his arm around her, pressing her back against him, so they were both facing Fern and Daughter of Strike. Stalworth bent down to whisper something in Belle's ear and, as she opened her lips to respond, he took his free hand, ablaze with fire, and pressed it onto her mouth.

Daughter of Strike's fingers dug into Fern's shoulders as she hid her blue eyes behind her sister's back. Fern did not blame her—it was a horrifying image to behold, Belle having no choice but to inhale pure flame, her eyes screaming in the way her lungs couldn't. It also saved Daughter of Strike from having to witness another guard break through the fog, his sword diving straight for Stalworth's back. The demon did not stop, his eyes fixed on a point on the ground—the same space that had been baptized in his tears. The guard removed his sword, taking a gush of Stalworth's blood with it, before plunging it back into the demon.

The fire in Stalworth's eyes dimmed slowly, matching the dying flame that enveloped his hand. When the blade was withdrawn again, Stalworth fell to the ground, dropping a limp, golden Belle before him. The last noise that could be heard was their bodies hitting the gravel in unison, then a complete silence from in and outside the fog.

Fern released the cloud, letting the light breeze take it away, creeping around the palace and pushing toward the Seas. As beings became visible, some had a look of fresh confusion, while most had already moved to guilt as they stared at their bloodied hands and weapons.

Daughter of Strike finally dared to look, letting out an agonized cry as she shoved Fern out of the way to fall to the ground between the only two beings who ever meant anything to her. She placed one hand on each of them, her head moving back and forth to look at each in turn through her cascade of tears.

Fern, on her knees from sheer fatigue, watched the scene with an aching heart. This was *her* doing. She brought this upon her sister. While she owed her sister nothing, she certainly did not deserve to lose *everything*. A warm hand pressed onto Fern's shoulder and a fear she had been holding inside melted. She reached up and placed her hand on Kraai's but was unable to stop watching her sister's mourning. Kraai's hand tightened at the same moment Fern was startled to her feet. They both waited with bated breath to see if it would happen again, and it did—Belle's eyelids moved once more, but this time they shot open.

The golden siren's body seized, her mouth wide, but no noise escaped. Her nails dug into the burned flesh of her neck, desperate. Daughter of Strike first flinched away, then fell forward to try to help her grandmother. She placed her hands on Belle's chest, and they rose and fell with the siren's breath. She wasn't fighting to breathe—she was fighting to sing.

Fern turned around, throwing her hands onto Kraai's ears, but he pulled her hands down, holding them gently in his. "She cannot sing." His eyes widened as he stepped toward the scene. "Stalworth burned her throat so she cannot sing. That is why everyone stopped—her power was in her song, but she no longer has a song."

Belle was frantically trying to find her voice, moving her lips to scream while making no sound, clearly more concerned about her inability to speak than about the physical agony from her wounds.

Daughter of Strike looked back at Stalworth again, then bit her lips together as she smacked her grandmother across the face, the slap echoing off the palace walls that surrounded them. When Belle finally looked at her granddaughter, the former princess snarled and said, "You no longer speak for me and you no longer speak for the Dark Region."

Belle rolled over, covering her mutilated face, and silently sobbed as everyone turned their attention to Stalworth. Surely, he would spring back to life as Belle did. He was strong, determined. He had been hit with an arrow, sliced and stabbed with a sword, and still stood to disable Belle—what was one more blow to take him out? As more moments passed, hope fell away as he continued to lie in a heap on the ground.

Fern built as much charge as she could in her hands, but she had so little left within her. When she placed her hands on his chest, his muscles twitched, but settled back to lifelessness in an instant. Fern fell away, collapsing into waiting arms. Even now Kraai could read her so well, knowing exactly when and where she would fall.

Through blurred eyes, threatening to close under the overwhelming weight of gravity, she saw Daughter of Strike copy her actions, though her charge was much greater from all she suffered in the past few minutes. She threw her power into his chest, waited for consciousness that never came, then tried again and again and again, her tears more distressed with each try. It was during the eighth or ninth attempt that Fern was finally stolen away by exhaustion.

Chapter 28

"The tribunal has met to discuss your trial," one of the seven judges said from their elevated table. "We believe it is a valid trial and will grant your request to be named."

Fern locked her jaw as a yawn threatened to push its way through her lips. She had a name already—a great name, in fact. It singled her out as belonging to no region. But now she would be named, just like her mother and father had been, like her grandmothers and grandfathers, a rite of passage in the Dark Region. Since her sister had yet to submit her trial, this name would make Fern the heir, and with no being on the throne now, the name would make her queen.

"The magic reported in your trial is quite rare, especially at the scale described," the elf continued, not looking away from his parchment. "We would not have believed it had it not been for multiple witnesses giving validity to the claims. Striking down attackers with lightning, as your father had done before you, but with more control over that power; taking on dozens of guards to usurp power from Belle after convincing your sister to give up her claim; manipulating energy and heat—all very impressive, but not the attributes for which you showed the most promise." Despite the enthusiasm of his word choice, he sounded almost as bored as Fern felt. "The tribunal has come to a unanimous decision as to your name. Based on the manner in which you defended yourself and those who fought for you, creating a fog that filled the entire palace courtyard, incapacitating those under the siren's song, I decree that you shall henceforth be known as Mist."

All seven men at the table repeated the name in unison. "Mist."

The elf stood, his white eyes finally meeting the newly-named woman's green. "Mist, being the first named child of Strike, you are now to be recognized as the rightful heir to the throne of the Dark Region."

Fern knew what she had to do. Closing her eyes so they would not see them roll, she gave a shallow curtsy to the judges. "I thank the tribunal for this name," she said, leaving off the customary part about carrying it proudly. She did not open her eyes again until she had turned toward the archway. His shadow was visible in the torchlight that radiated from the hall. As they passed each other, his hand brushed against hers, their pinkies curling around each other for half a moment before he was ushered into the room. Fern lingered at the end of the hall, daring the guard to make the new queen move when he returned to his station.

In the echo of the stone arch, the voices of the tribunal members could be heard telling Kraai he would be named tonight, as well. Fighting the urge to stay and hear his naming first-hand, Fern left through the path on the left—the hall for named individuals only. Kraai took this tradition much more seriously. In his short relationship with his father, he discovered that what he wanted most was to see his son named. When Fern escaped into the cool night air, all those waiting outside for their own loved ones stared, startled, before bowing to her.

Even Kraai's mother gave a curtsy. When she rose, she asked, "Do I get to help you pick the dress for the coronation?"

Fern linked her arm in Iris', turning to face the doorway. "We should hold off on a coronation for now and see how the next few weeks go."

Iris gave a sidelong glance and a conspiratorial smile. She could never read emotions well, but she was awfully good at picking up on when Fern or Kraai had some kind of plot brewing.

Fern did not have to wait long before Kraai emerged from the door, his shaking hand over his mouth. Concerned, she and Iris both rushed to meet him. "What is it? Did they not grant you a favorable name?"

His eyes pressed shut, he bit his lips together before inhaling deeply. "It is very favorable."

Iris brushed Kraai's hair out of his face. "Then tell us what happened."

Fighting back sobs, he was able to collect himself long enough to say, "One of the judges knew my father. He asked if—" He was stopped by a shake in his breath.

"If you wanted a name to honor him," Iris finished.

Kraai nodded. After a few breaths to regain his composure, he said, "In the Dark Region, I will be known as Flight." His self-control threatened to leave him again, but he raised his head, letting another tear fall. After a hug from Fern and his mother, he said, "We should go."

In the three days since what happened outside the palace, Stalworth had been honored in a ceremony attended only by Fern, Kraai, and Daughter of Strike. Fern had invited her parents, but her father had to remain dead to the region, while her mother was unable to overcome the sheer terror of returning to the palace. Stalworth's body was burned in the palace courtyard, in the exact spot he had fallen to the ground in tears when he regained his memory.

Belle had been forced back into the water, unable to return to land again, as she was unable to say the words required for the transformation. Daughter of Strike would join her in the Region of the Seas once she received a name, but she had other plans for where she would live when she got there, all stemming from a discussion with the sailors who came to transport her grandmother.

Now all that was left was to say goodbye to Flight. It had taken some time to find an elf willing to transform Kraai's father from his crow form so he could be honored as most knew him. Despite only knowing his father for a short time, Kraai was incredibly affected by his death. Iris, too, held a deep love for him still, even after nearly twenty years apart.

Fern took this opportunity to show support for these two who had both risked so much for her and for her family—the family she longed to return to, in the home for which her heart yearned. "Yes," Fern said. "We should go."

Epilogue

Mercy's legs wobbled beneath her—it had been almost two years since she had spent any substantial time on land. As the newest crewmate on the *Satisfaction*, she was always required to man the ship when in port, letting the more senior sailors engage in the debauchery they craved. She did not mind this, as she had spent the first eighteen years of her life surrounded by stone. The creak of wood under the metal deck was a song far more beautiful than any tune played in the public houses.

But now she had been summoned by the Council of the Seas. Captain had put her name forward to represent his sailors—he knew she had a mind for politics, as well as close associations with powerful beings in two other regions. After walking for hours on the dusty road that formed the border between the Seas and the Null, she was approaching the meeting place. The other council members were already waiting—two water elves with seaweed and shells tangled into their hair, three water demons from the coastal towns, and two women who glowed with siren auras. Mercy was greeted with cordial nods from most, but the sirens remained still, their eyes narrowed.

The elves opened the portal, a black hole bored into the air itself. One of the elves went first, his body disappearing as it passed through the two-dimensional oval. The second elf gestured, indicating he would be going last.

Mercy looked around, waiting for someone to move. Both groups whispered amongst themselves, then looked at her. She shrugged, a smug satisfaction growing in her heart as she realized that her presence made each group uncomfortable—the water demons due to their troubled relations with sirens and the sirens due to the fact she was instrumental in removing them from power in the Dark Region. She loved making beings nervous, including herself, so when she stared down a portal of pitch black that gave her medusas in her gut, she leapt toward it, bouncing through with a spring in her step.

The ground on the other side was further down than she had anticipated, creating a need to overcorrect her balance, barely avoiding a fall into the mess of ferns below her. She looked around—they were in the middle of the Null, each region so far in the distance that she would not be able to tell which direction was which if it weren't for the glow of the setting sun. In the location of the exact center of the Four Regions stood a heavy wooden rectangular table, with beings seated on three sides.

The side closest to the Dark Region was topped with metal. Occupying its one seat was the queen, dressed in her wonted red, giving a sharp-toothed smile to the new arrival. Mercy had met her before—she had returned to the Dark Region just as Mercy was leaving, sending shockwaves through the region even greater than those when Belle was ousted. The rumors of her evading the spell of the Golden Veil reached every region, only adding to the widespread admiration and fear of the vampire. She had confided in her granddaughters, however, that while the Golden Veil penetrated thousands of feet below the ground, the sea dove tens of thousands. Useful information for a vampire with no need to breathe air, or for sirens who can breathe underwater.

Seated on the side toward the Region of the Mountains were six somber faces, belonging to an assortment of dwarves and elves, and one amused smirk belonging to Mercy's own reflection, save for the green eyes. She had been named in the Dark Region, but still went by Fern—the name given to her by her mother. By *their* mother. Fern was adamant that Mercy travel into the Mountains to meet her, as well as the rest of Fern's makeshift family, but the sailor had other plans. Perhaps one day she would, but she wanted to make her own way for a while, away from the influence of familial authority figures. Each member of the Council of the Mountains had a guard standing a few paces behind them, including a familiar face behind Fern. Kraai gave a warm smile in greeting, which Mercy reciprocated with an added wink.

When all the members of the Council of the Seas were seated, their own guards arrived. There was one for the elves, one for the water demons, one burly demon clearly under the influence of the sirens' song, and Nimble—an elf and fellow crewmate on board the *Satisfaction*. While he was not as muscular or large as the other guards, he was incredibly agile, and was able to slip Mercy out of trouble more than a handful of times. He was incredibly dedicated to her safety—something about the relationship of his father with her grandfather when they sailed together.

Mercy's eyes finally fell on the side that was closest to the Light Region. Three guards hovered behind The Monarch, but he did not seem as if he would need them. His massive frame took up almost the entire side of the table. It had been assumed that they would change to a more delicate form the winter after Belle had been returned to the Seas, but he was still immense and intimidating. The prevailing theory was that war had not been prevented after all.

Mask looked to each side, scanning the two Councils with a warm pause for each of her granddaughters. She then made hard eye contact with The Monarch and, with unmistakable venom in her tone, asked, "Shall we begin?"

About the Author

Andrea Fink was born and raised in the Pacific Northwest. She studied Environmental Science and Resource Management at the University of Washington, then went on to get her teaching credentials. She loves Husky football, playing D&D, and will never say no to watching the movie Airplane! She lives just north of Seattle, Washington with her husband and daughter. Despite having no background in English or creative writing, she wrote a fantasy series. As of publication, she still has not completed a transatlantic crossing, become a confectioner, been an extra in a movie, lived abroad, or voiced a cartoon character.

Facebook: Andrea Fink, Author
Instagram: @andrea.as.an.author
TikTok: @andrea.as.an.author
Website: andreafinkbooks.com

To the Reader

Thank you for going on this journey with me. Emily, Dirge, and Fern all hold such special places in my heart and I am so glad I get to share them, and the world in which they live, with you.

Sincerely,

Andrea Fink
Author of *Mask*, *Wave*, and *Mist*

You're curious. I like you.